# SUDDEN DEATH

*Also by Malcolm Hamer (with Jill Foster)*

The Family Welcome Accommodation Guide
The Family Welcome Pub & Restaurant Guide
The Family Welcome Leisure Guide

# SUDDEN DEATH

Malcolm Hamer

**HEADLINE**

First published in 1991
by HEADLINE BOOK PUBLISHING PLC

10 9 8 7 6 5 4 3 2 1

British Library Cataloguing in Publication Data

Hamer, Malcolm
Sudden death.
I. Title
823.914

ISBN 0-7472-0361-X

Typeset in 11/13½ pt Times
by Colset Private Limited, Singapore

Printed and bound in Great Britain by
Richard Clay Ltd, Bungay, Suffolk

HEADLINE BOOK PUBLISHING PLC
Headline House
79 Great Titchfield Street
London W1P 7FN

**To Jill**

# Acknowledgments

My sincere thanks to the following for their help and advice: Peter Coleman, Richard Hills, Philip Olsen, and Peter Soilleux.

# Chapter 1

Only England has mornings like these. I walked quietly past the clubhouse, towards the first tee of the Royal Bucks Golf Club, and paused. In early May at 6 a.m. there was hardly a sound, but the sun was already up and giving the hint of a beautiful day to come. A perfect day for golf, as the club golfer invariably terms it. The outline of the fairway was almost pernickety in the way it was defined against the darker green of the semi-rough and the denser patches of the real rough. The bunkers ate into the fairway at around the 240-yard mark to cool the aggressive ardour of the professional golfer who might try to cut the slight dogleg and set himself up for an easier shot into the two-tier green. These bunkers, beautifully trimmed around the edges and beautifully raked, looked innocent and defenceless – an illusion, as I knew, brought on by the fresh and shining morning.

The sun was setting a glittering scene for the first hole, enlivening the damp leaves on the backdrop of ancient and stately trees, whose different designs gave character to each and every hole on this, one of the loveliest golf courses in southern England. It would not be so attractive to many of the professional golfers in the field of nearly 150 who would shortly begin to contest the World Wide Insurance Golf Championship.

The beauties of the course couldn't hide its tough and unremitting nature, which demanded accurate striking of the ball on virtually every hole. It had been laid out some fifty years before by one of those famous Scottish golfers who had dominated golf in the first couple of decades of the century. He had used all the natural contours of the ground, the heather which abounds in this part of England, and the hoards of mighty trees – all even mightier now – to produce a hard but enjoyable test for the club members.

1

There was plenty of room on the course and it was relatively easy to lengthen it enough to test the professionals. New tees lurked in the trees on several holes, and were skilfully placed to bring into play the same hazards which threatened the club players from their tees.

There were already several cars in the VIP car park, and prominent amongst them was a new Rolls-Royce Corniche with the number plate BS1. This obviously belonged to Brian Summers, the chairman of World Wide Insurance. He was a fanatical and not very competent golfer and a member of the Royal Bucks Club. He had started sponsoring the tournament half a dozen years ago, and loved the prestige that 'his' tournament gave him amongst the other members. Some of them had no doubt spent most of the preceding year trying to wangle an invitation to play in the pro-am.

Above all, Brian Summers delighted in rubbing shoulders with some of the world's best golfers, and his big day was the pro-am, which usually takes place the day before the tournament proper.

You might think that the function of the pro-am is to enable the professional to take a good look at the course under competitive conditions. Wrong. For a start only about thirty or so take part, since it is organised in four-ball teams, with one professional, a celebrity who is normally from sport or show business and two amateurs.

The main purpose of the pro-am has nothing to do with golf. It is the day on which the sponsor entertains his major customers. The day on which he pours as much food, drink and bonhomie into them as possible; and into the gentlemen of the Press, too. The chairman can then, whether it is justified or not, tell his board of directors and his shareholders how successful the whole exercise has been in terms of customer relations and exposure for the company and its services. He can then happily lay his plans for next year's shindig.

I walked down the first fairway in a relaxed and peaceful mood, despite my early departure from my bed. I paused by the first green, where one of the greenkeepers was raking a deep bunker. It was Mark Spicer, the son of the Royal Bucks secretary, and he was earning some extra money during his time off from university.

He leant on his long rake and grinned up at me.

'Did you see some of those swings yesterday?' he asked. 'My

God, they weren't just hitting it sideways, some of them weren't even making contact. Why do they bother?'

Mark played off a low handicap, and he had a point. It seems that no businessman, even if he hasn't touched a club for years, can resist an invitation to a pro-am. The results are often more comic than the antics of the television comedians and personalities who are out in force on these occasions.

'And did you see the gear?' Mark laughed and we compared notes on the most garish sights we'd seen. The prize went to a pop singer who had attired himself in tartan trousers, a flower-patterned shirt and a sweater with zig-zag stripes.

Mark and I agreed to have a game together soon and I moved off down the course, and mused on the ways in which the pro golfers cope in their different ways with the unusual demands of the pro-am.

The superstar is doubly lucky in that a certain aloofness – a concentration on tomorrow's battle for supremacy – is expected. Lesser players can try the same tack but run the risk of being berated by their amateur partners for being unfriendly or even unprofessional. On one famous occasion an aspiring pro, later to play in the Ryder Cup, was so incensed by the antics of his pro-am partners that he left the course in mid-round. He was fined and warned severely by the Professional Golfers Association, but there was many a wry and sympathetic smile about the incident amongst his fellow professionals.

Another way to cope with the day is for the pro to enter totally into the spirit of it all: like the perfect publican, he must try to be arbiter, philosopher, psychologist and friend, all rolled into one. In addition he must be the team captain, strong and sympathetic. He must listen attentively to the tales of how the amateur would have broken sixty five in a competition last Saturday if he had not had such disgusting luck on the greens. He must give lessons on the golf swing on the way round, encourage, cajole, crack jokes, tell tall golfing tales and generally be Mr Golf Personality. This is the best way. His reputation as a really nice guy will be assured, amongst two club golfers at least, and he might even get into the pro-am prize money.

One of the professional golfers had cracked under the strain yesterday. Jack Mason. I had seen it happen at close quarters because I am his caddie.

The golf fan, if he notices the caddie at all, probably just sees him as the anonymous person who carries the superstar's bag and is, incidentally, a walking billboard for the sponsor. Some caddies are just that, and the old tradition of the itinerant caddie who sleeps rough and dresses in cast-off clothing is still abroad. But many caddies offer a great deal more and look upon themselves as vital components in the professional golfer's armoury.

At this early hour I was taking a final look at the layout of the course. I already had two vital tools of the caddie's trade in my pocket: notes on the measurements and characteristics of each hole, which I had checked and rechecked on the practice days; and a chart, issued ahead of each day's play by the PGA which told me where the hole would be cut on each green.

Despite these I always took a last look at the course on the first day of a tournament. It was a superstition of mine. I was reminding the golfing spirits that I would not be caught napping.

These measurements were vital to Jack Mason, who relied upon me to confirm where he should hit his shots and how hard. A pro knows within a few yards how far he can hit the ball with each club – unlike the club golfer who has a wide variation from day to day, and even from hole to hole.

Later in the day I would tell Jack the exact distance that the first bunker was from the tee. Depending on the direction and strength of the breeze, Jack would opt either to carry his drive right over the bunker to set up an easy shot into the green or, more likely, for a conservative drive down the left side of the fairway and a mid-iron to the heart of the green.

Just as important is the chart which shows the position of the hole on the green. Some greens can be forty yards long, so the pin position can often mean a difference of two clubs. I checked the first one on my chart – a none-too-generous position near the back and on the left. It would be difficult to hit the ball close since a big bunker, cut into the front left edge of the green, was a threat, especially since the fairway sloped slightly towards it.

I went on my way, gazing anew at the beauties of the course. I noticed the leather of my shoes darken as it picked up the moisture from the grass. I was really looking forward to my breakfast.

The greenkeepers were already sweeping the dew off the greens with elongated poles – the final polish to an immaculately groomed course. In less than two hours the first shot would be hit – and the first tales of glory or misery or 'if only' would be told. Perhaps a new young star would make his insistent mark on the golfing heavens; or, more likely, one of the top dozen or so established golfers would add to his bank balance.

As I strolled down the next fairway and skirted a mass of heather which cut into the fairway on the angle of the dogleg, I wondered how my boss, Jack Mason, would fare in the tournament. He was approaching the awkward age in a professional golfer's career. After a short but successful amateur career he had been a steady winner of golfing titles in Europe and Africa; had flirted with the American tour in the seventies, but without the conviction to make a real marriage of it; and had been good enough occasionally to carry the hopes of British fans into the Open Championship. This invariably led to a first round in the high seventies followed by brilliant but despairing rounds which carried him well up into the place money. He was another 'if only' character, who nevertheless had played several times in the Ryder Cup against the USA with distinction.

His game was sound in all departments and his putting was particularly good, but his temperament was erratic. If he had a hangover from too much of the strongest real ale to be found the night before – Jack was a formidable seeker-out of head-banging beers with frightening names – or if the play was too slow, or if he disapproved of a local rule, or a local official, or a new initiative by the PGA, or . . . I could go on for minutes on end. This was one of the many reasons why he was such an immensely likeable man. He made short shrift of fools and knaves, but was human, too, and generous with his money and his time. Many of the younger professionals sought him out to have a look at swings and putting strokes that were out of tune, and he rarely if ever refused them his advice.

His attitude to any form of authority was irreverent to say the least, and a story still went the rounds of how, at the age of fifteen, he won a sporting scholarship to a relatively new and very expensive boarding school.

When he arrived with his parents for the interview the headmaster took him to a field where a few golf holes were laid out, handed him a wedge and a bucket of balls, and told Jack to hit some shots at one of the greens while he organised some tea for his parents. Jack hit a few shots and when the headmaster had disappeared around the corner he strolled down to the green and dropped three or four balls into the hole 'just to make sure'.

But Jack always gave good value and, apart from winning the British Boys' Golf Championship, he played rugby, cricket and tennis for the school and even managed to play county tennis as well.

Like most intelligent sportsmen, his was a complicated psychology which was highly tuned to provide feasible excuses for not winning every week. This is no criticism – virtually every sportsman has the same ability to turn a slight irritation or misfortune into a reason for defeat. Only the really great champions refuse to be sidetracked by any of these minor problems.

This can make those rare beings quite boring – an accusation you could never level at Jack. He was perhaps a little too intelligent for the daily grind of professional golf, without having that last cutting edge of brilliance which would have brought him an Open Championship. The X-factor, what the film people call 'bankability' when talking of superstars like John Wayne or Paul Newman or Barbra Streisand, was missing.

How Jack Mason would perform on any given day was, more than with most sportsmen, in the gift of the golfing gods. But it was one of my self-imposed duties to try to even out the peaks and troughs of his capricious temperament and make sure he produced his best golf when it mattered.

I was now approaching the eighth green, a plateau with four deep bunkers cut into the face and sides and a pronounced slope at the back if you overshot. At 170 yards it would not do to be less than accurate. I had caught up with the advance guard of greenkeepers, and greeted the head greenkeeper, a fit-looking, lean man with a rather scholarly stoop and a trim grey beard. I knew Tony Milton well from my brief days on the amateur golfing circuit. In his unobtrusive way he had shown his interest in my faltering attempts to climb the golfing ladder, and had even carried my bag in the Amateur Championship. As befitted a man who had been an assistant professional in his youth he had great sympathy for those afflicted by golf mania.

'Morning, Tony. A lovely day for golf.'

'Hello, Chris,' he said, in his quiet and welcoming way.

'How are the greens?' I don't know why I asked. No greenkeeper in the world would admit that his greens were anything but perfection, especially for an important tournament.

'Perfect,' he said. 'They'll hold a properly hit shot, but they'll be quick enough to test even the Swede, and they'll put the wind up some of 'em.'

The Swede was Bjorn Carlssen and he was the current leader of the European Order of Merit – a brilliant player in his mid-twenties, who could hit the ball miles and putted like a dream. As brilliant as he was on the course, so he was anonymous off it. There was nothing in the least bit objectionable about him, but he looked as though he had a computer where his heart was, and rushed home at night to plug in to a socket and recharge the batteries. There was no doubt that he was the first of an avalanche of Swedish players who might do to the golf circuits of the world what they were already doing to the tennis circuit. I wondered if I should learn Swedish (impossible, I'm told) and then remembered that most of them speak reasonable English.

'Your governor was at it again, then, yesterday,' Tony said. 'Up before the PGA committee, do you think?'

'Apparently not. Oliver warned him after his round, and offered the option of two hundred and fifty pounds into the Pro Golfers' Benevolent Fund, or an official reprimand and a fine. He chose the Fund – he reckons he'll get the money back one day.'

'He'll drop himself right in it, one day. He's got a mouth like Hell Bunker,' Tony said.

'But never as dry. Well, I must get on with it. See you later, Tony.'

Yes, Jack had certainly cracked in the pro-am, and had been given a sharp reprimand by the tournament director, Oliver Moreton, no doubt much to the latter's enjoyment.

Jack as always had an excuse. The hackers were surpassing themselves in the inventive ways they hit the ball badly, and often, and in the wrong direction. It was a tiresome and protracted round, and Jack had an evil hangover from too much Bonehead bitter during the previous evening.

If Jack had just returned in pristine health from a month at a health farm he might still have had trouble in coping with two of his partners. One was a rather patrician young man from a firm of London stockbrokers who played off a single figure handicap at Sunningdale and was a special guest of the chairman of the sponsoring company. He was dressed in traditional subfusc brown with a ragged sweater and a Viyella check shirt that his father must have handed down to him, and addressed Jack as if the status of professional golfers had not changed since the thirties. The celebrity was a monosyllabic professional footballer who had been transferred from a Scottish club to a fashionable one in London. He had acquired an agent of dubious reputation, a new hair style of highlighted curls, and the reputation of being a very trendy dresser. He was a novice golfer but at least he didn't talk much, and had an innate respect for a fellow professional sportsman.

The fourth member of the four-ball was neither silent nor relaxing to be with. He was, we gathered within seconds, the marketing director of a record company, and he knew everybody. Last year he had played in the pro-am with the Open Champion and Terry Wogan, and they should have won it, and next week he was playing in California with Trevino. He was of course on first name terms with everyone from the Prime Minister downwards whom he probably and inappropriately called 'man'.

Before we got to the first tee I could see that Jack was already on edge – or more on edge, rather, because a hangover had already eaten into his small reserves of patience and equanimity.

Jack's tactic was to keep as far away from his team-mates as possible – not difficult, because he was hitting the ball pretty straight and the Sunningdale amateur, who was also fairly straight, didn't really want to talk to a pro golfer. We could hear the constant drone of the record producer in the heather and the woods, and quite often when the others were chipping or putting. By dint of a couple of birdies and a fortunate eagle on the long fourteenth hole, Jack was looking good for a share of the prize money. The fifteenth hole is short but dangerous; its plateau green is ringed by bunkers at the front and sides and the trees press in at the back in a claustrophobic way – a nightmarish hole if you are playing badly.

'Well done, Mason,' said the stockbroker curtly after Jack's eagle and Jack raised his eyes to heaven but said nothing.

'Yeah, great putt, man,' said the record man.

Jack teed the ball up, after a short discussion with me about the merits of a six or a seven-iron. A high six-iron was the mutual decision, since there was just a gentle breeze to hold the ball up and give it a good chance to stop quickly. Jack settled into his stance, and relaxed as much as possible over the ball. He swung back and, just as his legs began to shift his weight forward into the shot and the downswing began, the record man shouted, 'Hey, Wally, how ya doin, man?' He had seen a friend fifty yards away.

Inevitably Jack came over the top of the ball, hit a combination of a pull and a hook and the ball went crashing into the trees left of the green. He dropped his club and, as the culprit began to mouth his apologies, picked up the large wooden tee-box and bellowed:

'If you open your big mouth again I'll ram this sodding box over your head and kick you all the way back to the clubhouse.' Unfortunately, a member of the tournament committee heard this picturesque statement of Jack's intentions – not difficult, you could probably have heard it twenty miles away at the PGA headquarters – and of course the stockbroker was a close friend of the sponsor.

The rest of the round was played in almost total silence, and Oliver Moreton duly took Jack on one side in the clubhouse and, in my view but not in Jack's, did what was necessary.

This tournament was my first outing of the year. I usually confined my caddying career to the main British and European season, with the odd foray to the United States or Japan or exotic places like the Philippines if my current boss was lucky enough to be invited, and if I was lucky enough to be invited by my boss.

I had drifted into caddying, much to the disgust of my father who had other ideas about careers for his eldest son and heir whom he had sent to the best public school he could afford (a slightly philistine, second division one near Brighton) and supported through university (Sussex-by-the-Sea). Despite playing all the usual team games at school it was the game of golf that captivated me.

The headmaster may not have been able to groom many boys for Oxbridge scholarships, but he did love his sport. So, apart from building tennis and squash courts, he managed to fit five holes of golf into a part of the school grounds and encouraged the boys to have a go.

We did more than just have a go when a golfing blue from Cambridge, whose other forte was history, joined the staff. He not only gave us a basic and very sound idea of the golf swing but enlisted the help of a young and enthusiastic local club professional. With all those holidays in which to practise and play – almost from dawn to dusk at times – my handicap rattled down, and I went to university with a handicap of two. By now, rather than dreaming of becoming Regius Professor of History, I was planning my speech to the cameras when I won my first Open Championship.

I strolled on down the edge of the ninth fairway in the gradually strengthening sun. It was picking out the spaces through the trees and making enchanting patterns among the bronzes and browns and greens, and occasionally highlighting spider's webs, laden with moisture. The many grey squirrels were out and about, busy, and unaware of the interruptions to their habitat which the golf fans would bring.

An even more pleasant prospect for club golfers is the presence of the refreshment hut in a little clearing between the ninth green and the tenth tee. On warm days a long and cooling drink, or a mug of tea, is impossible to resist. On winter days, usually after unsuccessfully battling against the spiteful thrusts of nature, a bacon sandwich and a mug of Bovril laced with sherry is guaranteed to soothe the injured spirit. The golfer, his strength renewed, is then eager to do battle with the remaining holes.

I checked the position of the pin, rather generously placed in the right centre of the green, and moved on towards the tenth hole. I was passing to the side of the refreshment hut and noticed that the door was slightly ajar, which was unusual because the genial Len who ran the place did not open his hut during a tournament as all the catering was franchised out.

I walked towards the door in the hope of a cup of tea. Len wasn't there, and the man who was would never drink a cup of tea again. Not with the shaft of a golf club driven through his neck and pinning him to the wooden floor.

10

# Chapter 2

The shock delayed any panic and I forced myself to walk across to the body and look at the face. Despite the caked blood and the chalky bruised skin I recognised the victim.

I couldn't bring myself to close the staring eyes, and that's when my courage dissolved. I knew that a dead man could not harm me, but didn't hang around to test the theory. I raced for the door and high-kneed it through the trees. Tony Milton and his assistant, thank goodness, were coming down the ninth fairway on an electric buggy.

'What's up, Chris, seen a ghost?'

'Froggy Davies is dead, in the hut,' I gasped out, but I was so breathless, from shock rather than running, that they didn't understand me. I repeated it, twice, before they got the message.

Tony gaped at me. We all knew Froggy, a caddie who had worked the circuit since the late fifties and had carried for many winners, including a couple of Open Champions – American, of course – in the mid-seventies. All his money went on beer, whisky and cigarettes, and whatever was left on the horses. He was much respected for his knowledge of golf courses, but was a throwback to the days when caddies wore old macs or tweed overcoats, slept rough in the summer, and in October committed a misdemeanour mild enough to ensure six months in jail to see them through the winter and send them out sobered up and refreshed for the new golf season.

Froggy was sufficiently a part of that tradition to scorn the smart and colourful clothes that the younger caddies wore as mirror images of their masters. It was only the threat of banishment from the game that persuaded him to wear the sponsors' bibs at the tournaments. It was never entirely clear where he bedded down at night after he lurched from the pub with various caddying cronies of a like mind. He wasn't the prettiest sight you would see on a golf course but, since he always turned up at the practice ground the following morning more or less on time and more or less clean-shaven, it was obvious that he patronised his own circuit of cheap guesthouses. Strong drink, and a frequent excess of it, made him unreliable at times, both in his judgements on the course and in his time-keeping.

There was one touching period in his life when he had tried to reform. He was carrying regularly for a top-class American golfer who eventually won the Open. This stylish player, in his forays to the British circuit, relied heavily on Froggy's local knowledge but was offended by his sinful lifestyle. Since he was a member of some obscure American religious sect which eschewed tobacco, alcohol and premarital sex, he tried to convert his caddie. Froggy, mainly for the sake of his generous retainer and the equally generous bonuses which glittered on the horizon, swore off drink, tobacco and even gambling. He lasted about ten days; through the week prior to the Open and until a couple of days before the tournament began. On the Tuesday his American boss had a practice round in the morning, practised for a couple of hours, pronounced himself satisfied and arranged to meet Froggy at ten o'clock the next day.

One of his more persistent cronies persuaded him to have 'just a little flutter on the four o'clock at Newbury'. Unfortunately for Froggy the outsider romped in, the unexpected bonus of nearly £100 led to 'just one drink' to celebrate, and by throwing out time that night all the money had gone and Froggy was legless. He didn't make it to the course on the next day, was sacked, and always maintained that if he hadn't given up the drink for those ten days or so and 'dried out' he would not have got so drunk, would have been on the course at the appointed time, would not have lost his job, and would have have carried for yet another Open Champion. So it was all the straitlaced American's fault.

He never reached such eminence again and had caddied, less reliably and more cantankerously, for a succession of middling golfers.

We had reached the hut and I didn't know what to do. I hoped Tony would know. He did and took the initiative in his firm but unassuming way.

'You stay outside, Jack,' he told his assistant, and he warily put his head round the door and then went in. I followed, even more warily, and my eyes confirmed what I did not want to believe.

'Right, let's get back to the clubhouse and ring the police. Hop on the back of the buggy, Chris.'

We took the shortest route back to the clubhouse. Tony went as fast as he could, and I was concentrating on staying on board as we rattled over the bumpy paths. We were all too shocked to say anything more than 'Poor old Froggy' and 'Who on earth could have done it?' Violent death, thank God, is a stranger to most people, and all three of us were knocked sideways.

It was only just after seven o'clock and the course was coming to life. The early starters were already on the practice ground and the putting green. We drew up by the main entrance and Tony and I went through the swing doors at speed and headed for the secretary's office.

It was already chaotically busy with officials and administrators knitting together the many responsibilities which would eventually make a successful tournament. Without ceremony, we headed past all these busy people and knocked on the half-open door of the secretary's office.

James Spicer had been a major in an infantry regiment and looked the part in a well-cut tweed suit, burnished brown brogues and his regimental tie. But his years in charge of a thriving and successful golf club had softened his hard-edged military manner, and he had trained himself to adopt an informal, 'civilian' manner.

'Morning, Chris. Hi, Tony. What's the problem?' Yes, he could see that there was a problem.

Tony took the lead, and with a succinctness that would certainly have satisfied any military man, said:

'We must call the police. Froggy Davies has been killed. He's in the hut by the ninth.'

Spicer got to his feet and stared at us. His mind had no doubt been on a myriad of problems, from the amount of lavatory paper required in the clubhouse to the quality of the claret in the sponsor's dining room.

He started to speak, but was interrupted by the slightly flat tones of the London suburbs:

13

'And what the hell will this do to my tournament?'

The speaker rose from his chair at the side of the room. He was smallish and dressed in a dark, lightweight suit with a rather violent striped shirt and the Royal Bucks Golf Club tie. He was tanned, fit-looking and fortyish, and had dark frizzy hair which might have been permed. This was obviously the sponsor, the chairman of World Wide Insurance, Brian Summers. I had occasionally seen his photograph as I skimmed the financial sections of the newspapers.

James Spicer, his military persona now well to the fore, ignored the question and picked up the phone.

'Put me through to the police office, please,' he said to someone in the outer office. While he waited he asked us a few basic and searching questions about our discovery. He then summed up the situation in brusque style for the policeman at the other end.

At every major tournament there is a police presence, partly to control the crowds, partly for security reasons since a lot of money is collected at the gate; and occasionally to deal with spectators who have lingered too long in the beer tents.

James Spicer put down the phone and turned to Brian Summers.

'First, Brian, there is no reason why this should affect the playing of the tournament. We shall carry on as if it has not happened. The major problem will be the Press, who will be here in their droves, and television who are already here.'

'Chris, what have you got to do with all this?' Under pressure the secretary became more and more military, and his question sounded almost like an accusation.

'I found him, when I was walking the course,' I said apprehensively.

'Well, you must be prepared to make a statement to the police. And you too, Tony.' He turned back to me. 'Let's see, what time is your man off the first tee?' he consulted a piece of paper. 'Eleven o'clock, so you should be OK. Your partners are Jose Miguel and Brian Harley.'

The first was a steady performer who was invariably among the top twenty money-winners at the end of each season. 'Steady' summed him up: he was adroit and unspectacular in all departments of the game. It was only when you looked at his score at the end of a round that you realised that somehow he was three under par.

Brian Harley was the reverse. When he had come on the scene about fifteen years earlier he had been a spectacular hitter of a golf ball and a brilliant putter: a fearsome blend of talents in a golfer – if they combine regularly. They did for a couple of years, and he won several tournaments and appeared in the Ryder Cup at the age of twenty-two. His game then deteriorated and he was rarely in the top fifty in a tournament, let alone the top ten. Later there came a reprimand for a breach of rules and, not long after, a six-month suspension for a further misdemeanour. He drank too much and was usually overweight but, to his credit, had dragged himself back into the top thirty on the circuit in the last couple of years. This year he had begun brilliantly on the Safari circuit in Africa, had won two tournaments and headed their Order of Merit. His form had continued with a win by several strokes in the Madrid Open and a high finish in the Italian Championship.

James Spicer interrupted my thoughts.

'Good God, Froggy carries for Harley. Where is he staying?' He picked up his phone again.

'Anne, bring us all some coffee please, and ring Brian Harley wherever he's billetted.'

Five minutes later the coffee arrived and so did a call from Brian Harley. Spicer told him the news and asked him if he would like a local caddie to be booked. Apparently not, Harley would make his own arrangements.

At this stage two men, unknown to any of us, were introduced by the industrious Anne, whose excited curiosity was increasing by the second.

'Inspector Drew and Sergeant Aitken,' she announced, and hovered by the door.

'That's all, thank you, Anne,' said the secretary, 'except for two more coffees.' Disappointed, she withdrew.

Inspector Drew was not a man who would stand out in a crowd. All detectives wear raincoats and his, a dark one, covered a charcoal-grey suit, a white shirt and an unidentifiable club tie of the striped variety. He could have been a computer salesman. His face was ordinary, slightly florid, but enlivened by bright and very blue eyes. His assistant, who was about my age, affected a more stylish dress, with an off-white raincoat which looked like a Hong Kong copy of a Burberry and a mid-blue suit with lapels which were fashionably narrow.

The Inspector took charge.

'I shall need statements from both of you,' he said, turning to Tony and me.

James Spicer explained that we both had pressing jobs to do and the Inspector agreed to take my statement immediately and that Tony could go off and make his final checks of the golf course and make his statement later.

'Right, let's get this done before the Press get wind of what's happened,' said Inspector Drew. 'Please may we borrow your office for a few minutes, Major Spicer?'

For the first time I had to tell my story logically, and the effort which this entailed, under the critical questioning of the Inspector, dispelled some of the depression which I felt. Less than one hour had passed since I had found Froggy's body, but it felt a lot longer.

'How well did you know Froggy Davies?' the Inspector asked.

'Mainly by repute. He was one of the old school, not exactly sleeping under hedges, but an itinerant caddie. You never quite know what they do or where they go in winter, though I'm told Froggy had a sister in the Birmingham area.'

'Would a caddie like Davies make a lot of money?'

'In general, no, Inspector. He wasn't out on the Safari circuit with Brian Harley so wouldn't have picked up his bonuses.'

I explained that a caddie is normally paid a retainer by the professional, plus a bonus of five percent of winnings, sometimes a little more. Not many caddies can make a decent living this way. It's fine if all year round you carry the bag of a genuine superstar, who might win £500,000; but a caddie who works for a golfer who is outside the top twenty in the Order of Merit will not exactly be reaching for the champagne every night.

'So how much would Froggy reckon to make in a season?' asked Inspector Drew.

'Difficult to say,' I replied. 'Last year he mostly caddied for Lars Persson, who finished around twenty-fifth in the Order of Merit and so he probably made less than five thousand pounds. And that would mostly have gone on booze and horses. But the way Brian

Harley is playing at the moment he must have been hoping to double that at least.'

'Do you think another caddie could have killed Froggy in order to get the job with Harley?'

I didn't like the way the questions were going, and in particular the concentration that was now all too apparent in Inspector Drew's eyes. Talk about the Ancient Mariner.

'Possible, but unlikely,' I said lamely.

'How much did you earn from caddying last season, sir?'

I didn't like the way he slipped in the 'sir' either.

Jack had had a good to middling season and with pro-ams and the occasional exhibition match I had earned nearly £8000.

At this point Sergeant Aitken came in and muttered something in the Inspector's ear.

'You'd better get back to your tournament, Mr Ludlow,' he said. 'But I would like to see you again this evening to take a fuller statement.'

Off I went to resume normal existence and my first priority, since it was now nearly nine o'clock and I was due to meet Jack Mason at a quarter to ten, was breakfast. I felt slightly ashamed that my priority was breakfast, but excused it on the grounds that shock probably induced hunger. I was on my way towards the main door of the clubhouse when I saw a cluster of men who could only be journalists. They surged forward but were held back by two very large and determined security men. I knew the clubhouse well from my amateur days and I quickly turned left, went through the main lounge (to the horror of one member who recognised me not as a former amateur golfer but as a caddie, God dammit), through the back of the already busy bar and through the goods entrance, or exit in this case. I breathed again, and decided to walk a few hundred yards down the road to a Happy Diner for a rapid sandwich and a cup of tea. I had some fruit in my car and this would sustain me during the round.

'Can I buy you breakfast?' asked a voice behind me.

I turned and the expletives died on my lips. It was a journalist, but Toby Greenslade was one of the rare ones who could write entertainingly about golf, and was a companionable and amusing fellow as well.

'I heard about Froggy,' he said, 'and that you found him with the shaft of a golf club stuck through his gullet,' he finished brightly. 'Will you give me an exclusive interview?'

'Sod off, Toby,' I said in friendly fashion. 'I want my breakfast and then to get on with my job.'

'I'm told that he may still have been alive when the murderer, or murderers, hammered the shaft through his neck and into the floor of the hut. Nasty, eh?'

We were by now seated in the Happy Diner, and I was still rather amazed that I could face a bacon sandwich. But down it went and it stayed down.

I tried to change the subject. 'Who's going to caddie for Harley, by the way?'

'Derek Jefferson, apparently,' replied Toby.

He was the managing director of Supersight Golf, and had been selling golf clubs for as long as most people could remember. He had been sales director for the major British manufacturer and had left two or three years ago when they were absorbed into a large industrial conglomerate. It was said that he was not enamoured of the tight business disciplines which they attempted to impose. He had started Supersight and had made quite an impact on an already highly competitive market with some clubs and putters which were a shade too gimmicky for me, but were tailor-made for the average club golfer, who will buy anything if it is 'guaranteed to add fifteen yards to your drive'.

However, Jefferson had done well, in no small way due to his own considerable abilities as a salesman. He was a large and out-wardly jovial man in his early fifties, with a gift for generating publicity for himself and his products. At tournaments and trade shows he always offered 'open house' and you could eat and drink all day at his expense if you wished, and many did.

'Have you seen the new Supersight putter?' asked Toby. I hadn't. 'Apparently you can't miss, but only Brian Harley has got one so far, and this is mainly why he cleaned up on the Safari circuit. All the other pros are going mad to get hold of them, but Jefferson says this is the only one – a prototype in the real sense – and it won't be in production for several months.'

'What's the secret?' I asked.

'Well, if there is a secret, only Harley knows it. It looks fairly ordinary, although it's one of the "big head" designs and it seems to be made of some sort of high-tech composite of plastic and metal. But Harley never lets it out of his sight. He sleeps with it, I'm told. That must give some of the girls a shock – a pleasant one, perhaps.'

I grinned at Toby. Brian Harley, with a failed marriage behind him, was one of several golfers on the tour who were renowned for their ability to pull the women. Interest in golf has grown so rapidly in the last ten years that it has reached out beyond its traditional confines and become glamorous. And the appeal of the professional golfers has grown with the sport, so that they are much sought after, not only in boardrooms but in bedrooms, too.

'Do you fancy Harley's chances?' I asked Toby.

'The way he's putting he could win anything, even though the rest of his game is no better than average. But he's so confident on the greens that the rest of his game doesn't seem to matter and, of course, as Willie Park said, "the man who can putt . . ." '

' ". . . is a match for anyone." ' I completed one of the great truths of golf.

Every professional knows that if he holes a few of those vital putts of eight feet or more, it can transform his whole round and maybe make him into a winner. Not only is his score likely to be several shots better, but a little success on the greens can infect a golfer's whole game. Suddenly he is more relaxed and confident and those horrible little worms of self-doubt which are perpetually burrowing away in a golfer's head are banished – for a few holes, anyway.

This is why professional golfers spend hour after hour on the practice greens in an effort to find that Holy Grail of golf – a consistent and ever-repeating putting stroke. Like the Holy Grail, it is a dream, a tantalising illusion. Now you have it and now you don't.

Putting is one of the enigmas of an extraordinarily difficult game. You have all heard the club golfer who says of his opponent, after losing a match, 'he putted like God.' What he really means is that he putted like the devil and it was grossly unfair; there is even a feeling that it is 'not quite golf' to win by superior skill on the greens.

The careers of many great champions have been blighted and eventually ruined by their putting. Look at Ben Hogan, a legend and a perfectionist who gave up the game when he was struck down by the dreaded 'yips'. Another past champion graphically described this as the moment when the golfer blacks out and hasn't the remotest idea that he is holding a putter at all. Every golfer in the world experiences that awful feeling of helplessness when he stands over a putt and knows that he has not the slightest chance of getting the ball near the hole, let alone into it. Conversely, a golfer occasionally has a phase when the hole really seems larger and it seems possible to hole almost every putt.

Obviously Brian Harley was going through one of those phases, and felt that he could one-putt every green. Lucky fellow. Before much longer fellow professionals would be wanting to touch his clothing just in case some 'fluence' would rub off on them.

'You know, by the way, that Brian's got a new agent, do you? Oh yes, he ditched Graham who's looked after him for over ten years through thick and thin, and mainly thin, in favour of Mike Martinez.'

This was news to me, although I knew Graham Fearnley, who was Jack Mason's agent and looked after quite a big stable of European golfers. He was really the only opposition to the powerful American golf managers, of whom Mike Martinez was the most successful, with clients in tennis, baseball, motor racing and with worldwide television interests as well. Many people thought he was too powerful, especially when he was able to set up his own sponsored tournaments, sometimes in opposition to official ones, into which he put his own clients and then sold the television rights around the world. He was powerful all right.

'Toby, I don't understand why Martinez would want to sign up Brian Harley.'

'Neither does anyone else, but of course Graham's furious now that he's started winning, because for the first time for years he could have set up some good contracts – and not least collected some commission on the bonuses paid by Hi-Flight.'

Toby was referring to the clause which was usually written into contracts between golfers and the manufacturer who supplies their equipment. Hi-Flight, as well as paying Harley an annual retainer to play with and publicise their equipment, would pay bonuses for wins in official tournaments.

Toby continued. 'Martinez pulled him out of the Hi-Flight contract and signed him up with Supersight.'

It sounded as if Martinez' legendary foresight had paid off yet again. He was famous for picking sportsmen young and preparing them for success; but in this case he had picked an apparent no-hoper like Harley, who immediately confirmed his judgement by notching up three tournament victories.

I was going to be late for Jack Mason and made for the door. I asked Toby to do me a favour and tell the Fleet Street 'dirty mac brigade', who covered crime and other seedy activities, that I had given him an exclusive.

# Chapter 3

I made it to the front of the clubhouse just in time to seize Jack's bag and head for the practice ground. Toby hadn't had time to try the 'exclusive' story on the dirty mac brigade and they clustered about me and shouted the usual obvious questions. I kept my head down and the heavy bag well to the fore as a protective shield. You may not realise, as you watch the humble caddie walk the fairways, how heavy that bag is. On its own it's weighty enough; but then you must add fourteen golf clubs, a dozen or so balls, an umbrella, a set of waterproofs, spare sweaters, caps and visors, half a dozen golf gloves, a book of rules, tins of sweets, bars of chocolates, apples, bananas and other fruit and, in Jack Mason's case, sometimes a couple of bottles of strong beer. It all weighs about forty pounds, and I carefully bumped, to good effect, into several of the more persistent reporters.

Jack was a good ally and more or less scared them off. When told to sod off by a man well over six feet tall, about fourteen stones in weight, with a four-iron in his hand, and known to be of uncertain temperament, even the most hardened reporter will do just that.

We reached the haven of the practice ground and went past the barrier. The tournament was, as far as we were concerned, about to begin.

Jack began his practice in his usual fashion by hitting a few half shots with the short irons. The objective was to try to reproduce a smooth and consistent swing; to trigger the muscle memory to produce such a swing automatically. A professional golfer tries to pull off a confidence trick against his own body.

During the approaching round the time would come, inevitably, when he would have to play a shot under immense pressure. It might be a recovery shot from deep rough with a minute margin for error; or a pitch shot from a bare lie over a bunker to a flag in a very tight position; or simply a six-foot putt to save par. These are the examinations that a golfer's hours of practice are designed to pass. The mind must try to lull the body into the automatic response that has been instilled during practice. At his best, the golfer gets 'outside himself'; he is a detached observer of his own actions and the shot is hit automatically. A conditioned reflex.

This was what Jack, and most of the other pros on the practice ground, was trying to achieve. He was now on to the mid-irons and these were flying high and true. He hit a few three-irons and three-woods and that was it. We walked over to the practice putting green and set about his putting. His stroke looked pretty smooth to me and he was obviously confident.

There was a better than average crowd watching us and a fair number were Press photographers who were intent on getting pictures of the unwitting discoverer of Froggy's body. But at least they were kept under control by several large gentlemen from the security company. There was also a surprisingly large contingent watching another golfer at his putting practice. I was about to ask Jack who it was, when the penny dropped. It was Brian Harley, but a new and obviously improved Brian Harley. For a start, he was considerably slimmer – around two stones had disappeared, I guessed – and was dressed in very jazzy style with the Supersight logo very much to the fore. Which was just as well because Derek Jefferson, the managing director of the firm, was there as the stand-in caddie, and was similarly dressed in Supersight clothing.

Many eyes were on his putter, which looked very *Star Wars*, with its large, rather bulbous head in some sort of black metal and plastic and a black shaft which looked slightly thicker than normal. Like Jack, he was trying to concentrate on smoothing out his stroke, but several reporters were waiting to ask questions about his dead caddie and Harley knew it.

A few minutes before we were all due on the first tee a tall and sturdy figure, crowned with a near-bald, sun-tanned head, appeared through the crowd. He was Oliver Moreton, the PGA tournament director, and he motioned Jack, Brian Harley and Jose Miguel and their caddies to the centre of the practice green and out of hearing of the cluster of Press men.

'You all know about Froggy,' he began briskly. 'I am glad to see, Brian, that you have such an excellent replacement,' he continued, a little ironically, with a glance at Derek Jefferson.

'You will all have to put up with a certain amount of unwelcome attention from the Press, but I have warned them that we will not tolerate any interference with your golf. So, carry on as usual, and good luck.'

He strode off in his usual busy fashion and left us to 'carry on as usual'. I wondered how Harley would cope. The tournament did, after all, offer a lot of prize money with £60,000 to the winner, and was therefore very important in the battle for inclusion in the Ryder Cup team. Harley was coming into it as an early-season form horse and was therefore in the news, and now his caddie had been murdered so he was very much in the news. Quite difficult to 'carry on as usual', I thought.

The first tee was packed and the cameras were clicking like type-writers. After the announcer had introduced the players and called for quiet, Jack Mason did an unusual thing. He walked over to Brian Harley, who was first to drive, and shook his hand. 'Good luck, Brian, and now let battle commence,' he said.

It was a generous gesture to try to ease the tension and relax a fellow professional. Nevertheless Brian Harley hit a sketchy drive down the right-hand side of the fairway and his shot to the green was partly masked by encroaching trees on the right. But he got the ball near the left edge of the green, flicked it confidently over the bunker to about four feet and holed out with ease. Jack had a conventional par four – a good drive, a smooth four-iron to the middle of the green and two putts. It's an easy game, really.

On the walk to the next tee, I nodded to Derek Jefferson and asked: 'When is this famous putter going into production?'

'Later in the year, we hope. Brian's got the prototype but it needs a lot of testing still.'

'The way Brian's putting with it you seem to have something good, don't you?'

'Maybe,' he said guardedly, put Harley's bag down, and got out his driver.

Again, Brian Harley hit a less-than-perfect drive, but his two-iron across the angle of the dogleg put him on the front edge of the green. His two opponents were safely on in two. Derek Jefferson held the pin for Harley's approach putt of about fifty feet. It was downhill, and with a left-to-right break of several feet. Nasty.

It didn't bother Brian Harley because he holed a very unlikely putt and went one under par after two holes.

By the turn, this had become the pattern of the round. Jack was very much in the groove, rarely deviating from the fairways and the centre of the green, but was a mere one shot under par, while Miguel was one shot better. Harley, however, was all over the course, but his short game and especially his putting was brilliant. He was four under par, and never looked like missing a putt.

Fortunately for the players, only accredited golfing journalists were allowed to encroach on the fairways and everyone else was kept firmly behind the ropes and barriers which ran along the perimeter of each hole. The golf journalists knew enough not to ask any leading questions in the middle of a round, and they were sufficiently wary of Jack's temperament and his considerable command of the pointed rebuke. There was, nevertheless, an unusually large crowd, including one or two golf journalists who rarely saw a golf course. They usually watched the action on the television in the Press tent or, even better, in the champagne tent. They had obviously received strict orders from their editors not to miss a story.

We skirted the now-notorious refreshment hut, which was marked off with those fluorescent orange ribbons that usually signal a particularly nasty accident, and which was now guarded by two policemen.

'Was that where . . . ?' began Brian Harley.

'Yes, it was,' I said quickly, 'and it was not a pretty sight.'

I hoped nobody would pursue the matter, and the golfers had other things on their minds anyway.

But Derek Jefferson wanted to know more and asked how Froggy was killed.

'He was stabbed through the neck with the shaft of a golf club,' I said, with no attempt at, or wish for, subtlety.

I watched his face as he blinked rapidly and he looked at me in disgust, or was it disbelief? He muttered something, turned his back on me, and strode on to the tenth tee. There were no more questions on that subject during the rest of the round.

The second half of the course is a more difficult proposition, with five very difficult par fours to test the golfer's nerves and his abilities. Any thought in his mind of trying to protect a good score will rarely be successful; he must meet the challenge squarely or drop shots. Jack dropped a couple of shots with poor putts but got them both back with a superb eagle at the sixteenth – an uphill par five with a difficult green, long and narrow and well protected with bunkers. Jose Miguel had been his usual model of self-effacing but steely efficiency and he seemed to have conjured another two birdies from the course without anyone noticing, although he too had dropped one shot. Brian Harley had made his one mistake at the sixteenth by finding both a fairway bunker and one by the green and was still standing at four under.

The two finishing holes are designed to test the last reserves of the golfer's confidence. They are both over 450 yards and their design, as they curve through the protection of the heavy trees with a scattering of bunkers on the angles of the fairways, induces tremors in even the most hardened competitors.

Harley was in trouble off the seventeenth tee. His swing was taut and abbreviated as, despite what his golfing mind was telling him (swing slow, swing smoothly through the ball), the darker side of his mind made him try to steer the ball. The ghost had definitely got into the machine. His drive went low up the right side of the fairway and faded impotently into the heather. He managed to hack it forward just to the angle of the fairway, and had still not reached his opponents' drives which were about thirty yards ahead. He was now faced with a shot of about 230 yards, with the prospect of dropping one shot at best, but possibly two. In the circumstances, he made a fair pass at the ball and got it into a reasonable spot about fifteen yards short of the edge of the green and about thirty yards from the hole. This is the shot that the club golfer dreads and that the professional, with his adroitness with his chipping and pitching clubs, loves. I was duly astonished when Harley asked for his putter and sent Derek Jefferson ahead to hold the flag. With fifteen yards of quite lush fairway to cover before the ball even reached the putting surface, the margin for error was dangerously small. He gave the ball a very sweet hit and off it went. It reached the green at a good speed, took a right-to-left swing, and disappeared into the hole. I looked at Jack Mason who just shook his head, gave one of his sourer smiles, and then also holed out for a four.

The drama was not quite over because all three players managed to hit the last green in two shots, and Harley, by dint of a nice kick forward when the ball pitched, was no more than six feet from the hole. Jack and Miguel got their pars and it was Harley's turn to go for a closing birdie to put him well up the leader board. He asked his caddie to hold the pin. This was highly unusual, since most golfers prefer their caddies to be well out of the way for such crucial short putts. It looked positively eccentric as Jefferson stood alongside the hole. I wondered how Harley would relish a putt back over Jefferson's footprint – a substantial one since he was a good fifteen stones in weight – if the putt hit the hole and bounced left. My speculation was irrelevant – the putt went straight in the middle of the cup.

There were handshakes all round and the usual 'well playeds', and we headed for the PGA hut where the scores are checked and handed in. It is extraordinary how often professional golfers record the wrong score or add it up incorrectly. The PGA therefore allows them a sort of cooling-off period at the end of a round to check each other's scores thoroughly. The rules on incorrect scores are simple and Draconian: if you sign for a score which is lower than your actual score you are disqualified; if you sign for a higher score than your actual, the higher score stands.

We waited near the PGA hut, and I particularly wanted Jack's instructions, if any, for the rest of the day. Sometimes he wanted to practise, and might well require an hour or so on the putting green, or sometimes he fancied a pint or two of some obscure real ale that he had heard of in the vicinity. Not today, however.

'That's fine, Chris,' he said, 'I'll see you at about one thirty tomorrow.' He had a late starting time at three o'clock.

He turned to Brian Harley who was talking to Jefferson. 'Well putted, Brian, you bugger. Let's have a look at that putter of yours. I reckon I need one of those,' he said.

Jefferson deliberately put the leather hood on Harley's bag and zipped it up.

'Sorry, Jack,' he said, 'that's the only one available and is for Brian's use only. We might have some more prototypes in a couple of weeks and you're welcome to one of those.'

'Suit yourself. Are you worried I'll take away the magic, or what?' he asked sarcastically. But Jefferson just nodded, not in his usual jovial manner, and walked off with Brian Harley.

I guessed it was the shock of Froggy's death, and the tension of caddying for one of his contracted professionals. Certainly it was unusual to refuse another golfer a practice with a new putter because professionals are notorious for trying each other's equipment, and for swapping clubs. But I put it down to a natural wish on Jefferson's part to protect what for him was a considerable investment in a new club and, if Harley's new agent had exacted his usual pound, or stone rather, of flesh, a considerable investment in a golf pro.

As we walked off towards the car park, a woman's voice shouted my name.

'Chris, a message for you.'

I turned towards the voice and saw a slender young woman hurrying towards me. She was dressed in the gear which the PGA encouraged for their female employees, dark trousers with a pastel-coloured sweater. She looked familiar, and I was soon looking into the green and expressive eyes of Sally Drayton, who had been a fellow student at Sussex University.

'What on earth are you doing here?' I asked.

'I'm working for Oliver Moreton,' Sally said.

'And I work for Jack Mason,' I said and introduced them. Jack who, despite his stable and untroubled domestic life, was not averse to an occasional dalliance with a pretty girl, loomed over her in genial fashion.

'Nice to meet you, Sally. And a word of advice – just you be careful of that old goat, Moreton. And Chris, I'll see you tomorrow.' Diplomatically, he took the golf bag from me and headed for the car park.

'How long have you been with the PGA?' I asked.

'Oh, about three weeks. I'm Oliver's personal assistant.'

'Not too personal, I hope,' I said pointedly. At Sussex University I had harboured hopes of getting very personal with Sally Drayton. She was *the* female student of her year. Apart from her looks, and especially those deep green eyes, she was cheerful and friendly and seemingly unaware of the effect she had on the unsophisticated young men around her. Not for her that studied aloofness which so

29

many attractive women mistakenly affect. She had on several occasions fobbed off my clumsy advances with great ease and much friendliness. So much so that even when I had abandoned hopes of luring her into my narrow and uncomfortable bed, we frequently got together for a drink or a cheap meal.

But after university, despite our protestations of eternal friendship and vows to get together, the gaps between our meetings and our phone calls had got longer and longer. The last communication had been a letter from somewhere on the west coast of America, and my eventual reply had been returned 'not known at this address'. That was about five years ago.

'Where are you living these days – in London by the sea?' I asked her. Her parents used to live just inland from Brighton in a converted windmill.

'No. My parents are still there, but I've just bought a little flat in Fulham.'

'Well, I live in Putney, so do you fancy a drink or a meal, or something? Preferably the something,' I said with a hopeful smile.

'A drink will be fine, Chris,' she said and her friendly grin took any primness out of the remark. I knew that it would at the very least be fun to fail again, however effortlessly, and we agreed to meet at a pub in Barnes on the following evening.

'By the way, a message for you. Inspector Drew wants to see you at five o'clock at Richmond Police Station.'

I had almost forgotten about him and immediately felt depressed as I trudged off to find my car. Apart from having to go over the unpleasant details of Froggy's death yet again, I had a nasty feeling that Inspector Drew's bright and suspicious eyes masked darker ideas about my role in Froggy's murder.

At five minutes to five I parked my car alongside Richmond Police Station, and on the dot of five o'clock was shown into Inspector Drew's office. Without any preamble, except the customary offer of a cup of tea which I declined, the Inspector began to take me in painstaking detail through my account of my discovery of Froggy's body. After this, more questions.

'Would it surprise you to hear that Froggy Davies was stabbed with a golf shaft that is specially made for Supersight?' asked Inspector Drew.

'I didn't stay around long enough to check the make, Inspector,' I said, pointedly.

'Of course not. But you understand that someone went to a deal of trouble to sharpen it, well in advance, and so must have planned the murder. It obviously wasn't just a quarrel which got out of hand, or robbery with violence.'

Inspector Drew was looking at me very closely, and I felt rather like a naughty schoolboy under the stern gaze of the headmaster. Uncomfortable.

He continued: 'Someone with a very sadistic outlook committed that murder; someone who obviously doesn't like Supersight and its owner, or who possibly doesn't like Brian Harley.' He paused again and gazed over my shoulder and I wondered what was coming next.

'Would you also be surprised to hear that Froggy Davies had given his sister nearly two thousand pounds in cash?'

It was certainly a day for surprises, because Froggy had probably never seen so much cash in one lump, let alone earned it.

'Well, he has been caddying for Harley in Europe, and he did win one tournament and finished equal second in the other. So, his bonuses would have brought him over two thousand pounds.'

I was thinking to myself that he would have blown most of it on horses and strong drink. His mind would gleefully have converted the money into his own units of currency – large whiskies and five-pound yankees.

Inspector Drew was obviously a mind-reader, too. He said: 'You are thinking what I'm thinking, aren't you, that Froggy would normally have squandered the lot?'

'Well, maybe he'd seen the error of his ways,' I said lamely.

'Maybe not,' said Inspector Drew, grimly.

The Inspector left it at that and as I was waiting expectantly for the interview to end, he said: 'Why does an educated man like you spend his time caddying? You went to a good school and then to a reasonably good university, didn't you?'

Shades of my father, I thought, but replied amicably: 'Because I enjoy it, and remember that I don't work at it the whole year, so I don't get bored.'

'Not even with the company of people like Froggy Davies?'

'I don't spend much of my time with the other caddies, Inspector. I have the occasional drink with my current boss, Jack Mason, but otherwise have my own friends.'

'So would the other caddies regard you as stand-offish, a bit of a snob perhaps?' he asked.

'Some of them.'

'Especially when they see you getting into your Porsche, and driving off to the flat you own in Putney?'

There was a harshness to Inspector Drew's questions, despite their quiet, almost conversational delivery, and I tried hard not to become uncomfortable under his eye.

'Look, Inspector, Dave Wheatley caddies for Bjorn Carlssen, who guarantees him twenty thousand a year, and he earns at least double that. He's also got a Porsche, and a more expensive one than mine, and he's even sponsored by Carlssen's clothing company.'

'Yes, but he's a very successful caddie with one of the highest earners in the game outside the States,' said Drew. 'You are not. You carry for Jack Mason who won just over a hundred thousand last year in tournaments. So, do I assume that you have a private income?'

I explained that I worked during the winter for a golf-mad stockbroker called Andrew Buccleuth whom I had met during my year on the amateur circuit. I also kept my contacts and my work going during the golf season, even if I did it mostly by telephone. The telephone answering machine, and my clients' willingness to talk to me at unusual hours of the day and night, kept me firmly in touch.

My father had initially encouraged my interest in the stock market and I had jumped at the chance of a part-time job in the City. I had become something of an expert in the leisure market, and to many of the institutional buyers had some spurious extra authority simply because I could hit a golf ball further and straighter than they could. As the share markets of the eighties rocketed upwards so did my commission and much of it was reinvested.

I was happy with the arrangement because I did not want to be tied to a nine-to-five existence, and my employer remained happy, especially when I made regular appearances as his partner at various golf days – all good for business, of course.

We both suspected that it could not last, but it even survived the Big Bang when the leisurely practices of the City – short days, long lunches, and three-day weekends – supposedly ended.

Everyone was believed to be glued to their computer screens from seven in the morning until nine at night. Andrew Buccleuth certainly had his fair share of brokers and analysts doing exactly that, but he had a more relaxed view of the duties of a salesman – and especially of one who enabled him to win substantial bets on the golf courses of southern England.

Inspector Drew listened, and nodded. Not approvingly, because that world of brokers and bankers and speculators, piling their insubstantial castles of paper money ever higher, was foreign to him – and judging by the look on his face, anathema.

'Mr Ludlow, let me test a theory on you. You are a young man who is a part-time caddie and a part-time stockbroker, and you don't seem to be particularly successful at either job. You have heavy commitments, a flat on which you probably spent over a hundred and fifty thousand pounds, a Porsche to run, and a suitably lavish way of life, no doubt.

'You earned, by your own admission, less than ten thousand from caddying last year and, late in the year, there was quite a drop in the stock market. It caused a lot of financial pain to a lot of people, and especially to the fast operators in the City who were over-extended with investments in secondary stocks and flashy shell companies. And I can't say I have the slightest sympathy for them, and I would also guess that you were one of those caught with their financial trousers down.'

Well, Inspector Drew had certainly hoisted his colours to the mast. I began to speak, but was silenced by a stern look from the Inspector and a raising of his hand.

'So, perhaps a really cynical person would conjecture that you need the money that caddying for a golfer like Harley, who is obviously back in form and on the verge of some big wins and big money, would bring. And that being an intelligent man you planned the murder to divert any suspicion from yourself to someone who had some sort of grudge against Brian Harley or Derek Jefferson.'

I looked at Inspector Drew for several seconds while I tried to marshal my tumbling thoughts.

33

'A couple of points, Inspector. I have no wish to caddie for Brian Harley; I am happy working for Jack. Second, the motive – money – doesn't apply.

'You are quite right that the decline in the market caught a lot of people short. But I was lucky. About two months before, I sold almost all my shares in order to buy the flat. I wanted a manageable mortgage. So I put down a hundred thousand in cash and took out an eighty-thousand mortgage.'

I can't say that my revelations were having any effect on the Inspector. He sat unmoved.

'If you want proof, you can see my bank account and all my share-dealing records.'

'Yes, I will probably want to,' he said ominously. 'Well, that's all. For the time being.'

If the Inspector had planned to unsettle me for some reason, he had succeeded. As I walked across the car park I looked back at the police station and almost expected to see the figure of Inspector Drew looming at one of the windows – as in an early Orson Welles film. I actually felt guilty as I climbed into my Porsche, and then kicked myself hard, metaphorically, and told myself not to let a nasty-minded Police Inspector upset me. The car was, after all, three years old and had over 50,000 miles on the clock.

# Chapter 4

When I reached my flat on the ground floor of a huge house in a quiet road off Putney Hill, I reflected that it had been, to put it very mildly, a somewhat taxing day.

I was thinking about the relative merits of a bottle or two of Ruddles from the fridge or a glass or two of Sancerre or even, in the circumstances, something stronger, when there was a knock on my door.

There was a peremptory sharpness to the knock which announced the presence of Mrs Bradshaw, a lady in her early sixties who lived in the next-door flat. When I moved in to my flat she had to a certain extent taken me over, and treated me like an erring and somewhat unintelligent son who obviously needed the care and attention of a responsible adult. She insisted on cleaning my flat very thoroughly every Tuesday and Thursday, and often left me a casserole in the oven. I had never been able to persuade her to accept any money for her kindness and tried to reciprocate by doing any small repairs she needed to her flat, and by supplying occasional tickets for the theatre, for the tennis at Wimbledon, and for the races at Epsom. I also guided her occasionally in the stock market: she shared these tips and the jaunts with her friend from around the corner, Mrs Warburton, who was also widowed.

I opened the door and there was the commanding figure of Mrs Bradshaw. She was dressed in a sensible tweed skirt and a rather elegant cashmere sweater. Her widowhood had thankfully not reduced her circumstances too drastically and had certainly not altered her sense of style. Her hair, as always, was immaculately arranged.

'Chris, are you all right? I read about you in the evening paper. What a dreadful business. Is there anything I can do? Have you phoned your mother?'

Mrs Bradshaw had met my mother a couple of times and they plainly approved of each other. Indeed they had spent most of their time reassuring each other that, despite all my obvious failings, I was almost capable of looking after myself – under their joint and several supervision.

Right on cue, the telephone rang and I waved Mrs Bradshaw into my lounge. It was of course my mother, and she asked me the same questions as my neighbour.

I assured her that all was as it seemed, and that I was not under suspicion of murder, and that I was indeed doing all I could to help the police.

'How has Dad taken the news?' I asked.

I was anticipating severe disapproval from that quarter, because my father was bemused, to say the least, by my refusal to settle down into a job with a future, as he put it.

He had been very proud of my golfing prowess when it won me a place in the university golf team, and had even been heard to express his satisfaction when my handicap went down to scratch. Even so, I had been surprised when he agreed to back me on the amateur circuit for one year after I left the university. He could afford it – he was the owner of a successful computer software company. He put up some token resistance: he'd never had my advantages, it was time I got down to some hard work, and so on. But secretly he loved the idea, and it gave him a great kick to tell his friends and business acquaintances that he was supporting his son on the amateur golf circuit.

It was just as well that he didn't know my long-term aim was to be a pro golfer. My grand plan was simple enough, and was one of the traditional ways into the professional game. I would play the amateur circuit to get some hard competitive experience, enter the qualifying school in Portugal at the end of the year, and be a fully fledged tournament pro in the following season. Simple. This is the stuff our dreams are made of, but it didn't quite work out that way. My best finish was in my first major tournament, the Southern Amateur in the cold and rain of Royal Cinque Ports in March. I finished equal fifth and, although I got as far as the final qualifying round for the Open and won through two rounds of the Amateur Championship, that was to be my best result for the year. When I saw the potential ability of so many of my opponents and how young so many of them were, I realised that I would have to devote more time to practice than there was in a day just to become a moderate professional.

My comparative lack of basic talent came home to me on the practice ground before the first round of the Amateur. Alongside me was Sam Ratcliffe who, at the tender age of sixteen, had already had quite a bit of publicity. He was the son of a club professional in the Midlands, and had apparently first swung a golf club when he was about three. He was obviously destined for the professional ranks and as I watched him I could see why. His swing was slow and very compact, and at impact he was beautifully in control of the club. The power he generated with his simple swing was devastating. What really gave it away was the totally different sound his ball made when his club connected. Despite our difference in years, I felt like a boy alongside a man. It was then that I resolved to enjoy the rest of the year, accept that I simply did not have the talent to make the professional grade, and find a job.

My mother told me that Dad was on one of his frequent business trips to America and would be home in a couple of days. I promised to ring him, if he didn't ring me first, reassured her again that everything was fine and that she didn't need to drive over to look after me.

Mrs Bradshaw didn't want a drink because she was going over to Mrs Warburton's flat to play bridge.

'I noticed a man wandering around the garden a couple of hours ago and asked him what he wanted. He asked if this was your flat. Well, I didn't say it was, because you can't be too careful these days with all these burglaries. But I said I knew you and did he want to leave a message. He didn't, and said he'd call you and wouldn't leave a name. Very odd.'

'What did he look like?' I asked.

'Oh, about forty. Blue cord trousers from M&S, I would say, and a maroon sweater. Old training shoes. He was unshaven and looked a bit rough. I didn't take to him. He certainly didn't look like the sort of friend you would have, Chris.'

Mrs Bradshaw was certainly in the Inspector Drew class for observation.

'Well, he doesn't sound like anyone I know,' I said, 'unless he's a caddie who happened to be passing nearby and wanted to quiz me about any work available.'

'Perhaps so,' said Mrs Bradshaw. 'Give my regards to Mr Mason tomorrow, won't you. I shall be watching him on the television.'

She had become a golf fan when she had learned of my job and took a highly personal interest in Jack's performances. He, too, had become part of her vicarious family, and she sent him regular messages of encouragement.

'Now then, Chris, you take it easy and have an early night. You look very tired and I'm not surprised,' she said.

A few reassurances later and she was on her way to do battle at the bridge table.

I glanced at the answering machine in the corner and saw that the red light was glowing. I rewound the tape and prepared to note down any urgent messages. A couple of clients had called me, and I would have time to talk to them in the morning; and I had an invitation to a golf society day in a couple of weeks' time.

The final message was from Andrew Buccleuth, who told me that the shares in one of the leisure companies which I followed closely had dropped a further 20p during the day. I switched on my computer, which gave me access to the prices of all the stocks listed, to price movements of the market as a whole and of individual sectors – a splendid toy, and an essential one. Andrew was right – another fall of 20p. This particular company, with the unusual name of Garth Enterprises, had been quite a glamour stock over the past eighteen months or so, and had a mixture of interests in restaurants, pubs, snooker halls, and property. It was run by a couple of brothers who had started with one large pub in North London and had built the company, by dint of aggressive take-over tactics and shrewd property dealing, to a sizeable enterprise with a turnover of nearly forty million pounds.

Such was the heady nature of the stock market at this time, when share prices in obscure shell companies could shoot upwards on vague promises of exciting future developments, that Garth Enterprises had advanced from being a penny share to the dizzy heights of nearly £4 a share.

One of Andrew Buccleuth's analysts had looked carefully at the company since one of my big customers, a pension fund with vast resources to spend, had bought heavily into the company and so had several of my private clients. We had indeed given several recommendations over the past few months to buy the shares.

About five weeks ago, I had been invited to a presentation by Garth Enterprises, who were unveiling their plans for a golf course and leisure complex which would also include a hotel and the provision of some expensive houses alongside each fairway. God knows how they had conjured up the planning permission for such a venture, situated as it was on the borders of Essex in a green-belt area.

The presentation was smoothly and effectively done by the experienced PR company which Garth Enterprises employed. The inevitable lunch followed, since this is the opportunity for the PR executives heavily to plug the project to the assembled journalists; and to the City boys such as myself and the various stockbrokers' analysts so that we will continue to rate the company as a 'buy'.

It is permissible for journalists to get drunk at these affairs – and indeed encouraged – but not recommended that the executives of the company doing the presentation do so, and especially not the joint managing directors. The Stevens brothers, who had built up Garth Enterprises, got very drunk and very noisy. That's when I began to have doubts about the company. In particular I wondered whether the two brothers would have the capacity and the style to take their company into the upper echelons of the business world.

Stockbrokers issue circulars to all their major clients on a regular basis. They assess specific companies and make recommendations to buy, sell or hold the shares. We were about to issue one, with a buy recommendation, on Garth Enterprises.

I got back to the office and explained my doubts to the analyst. Even if there was a certain amount of personal intuition involved, these questions were real enough, especially with regard to the management skills of the company. Its long-term liquidity was also suspect. We agreed that these doubts were sufficient to justify a recommendation to sell.

Over the next twenty-four hours a flurry of selling, mainly triggered by our circular, sent the shares of Garth Enterprises down by 40p, and by another 50p on the following day. It was then revealed that the two brothers had been on the brink of a merger with a hotel

39

group, a highly respectable one with over fifty good solid hotels in the provinces. The depression in their share price had aborted the deal, and the net result was another 50p off Garth Enterprises shares.

My clients were relieved, but the brothers, George and Mike Stevens were not, and had made their feelings plain to Andrew Buccleuth in language that he did not normally hear outside the fringe theatre, of which he was a generous patron.

My mind was rattling away hard enough without the latest news on Garth Enterprises. I was trying hard to absorb the bizarre happenings of the day. So I manfully postponed the drink I fancied and put on a tracksuit. The drink, whatever it might be, would be all the sweeter after a run, and maybe the relative peace of Wimbledon Common on a mild and gentle spring evening would bring a measure of tranquillity to my mind.

It did, especially after lolling in the bath with the first of several Ruddles. A meal of fresh pasta and a glass of Sancerre ensured that I was sound asleep in front of the television's latest moronic soap opera by ten o'clock. I went to bed, slept like an oak, and woke at around eight o'clock. I could faintly hear the distant rumble of commuter traffic from my bedroom – a reminder of what I had temporarily escaped.

The three newspapers I took were sticking through my front door, which was at the side of the house. It's a bonus to have your papers delivered, but my newspaper boy, like all others, had perfected the art of cramming them in the letter box so that they were shredded as you pulled them inside.

I buy one of the newspapers for its financial pages, another for its news coverage, especially its sport, and the third out of loyalty to my favourite golf correspondent, Toby Greenslade. His talents were wasted on the tabloid for which he worked.

It had once been a middle-of-the-road paper with a big circulation and had traditionally reflected the views, or prejudices, of its middle-of-the-road readers. The advent of racier papers with topless models featured on the inside pages and a grim concentration on the latest doings of talentless television stars, equally talentless soccer stars and the Royal Family had taken away its market. As a result the *Daily News* decided to compete, and sentences of no more than five words and paragraphs of no more than ten did not really suit Toby's style.

A glance at the 'qualities' revealed that Froggy's death had certainly not made either the front or the back page, but I guessed that the *Daily News* might have a headline somewhere. I was unprepared for a full spread on the back page, where normally soccer was king – even in the middle of summer.

## TOP CADDIE SLAIN
## GRIM DISCOVERY BY UPPER-CRUST CADDIE

### An exclusive report by Toby Greenslade

The world of golf is in shock. Froggy Davies, caddie to the golfing superstars, was found murdered early yesterday morning at Royal Bucks Golf Club. He was stabbed through the neck with the sharpened shaft of a golf club. In the early hours of Thursday morning, the murderer skewered him to the wooden floor of a refreshment hut. Dilettante caddie Chris Ludlow, who was educated at Britain's finest public school and a top university (some poetic licence there, I thought) found the body on the morning of one of golf's biggest tournaments, the World Wide Insurance Championships.

In an exclusive interview with the *Daily News*, Chris explained that, while he was walking the course early that morning, he saw that the door of the hut was open.

'I glanced inside, and saw Froggy lying there in a pool of blood. It was ghastly, and a ghastly day for golf. Froggy was a splendid character, and we shall all miss him.'

The chairman of World Wide Insurance, Mr Brian Summers, told me: 'We greatly regret the death of Mr Davies, who was one of the unsung servants of golf. But I know that he would wish the tournament to continue, and we, as sponsors of this great tournament, have a duty to the sporting public to carry on.'

Mr Davies' employer, Brian Harley, who is lying second in the tournament after the first round, was unavailable for comment.

The police are pursuing their inquiries.

Unusually for the *Daily News* there was a tailpiece to the article, set in darker type, with Toby's name attached.

The death of Froggy Davies has certainly removed a real character from the golf scene. He was the genuine article, a caddie who followed the circuit for year after year and carried the bags of two Open Champions.

His death, in such strange circumstances, comes soon after beginning work for Brian Harley who, after so little success over the last few years, has suddenly come good. He has won three tournaments this year; got himself a new agent, the all-powerful American golf manager, Mike Martinez; and a new, and I'm told very lucrative, golf club contract. He also got himself a new caddie, Froggy Davies. To many of us inside the game of golf, Froggy seemed to stick out like a sore thumb in this world of smooth agents, six-figure endorsement contracts and marketing strategies. Someone obviously decided to do something about it, and we wonder why, and who.

This was strong stuff, even if it was wrapped up as mere journalistic conjecture, and obviously Toby knew or suspected something. I decided to telephone him in the hope that he was still soothing his habitual hangover with buckets of orange juice, followed by gallons of coffee. There was no reply, so I would have to contain my curiosity until I got to the golf course.

I had most of the morning to myself and made a few calls to clients, to a financial journalist whose opinion I valued and finally to Andrew Buccleuth. He passed lightly over the Garth Enterprises business and seemed more interested in Brian Harley's putter and the chances of his getting his hands on one. I said I would do my best for him.

I then decided to have a work-out on the weights. In my spare bedroom, which was the size of a ballroom, I had installed a clever piece of apparatus which, despite its compact size, allowed me to exercise most of the essential muscles. I started with five minutes of rowing and then went through the rest of the circuit, and then repeated the process. Forty minutes was enough, but after a shower and a breakfast of fruit and cups of tea I felt very sprightly and strolled out to the row of shops nearby. After browsing in the local bookshop and buying a few necessities for the flat, I decided to leave for the course. I hoped to catch Toby in the Press tent – a good bet since he kept his appearances on the course itself down to the minimum, on the grounds that his editor was not interested in golf but only in scandals that might be unearthed or invented.

I had parked my car about fifty yards down the road. There were only three spaces available on a concreted section of the front garden and I normally left these for the use of Mrs Bradshaw and the two families who lived in the second-floor flats. The parents invariably seemed to be laden with shopping, children, pushchairs, and all the other paraphernalia of parenthood.

As I got nearer the Porsche I saw that during the night someone had taken a sharp instrument to the bodywork. There were deep gouges in the paintwork down both sides and across the bonnet. It was no accident, and I knew I was looking at several hundred pounds worth of damage.

My mind turned back to the man Mrs Bradshaw had accosted in the garden, but I knew of no one who bore me that kind of grudge or, if he did, would take it out on me in such a petty and spiteful way.

Maybe I was just another minor victim of the class war that continues unabated, especially in large cities.

I comforted myself with a few thoughts of what I would do to the culprit if I ever caught him; realised that was highly unlikely, and headed for the golf course.

I parked my car at around midday and set out towards the Press tent. I was tempted through the doors of the trade show. Most big tournaments have a tent in which the major manufacturers of equipment and clothing display their wares. It is another opportunity to promote sales and to entertain customers, and bonhomie is the order of the day. I knew many of the manufacturers from my brief career on the amateur circuit, and was always fascinated by the gimmicks that appeared without fail every year. Revolutionary new . . . clubs, balls, gloves, and even tees; and all guaranteed to add twenty yards to your drive. If they all worked, every golfer would be driving the ball about a quarter of a mile. But I was as susceptible as any other golfer and loved to look at new equipment.

Supersight had one of the biggest stands and it stood, emblazoned with the company logo, in the centre of the tent. Derek Jefferson was there doing what he did best – the hard sell. He was telling all and sundry how his new range of clubs were the best in the world and would transform anyone's game. His new putter would take the world by storm because it was revolutionary and, as Brian Harley was already demonstrating on the pro tour, the most effective putter ever designed. So get your orders in well in advance for when the putter goes into production in a few months' time . . . His lighthearted and friendly manner enabled him to put over a very strong sales pitch without a hint of strain. It was a well-turned performance and, if the putter was really as good as Brian Harley made it look, there was no doubt that he would sell a huge number.

I walked on, exchanged some nods and greetings with other manufacturers, looked wistfully at the array of cashmere sweaters and went to find Toby.

At the entrance to the Press tent I asked the security man if Toby was inside and he pointed him out in the middle of the usual muddle of desks and papers, with telephones ringing and cigarette smoke drifting, and expletives exploding. No wonder the prose is not so peerless in our morning newspapers. I waved at Toby and he walked over.

He looked quite pale and rather untidy, with his tie undone and his hair ruffled. Very much the *Front Page* look today, I thought, or was the hangover worse than usual?

'Chris, dear boy. I badly need a drink and I need to talk to you.'

'Fine. Here I am. What's the problem?'

'No, I want to get away from here. Prying eyes and flapping ears.' He gestured over his shoulder at the other members of the golfing Press.

Much to my surprise, he led me towards one of the public beer tents. He was obviously in a worse state than I had imagined because to Toby a bar invariably meant a sponsor's tent where the booze flowed like water, and at no expense to the consumer.

Toby was a well-known golf writer, even if he wrote for a newspaper that was rarely, if ever, seen in the boardrooms of Britain. But he was, nevertheless, a witty and civilised man and was always welcomed by the public relations people who like nothing better than to pour alcohol down the usually receptive throat of a member of the Press.

The public bar was already doing a brisk trade. The metallic keg bitter was being poured rapidly into those disgusting plastic, pint glasses; and the sandwiches, a millimetre of filling between emasculated slices of white cotton wool masquerading as bread, and all safely encased in more white plastic, were also selling rapidly.

Toby appeared at my elbow in very quick time – nobody was more expert than him at getting served quickly in a crowded bar – with an extra-large glass of Scotch and a mineral water for me, my habitual drink when I was working. By the time we found a space to stand in comfort most of his drink had gone with a gulp.

'Chris, I've just had a threatening phone call,' he said.

'What, from your editor?' I said facetiously.

He ignored my remark and carried on. 'Just before you arrived a bloke came on the phone and said he had read my article this morning. At first I thought the unlikely had happened and I had a fan out there somewhere. But he then said that he and his friends didn't like the drift of my article at all, and for the sake of my health I would be well advised to leave the subject alone. It was his tone that got me. He was matter-of-fact about it, as if he were telling me what time it was. It really frightened me, Chris.'

'Did you recognise the voice? Maybe it was a joke. You know how the other journalists take the mickey occasionally,' I suggested.

'No, I certainly didn't recognise the voice. It was one of those featureless, slightly off-centre voices. You know – someone who lives in London or nearby. The vowels are not quite right – like football commentators on television.'

He wasn't joking. I could tell he meant it. He was deadly serious and I knew it.

I was at a loss, because Toby was so clearly shaken. Only one response came to mind. Automatic.

'Toby, would you like another?'

'Yes, but I'll do it. Expenses, dear boy.'

He made another foray to the bar and was back in quick time with another of the same.

'Chris, I really didn't know who to turn to; and that voice made me shiver. But I knew I could trust you, and that at least you would believe me. I haven't forgotten either how you rescued me from that drunken Scot in Champers a couple of years ago.'

Champers is one of Toby's favourite watering holes just off Ludgate Hill and within an easy stagger of his office. It is also on my way home from my stockbroker's office in the City. On the winter evening in question I was sharing a bottle of champagne with Toby and we were, inevitably, talking golf.

I was only half-aware of a looming presence next to me at the bar, until he joined in our conversation:

'Are you that bloody idiot who does golf for the *News*?' was his opening salvo; and things got worse when Toby, never able to turn the verbal cheek, even to a large and extremely aggressive drunk, proceeded to tell him his opinion of Scottish golfers in general and of unwelcome Scottish drunks in particular.

As the Scot pushed his way past me I grabbed him, put an arm-lock on him and suggested that he had a drink elsewhere. As I escorted him, none too gently, to the door, I thanked my lucky stars for the hours of self-defence training that I had undergone, at my father's insistence, from the age of twelve onwards.

'Why did you write that tailpiece to the article, by the way? I assumed it was just journalistic surmise but obviously, from the sound of your friend on the phone, it struck home.'

'Quite frankly,' said Toby, 'a lot of it *was* surmise. I was dropping a hint, trailing a cloak, in the hope of making the article a bit more interesting.'

'Yes, thanks for the write-up, by the way.'

'Think nothing of it. The only concrete information I had, and that was more sand than cement, was from Froggy Davies's sister. I managed to track her down and eventually got her on the telephone. By the way the sports editor really did "hold the back page" for me yesterday. I only wanted to get a few comments about Froggy. Was he pleased with his new job with Harley? You know, a bit of colour as sentimental as possible, with which to tickle the tear ducts of my faithful readers. Well, Mrs Newton, as she is now, was fairly monosyllabic until I promised that the *Daily News* would send her a little present. She then told me what she said she had already told the police and that there was no harm in telling me, to wit that Froggy had given her nearly two thousand quid to do up the kitchen and bathroom.'

I nodded.

'Oh, you already knew that! Well, why didn't you tell me?' asked Toby. I explained that this had come out during my long interview with Inspector Drew last night.

'Right. Anyway I suggested to Mrs Newton that this sort of thing didn't sound like the Froggy we all knew and loved because, with great respect, that sort of money would usually have gone only in one direction – to the publicans and bookies. She agreed, but said that before he began work with Brian Harley – after the Safari circuit but before the European Tour began – he had gone off for several days' training. This sounded very odd to me, because who on earth could hope, or even wish, to "train" an experienced caddie like Froggy. But she maintained that he went off to the Supersight factory with Brian Harley for several days.

'When he came back he said he was going to make more money than he or she had ever dreamed of. He gave her the money then, and said it was part of his retainer for the season.'

I interrupted Toby. 'The police assumed that the money he gave her was his bonus for the Madrid Open and the Italian Championship.'

'Quite. And that's when I began to get suspicious. For who would ever bother to give a caddie like Froggy Davies such a huge retainer up-front. You wouldn't expect to see him again for months – or weeks anyway until he'd spent the lot. And more to the point he didn't disappear on a massive binge, and he gave all that money to his sister. So he must have been convinced that there really was a lot more where that came from. It all rang very off-key and that was the basis of my tailpiece article.'

'And now you've been warned off, which confirms your suspicions.'

'Exactly.'

'Have you told your editor?'

'Not yet. I'm trying to decide whether to be a crusading journalist or a craven hack.'

'But you have told the police, of course.'

'Not bloody likely. There could be a great story in this.'

'Yes and you might not live to tell it. I don't know what to suggest except for God's sake be careful. Let me think – and let's meet up later. But I've got to meet Jack now. I'll see you later.'

'Good luck,' said Toby.

I mused on Toby's story as I walked towards the clubhouse and so intent was I on my thoughts that I nearly knocked over Sally Drayton as I passed the PGA hut. She looked as delightful as ever, trimly turned out in cream trousers and a bright red sweater and with the bumps all present and correct and in the right places.

'Good luck today,' she said, 'and don't forget about tonight.'

I'd rather have the good luck tonight, I thought, as I resumed my walk to the clubhouse.

Jack Mason appeared at the players' entrance and greeted me in his usual jovial way.

'Ah, the upper-crust caddie has appeared. Would you care to carry my bag, sir.'

I grinned dutifully and asked him how he was.

'Not bad. I slept well after a few pints of Sussex Devil at the local, and woke up to find my caddie famous.'

I said nothing about Toby's revelations, and Jack had other matters on his mind. He did his usual practice stint, during which I endured more jokes from the other caddies and from some of the players about my sudden fame. At three o'clock the same three players – Jack, Harley, and the self-contained Spaniard, Jose Miguel – teed off.

The wind had changed slightly and had strengthened and there was a hint of rain in the air. Rarely are two days the same in England, and this made the shot calculations on each hole quite different from the preceding day. Derek Jefferson had abandoned his executive suit for a caddie's bib and was ready to do his stuff again.

Despite losing a ball on the second hole, Harley had a respectable opening half of two under par and his putting was as consistent and accurate as before. He ended up with another sub-par round and the leader board showed him in a tie for second place behind Carlssen, who had played another superb round to be nine under par.

Jack had obviously had one pint too many of Sussex Devil because his swing was not quite as smooth and slow as usual. His

48

body was not as solid and stable as it should be and he was frequently off-line by a few degrees.

It was one of those days which all professional golfers have to endure, when their swing isn't quite right. Most of them know enough about their swings to make minor compensations and can work the ball around the course quite adequately since they can all revert to a 'bread and butter' swing, usually with 'bread and butter' results. Even when the swing is slightly out of tune, the really good golfer has such good feel for the ball and where it ought to go that he can produce a respectable shot most of the time.

Jack was certainly aware that this was one of his off days. Instead of the fairway he found the edge of the rough several times, and his irons were not flying straight at the flag. The consequence was that he returned a par 72 to recede into the pack. Miguel was his usual self and his efficiency left him in fifth place.

It was down to the practice ground in the gloom for Jack and myself but I managed to get a message to Sally to meet me an hour later than planned.

I was grateful that practice balls are now provided for the golfers, courtesy of a sponsor, of course. A few years back each golfer used his own collection of chipped and misshapen balls and the caddies were expected to stand at the end of the practice area and collect them. It was a very dangerous business, if up to thirty or so golfers were letting fly. Caddies were hit often and painfully and several took to wearing crash helmets, and one well-known caddie, who obviously had other priorities, used to wear a cricketer's box.

I was able to stand alongside Jack and offer some advice. He had been moving his body slightly as he came into the shot, and the club head was being thrown slightly off line. After half an hour or so he was happy that the fault had been corrected – for the time being.

I reached one of my favourite pubs in Barnes at nine o'clock. It is one of the few pubs in London where the landlord and his staff have mastered the art of pulling a really good pint of bitter: one with a creamy head which lasts right down the glass. I was making my first inroads into a superb specimen of the amber fluid when Sally walked in. Dressed as she was in a simple dark green dress, set off by a bright red scarf, she caused a momentary pause in several conversations. I grinned at her and kissed her lightly on the cheek.

49

'What would you like to drink?' I asked her.

'Oh, half a bitter would be fine.'

'OK. I don't want to rush you but I've booked at the bistro down the road for nine o'clock so we ought to have this drink and go.'

'Suits me. I'm starving,' she said.

A few minutes later we were seated at a corner table in the small bistro which I had known for several years. It has the advantage of offering a small choice of three or four dishes for each course, all cooked with skill by a cheerful Frenchman in a kitchen in full view of the customers.

I am always deeply suspicious of long and complicated menus; the chances are that the busiest thing in the kitchen is a microwave oven.

The food was served up by the equally cheerful owner, a middle-aged lady who did not believe in overcharging her customers.

'Hello, Monsieur Chris, *comment ça va?*'

My usual greeting from the cook from his kitchen on one side of the small restaurant.

'*Très bien*, Roger, *merci, et vous?*'

I was anxious to avoid too lengthy a conversation with Roger. Because I retained a few French words and phrases and could make myself understood in his language he had assumed a much wider knowledge than I possessed. He usually left me floundering in his voluble Gallic wake. So I waved and ushered Sally to our table.

Over the first course I made the usual polite inquiries about Sally's new job and asked her what she had been up to for the last half-dozen years or so.

Like me she had been disenchanted with the various jobs she had taken after university. Perhaps student life does not prepare anyone adequately for the daily slog of an ordinary job, and after two or three attempts to settle into a career in sales management and even in personnel, she had taken off for America.

'Personnel. My God, you must have been desperate,' I said. Sally grinned.

'I have an old friend who works for a publisher in New York and I stayed with her for a couple of weeks while I found a job. Eventually I joined a real estate company in New Jersey and did rather well. I was selling houses and apartments on a commission basis, and I think that my English accent stood me in good stead. It's surprising how the American middle class are still very pro English. I used to wonder whether they were actually taking in the meaning of what I was saying, or just listening to the accent.

'Anyway, after about six months I had saved several thousand dollars and decided to spend a few weeks drifting across the country to the West Coast.

'I eventually arrived in Los Angeles and got a job with a show-business agency as a secretary. I didn't particularly enjoy that, but the fact that I could play a reasonable game of golf led to an offer to do a sales job for a golf manufacturer just south of Los Angeles in a place called Tustin.'

I remembered that Sally had been on the brink of a place in the university ladies golf team, and I discovered that she now sported a handicap of four.

She went on. 'The new job mainly entailed selling the company's equipment to the big stores in the Los Angeles area and to some of the bigger golf courses. This suited me because I got plenty of invitations to play golf, and the only fly in the ointment was the sales manager. He was convinced that if he tried hard enough and often enough I would go to bed with him. Well, since he did not appeal to me in the slightest, the whole business became a terrible bore.

'He tried all the usual tricks. Would I stay on at night to go over some sales figures? You know the patter, I'm sure.'

'Absolutely not.'

'Anyway, he then insisted that I went with him to a trade show in San Francisco. When we arrived at the hotel I found that he'd booked us both into the same double room. I embarrassed him terribly – in my loudest voice – in front of all the people working on the reception desk, and a separate room was very quickly found for me. But I knew my days were numbered at that firm.'

I made a mental note not to suggest a dirty weekend away somewhere – well, not yet, anyway.

'So, I started looking around for another job and heard that Mike Martinez, the agent, was looking for someone to do some secretarial work and some negotiating, and that he preferred English girls for such work. I discovered at the interview that he's a

51

most amazing snob. He asked me if I'd been to Eton, but seemed more or less satisfied when I told him I was educated at Cheltenham Ladies College. So I got the job, which had the great perk of corporate membership at the Riviera course, which was just down the road from the office.'

My ears had certainly pricked up when Sally mentioned Mike Martinez.

'How long did you stay with his agency?'

'For about a year. I left a couple of months ago, at the end of March.'

'Why?'

'Mostly because I was homesick. And despite the wonderful climate, and being able to play Riviera whenever I wanted, I longed to see green fields and my folks and my friends, and hear the cricket scores on the radio, and escape from the constant pursuit of more money and better deals for the clients, who mostly didn't care anyway because they already had more money than they knew what to do with.'

I could partly understand Sally's comments because I heard at second hand from Jack Mason about the bickering that went on between manufacturers and the players' agents about contracts. It was a constant battle. On the one hand, the size of the guarantee which must be paid for a famous player's name and, on the other, how much support the player would give to the company. Personal appearances always seemed to be a bone of contention. Would the star turn up on time? Would he turn up sober? Would he turn up at all? And so on.

'You were presumably with Martinez' agency when they signed up Brian Harley?'

'Yes I was. I couldn't understand why they bothered to take him on, because he hadn't won anything for years. My immediate boss, Ed Grainger, hadn't even heard of Harley and he is actually the man who runs the golf division for Martinez.

'In fact he was very put out because Martinez simply told him one day at the end of last year that the agency had a new client but he, Martinez, was going to handle him personally and Ed Grainger didn't need to bother about him. Ed just muttered "Brian who?" and left it at that.'

I butted in: 'But of course Martinez was right again – Harley starts to win and Martinez gets him a fat contract with Supersight. By the way, have you any idea what that contract is worth?'

'No, I haven't,' said Sally, 'and Ed was also fed up by the way the deal was done. As the golf director he normally oversees all those negotiations although the contract is ultimately approved by Martinez.

'In fact, Ed knows far more about endorsement details these days than Martinez, who is mainly concerned with the big-time sponsors and the top brass at the TV companies. You know the form. Power lunches at Ma Maison or the Connaught. A day's golf with the president of this company or that company when the fellow who makes up the four and plays with the president of the corporation just happens to be last year's Masters Champion. All legitimate and very effective, and Martinez is very good at it. But Ed was very annoyed when Martinez negotiated the Supersight deal for Harley. Not a word. No consultation at all.'

Sally wanted to know how I became a caddie and I filled her in on my doings since we left university. She knew a little about my brief and less than glorious foray on to the amateur circuit.

I told her that my ability as a golfer had secured me a good job at a finance company and a certain amount of time off for local competitions. I was bored stupid by it and moved on to the marketing department of an American conglomerate. The experience of working for a number of American executives, who were too busy protecting their jobs and the inflated salaries that went with them to pass on any responsibilities to me, made a move imperative after about a year.

Various jobs followed in sales and marketing, with the shadow of my father always looming, together with his wish that I should work for his company. Not a course I relished.

'One spring day, rather like today, I was playing in a pro-am. The Irish professional I was partnering needed a caddie for the tournament, since his usual man had not turned up. I was between jobs, and I actually had enough to tide me over while I had a sabbatical. At the ripe old age of twenty-six, I had half-decided to take stock of my life so far and try to decide what to do.

'Of course, I agreed to carry his bag like a shot, and the Irish golfer gave me some very basic instruction in my duties over a couple of pints of the dark stuff from his native land. I enjoyed the experience immensely, since it opened my eyes, a little, to the huge differences between top amateur and top professional golf. My man, Jim Flanagan, was a middle-of-the-road, journeyman professional, but a *real* professional.

'As you know, Sally, he's no great shakes as a shot-maker but a wonderful putter – he has a great feel. And you know what Willie Park said.'

' "The man who can putt is a match for anyone," ' she replied triumphantly.

'Quite. And he was good enough to win the Open,' I said and tried not to sound peevish because she knew the quote. 'Anyway, Jim putted brilliantly in all four rounds, finished equal seventh, genially accepted a cheque for about six thousand pounds and then gave me his own cheque for four hundred. Well, I didn't want to take it, because I was vaguely thinking of my amateur status. But Jim insisted, insisted that I bought him a pint and asked me to caddie for him the following week at St Anne's.

'So my career had begun, even if at that stage I had no intention of prolonging it. Eventually Jim's old caddie came out of the woodwork again and I carried on for one or two other pros. I even caddied in the Open and that was simply marvellous. Even though my man, a very strong American, was blown away by the winds. And I eventually ended up with Jack Mason.'

We were on to the pudding course by now and I was attacking a delicious *crème brûlée* with great gusto, while Sally sensibly preferred the fresh fruit salad.

'Come and have coffee at my place,' I suggested.

'I don't drink it very often. It keeps me awake.'

'That's what I was hoping,' I said with a deliberate leer.

'Another time, Chris. I have to be up very early.'

She had.

'It's been a lovely evening.'

It had.

'Why don't you come round to my flat next week, and I'll cook you a meal.'

'I'd be delighted.'

Oh well, hope springs eternal, I thought as, after a brief and chaste kiss, we climbed into our separate cars. Like the golfer who hits his one decent shot on the eighteenth hole and cannot wait for the following weekend's game, I felt light of heart with the warm promise of another evening in the company of the delightful Sally Drayton.

# Chapter 5

Saturday morning dawned late for me, and I just caught the tail end of *Sport on Four*. I was glad to see that the weather was presenting its sunnier face today, although a breeze was scurrying through the tops of the trees. But a dry day would bring bigger crowds and add to the excitement of the vital third round of the tournament. I hoped that Jack Mason had restricted his intake of real ale last night and that he was feeling as cheerful as I was, though my happy frame of mind had a lot to do with Sally Drayton. As I put some oranges through the juicer, her image, bright and laughing, was in my mind.

I settled down at the kitchen table with a jug of fresh orange juice, a bowl of fruit at my elbow, and the newspapers before me. Toby first – and I turned to the back pages of the *Daily News*.

'HARLEY HOT IN PURSUIT OF COOL SWEDE' read the headline, and the first sentence ran: 'Brian Harley, the golfer who was on the scrapheap a year ago, continued his early season bid for glory yesterday with a brave round of sixty-eight to leave him one shot behind the cold-eyed Swedish ace, Bjorn Carlssen.'

I looked down the other scores and confirmed that Jack was in about twentieth place, so he would need a very special round today to force his way back among the leaders. I was ruminating on his chances when my phone rang in the hallway. I thought about letting it ring, but there was a faint hope that it might be Sally. It was the ace golf reporter, Toby Greenslade.

'Good morning, Chris,' he said briskly.

'Are you all right? No more nasty phone calls?'

'No, thank goodness. I trust that you have been reading my peer-less prose this lovely morning.'

'Yes, Toby. It didn't take long and I only spotted one word with more than one syllable.'

'Thank you, Chris. But I didn't ring you for a critical appraisal of my work. How do you fancy a trip to Birmingham?'

'I don't.'

'Let me tell you more, dear boy,' said Toby in the sonorous manner he adopts when he is either about to state an immortal truth, or browbeat you, or both.

'There is obviously more to Froggy's murder than meets the eye and, despite the bullying phone call, my editor, God bless him, wants me to do a little more digging. The place to start is clearly with Froggy's sister. I want to know why Froggy was so confident that his financial ship was about to dock. Will you keep me company on Tuesday? It'll be a nice change for you.'

It would have been easy to claim some other appointment, or a practice session with Jack, but the situation intrigued me and I was particularly happy at the thought of pulling a fast one over the shrewd and imperturbable Inspector Drew.

'OK Toby, you're on. I'll see you later at the course.'

'Thanks. And good luck today; you'll need it if Jack is to get anywhere near Harley, let alone the Swede.'

'Ah, yes, the cold-eyed Scandinavian ace.'

'Don't, Chris,' begged Toby. 'I'll see you anon.'

He rang off and I realised that I ought to leave shortly since Jack was due to tee off at midday. The phone rang again and this time it was my father.

'Are you all right? I've only just read about this old caddie you found murdered. I got back from the States this morning. What's going on?'

There was certainly a note of concern in my father's voice but it was overlaid with annoyance, as if I'd let him down by finding a dead body.

'Dad, I found Froggy dead – murdered – reported it to the police, made my statement, and that's it.'

'Well, if you mix with those types you'll become as bad as they are.'

My father, when he talked to me, always tended to ape some crusty old colonel of decidedly right-wing tendencies. He wouldn't dream of adopting such a persona in his own business world, and I knew it.

'Come off it, Dad, there is nothing wrong with the world of golf.

It's not full of coke sniffers like the music business; it's not full of yobs like football; and it's not full of crooks like horse racing. No doubt there are some of each in golf, but not many.'

'Well, as long as you're OK. Are you sure?' he asked placatingly. 'I tell you what, if it's a nice day why don't your mother and I come down to the tournament on Sunday? Maybe Jack will win some money.'

They knew Jack Mason and liked him despite his occasional tantrums both on and off the course. I promised to get them tickets and to let them know where and when to meet me on Sunday.

I had to make haste now or I would be late, so I threw my kit in the back of the Porsche, threaded my way through the traffic on the Kingston By-pass and then put my foot down on the M3, keeping a wary eye open for the police. As long as I kept just over 80mph I reckoned that, even in a red Porsche, the traffic police would turn a blind eye. Only the occasional sales rep, in his weekend mufti, went past me in his company Cavalier.

It was relatively mild and sunny when Jack teed off just after midday, in company with an Irish golfer who was a couple of places ahead of Jack in the Order of Merit. Jack was in an attacking mood and hit an immense drive over the angle of the dogleg on the first hole. A seven-iron and one putt later he had recorded his first birdie of the day.

It was a great way to start any round and the bright sunshine and colourfully dressed spectators lining the fairways and ringing the greens combined to give everyone a lift – Jack included. His swing was solid and deliberate. A mistake at the eighth, which cost him a shot, was only a momentary falter in his stately progress to a seven-under-par round at 65. This marched him well up the field, and when the final scores came in we saw that he was in equal third place behind Brian Harley and the inevitable Bjorn Carlssen.

The BBC was covering the tournament and their man on the spot had the dubious pleasure of interviewing Jack Mason after his splendid round. A dubious pleasure because Jack, as in most of his activities, was unpredictable. Despite all the homilies from the PGA that professional golfers must help the sponsor in every way possible, especially by cooperating with the media and especially with television, Jack had been known to stride straight past a TV interviewer without a word. On another famous occasion he had left the TV man floundering in his 90-second interview by answering every question with a single yes or no.

On this occasion he was in a jovial, even bantering mood, as I stood beside him facing the camera. Caddies were told to do this so that the sponsor's name printed on our bibs could be clearly seen by millions of viewers. This, after all, was the whole point of the exercise for the sponsor. I put on my best alert face, in case my mother was watching, and saw that the camera was in close on Jack, so the cameraman had neatly avoided getting the sponsor's name into his shot. Obviously a few spare fivers had not found the right pocket.

The TV interviewer, Stewart Hart, a former golfer of middling talent, spoke into his microphone: 'Well, Jack, that was a splendid round. You're obviously in great form. How do you rate your chances tomorrow?'

'I'm hardly likely to say that they're slim, am I, Stew?' said Jack. 'I wouldn't bother to go out there if I didn't think I could win. What do *you* think of my chances, Stew?'

This caught the interviewer unawares, because he was already rehearsing his next question in his mind.

'Well, another round of sixty-five should do it, Jack,' he said after a moment's hesitation, and then continued. 'Do you think you can win tomorrow?'

'Yes, I do,' said Jack firmly, 'with a little touch of luck on and around the greens. I'll do my best and aim for a sixty-three.'

Jack grinned amiably into the camera.

'Thank you and good luck to Jack Mason tomorrow,' said a slightly flustered Stewart Hart. 'And now back to Brian in the studio.'

'Was that all right, Stewart?' asked Jack innocently.

'You're an awkward bastard, Jack,' said the affronted Hart, and drove off in his buggy to do another 'on the spot' report.

On the Sunday I met my parents and, courtesy of Jack, handed over sponsor's tickets which allowed them into any part of the course and the clubhouse and also provided tickets for lunch.

Jack's round was not as vivid as the day before. He made the turn in one under par and was joined in a battle with the Spanish machine Jose Miguel and a few other golfers for the places from third downwards. A stroke dropped or gained was crucial. Apart from the differences of several thousand pounds between the final placings, Ryder Cup points were at stake.

Behind us, Carlssen and Harley were having their own private battle. They were already joint leaders, five shots to the good on Miguel who was one ahead of Jack. The relative positions of the players changed and changed again over the second half and, as we waited on the eighteenth tee, Miguel had edged yet again one shot ahead of Jack. We looked back at the tournament leaders on the seventeenth. Carlssen was safely on the green in two shots, but Harley was in trouble again. He played his third shot from the semi-rough to the left of the green, got it up fast over the bunkers and finished about six feet from the pin. His opponent got his par four, and then Harley lined up his 'arse-gripper' putt.

Derek Jefferson once again took the unusual course of holding the flag for such a short putt, but it didn't put Brian Harley off. He holed a very difficult putt with great confidence.

The crowd cheered their British player and hurried to the next tee, which we were just leaving. Both Jack and Miguel finished with par fours and headed for the PGA hut to check and sign their scores. Jack was £10,000 richer or, rather, a shade over £9000 after my bonus was deducted.

I waited by the eighteenth green with thousands of spectators to see the denouement, and my money was mentally on the dashing Swede. He obliged by hitting a vast drive about fifty yards beyond Harley's, who then got his second shot just on to the front edge of the green and about forty feet from the flag. With a much shorter iron, Carlssen placed his ball ten feet from the cup. Advantage Carlssen. In dead silence Harley surveyed his putt and Jefferson took up his usual position beside the pin. A final look, two practice swings with the putter and the ball was on its way. Everyone, myself included, held their breath as the ball swung the last couple of feet towards the cup and disappeared. Shouts and cheers of 'Great putt' greeted yet another brilliant shot. Harley raised his arms in relief and triumph. The stewards called for quiet but, even to the brilliant Swede, the hole must have seemed distant and minute. He missed easily and Brian Harley had won a spectacular victory.

I wandered off to find Jack Mason and my parents and saw Toby, who was obviously heading for the Press tent, the conference with the winner, and several post-tournament drinks.

'The man can certainly putt,' he said somewhat obviously.

'Yes, but why does his caddie hold the pin even on the short putts? And come to think of it why didn't he find himself another caddie after the first round?' I asked Toby.

'First of all, he kept Derek Jefferson on because he brought him luck and he likes the caddie to hold the flag because he can concentrate on his stroke better. Well, that's what he said.'

There are many theories about putting, most of them weird and wonderful, and here was another for the collection. No doubt when Harley's golden streak with his putter came to an end, as end it must, his theory would be consigned to the dustbin – at the same time as his current putter was hurled into a dusty corner of the attic.

I eventually found my parents in the sponsor's tent in a huddle with Jack and his delightful wife, Jenny. My father was obviously enjoying the company of the Masons; like most people he was gratified to be seen with a well-known golfer and to be ever-so-slightly in the spotlight.

'I was just congratulating Jack on his round,' Dad said. 'What a splendid effort.'

'Well, it was a decent pay day, anyway,' said Jack.

'And puts you further up the Ryder Cup list,' I pointed out.

'If I make it,' said Jack automatically.

I inquired after my brother, Max, who had finally agreed a few months ago to work for Dad's firm, and I established that he was in Paris for a few more days. One of the sons had done the right thing and had taken the pressure off me for a while. After I had arranged to meet Jack on the following Wednesday, the Masons left for home, and I had an early dinner with my parents.

Monday was usually a busy day for me, when I talked to my clients at length and often had lunch with one of my various contacts in the City.

Ritually I turned to the back pages of the *Daily News* to see a picture of a grinning Brian Harley holding the habitual poster-sized cheque beside the equally cheerful sponsor. 'BRIAN BOOSTS BRITISH GOLF' said the headline, followed by Toby's account of how the 'foreign invader in the person of Bjorn Carlssen was repulsed by British phlegm and determination in the person of Brian Harley.'

But he finished the article on a serious note: you could tell it was serious because it was printed in heavy type. After re-stating, in different words, his comments in Friday morning's edition, Toby ended: 'This paper reaffirms its commitment to unearth the unsavoury truth about the death of the caddie, Froggy Davies. We are happy to offer a substantial reward for information which leads to the arrest of the guilty person or persons. You can speak in total confidence to the Editor.' A special direct line to his office was then given.

I wondered how the redoubtable Inspector Drew would react to the *Daily News* initiative, and hoped I would hear a verbatim account of his first interview with Toby Greenslade.

After spending all morning talking to clients on the telephone, in place of lunch I nipped up to the golf club and played a few holes with one of the assistants. When I got back to my flat I decided to ring Toby. No reply, but that was not unusual at three o'clock, since he was probably in a hostelry somewhere. I tried his office at four o'clock and then his house at five, without success.

He had not been seen at all at his office. That was not unusual on the Monday after a tournament, so I decided to drive to his house in Clapham in the hope that I might intercept him either on the way in from a long lunch or on the way out for a pre-prandial drink. If not, a note would suffice to confirm our plans to head for Birmingham to see Froggy's sister on the following day.

Toby had been married twice and divorced twice but, without the problem of children to provide for, had escaped without too many financial penalties. He lived in a quiet road off the south side of Clapham Common in a small Victorian semi, with tiny patches of garden at front and back. His car was outside, so I was probably in luck, since Toby never went anywhere on foot. A trip to his local pub, which was two roads away, was invariably undertaken by car.

I rang the bell, bashed the knocker and rattled the letter box since this was guaranteed to provoke a tirade of the 'noisy young bastard' variety from Toby, who was probably in an irritable state, stranded as he was between the lunchtime and the early evening session.

There was no response, which meant that he might still be sleeping off a particularly heavy lunchtime session or perhaps was in the bath and couldn't be bothered to get out. I knew where he kept a spare back-door key and walked round the side of the house.

Whoever had been there before me didn't know about the spare key because the glass in the top half of the door was shattered and the door was open. Burglars, I thought, and then thought again as I remembered the threatening phone call. I suddenly felt cold and my stomach tightened up as I went through the kitchen, crunching over the bits and shards of broken glass, and towards the main part of the house.

There was nothing untoward in the lounge-cum-dining room which occupied most of the ground floor. With every nerve on edge and my heart pumping I put my foot on the first stair. It creaked and I stopped and then heard something: a sort of thin scratching from underneath the stairs.

Toby had a cupboard there in which he threw his golf clubs, normally with a high degree of disgust, and where he kept a dozen or so bottles of wine.

With all sorts of primeval fears about dark cupboards and traps and ghostly animals I put my hand on the handle, turned it, pulled and jumped back. Sprawled on the floor with hands and feet tied and sticking plaster over his mouth was my friend Toby. At least I assumed it was Toby. It was hard to tell because his face was masked with ribbons of caked blood, and his eyes were just slits in a puffy mess of red and black bruises.

'Oh Christ, oh Christ,' I mouthed in a panic and first set about getting the sticking plaster off him. I tried to pull him bodily out of the cupboard but could hear his agonies even through the gag. I eased the corners of the sticky tape off his cheeks, held the side of his head steady and pulled. I had to tug hard and at last freed him.

'Don't move me,' Toby groaned, 'get a knife, untie me. Don't move me.'

I ran into the kitchen and looked about wildly for a knife. It seemed an age before I finally saw his collection of Sabatiers on the wall by the cooker. I ran back and turned him, ever so gently, to get at his hands. More sticking plaster and more blood all over his hands. I cut through it on each side and did the same to the binding on his ankles.

To further pleas from Toby not to touch him I raced upstairs, grabbed a duvet and put it round him. The 999 call took a maddening amount of time, but finally the ambulance and the police were on their way.

I sat by Toby, and stopped myself asking the questions which were dashing through my head. Poor Toby would tell me what he could, when he could. I wondered what to do. My first-aid skills were non-existent. A cup of sweet tea? A brandy? At least I knew that was wrong. I wished Mrs Bradshaw would walk in. She would know exactly what to do.

Eventually he spoke.

'Two men . . . this morning . . . big. They didn't say a word. Just smashed my head and my ribs.'

The ambulance only took a few minutes, but it seemed like hours. The ambulance men took over, so calmly and reassuringly; and Toby was soon in the van and on his way to the nearest hospital.

The police were a minute or two behind but, before the inevitable string of questions began, I insisted on making and drinking a huge mug of tea. I could hardly pour the kettle because I was shaking. My fingers seemed to be made of cotton wool. I also insisted that Inspector Drew be called.

I followed the police car back to base and made a short statement about finding Toby, and then drove over to the hospital. Toby, surprisingly, had been put in his own small room and I guessed that the power of the Press was already being wielded in his favour. I was given a brisk homily by the sister in charge about how ill Toby was, and that my allowance was no more than ten minutes. I idly wondered why there are so many brusque Scottish women in the nursing profession.

Toby certainly looked in better shape than when I last saw him, but these things are comparative. He still looked as if he had escaped from a major car crash. His face was full technicolour with red and black the predominant hues, with stitches over one eye and underneath the other. He managed a very weak and soporific smile.

'Thank you, old boy, for rescuing me. I thought I was a gonner,' he said weakly and tried a smile which became a grimace. 'Christ, I hurt everywhere.'

'Have you any idea who did it?'

'None at all. I was upstairs and heard the window smash. They caught me as I came through the lounge door. I only got a glimpse of them. They were big and I registered the yob uniform – jeans and bomber jackets. The next moment I was on the floor and one was kicking me and the other was hitting me in the face.

'The terrifying thing was that they didn't speak. I thought they were going to kill me. Then just before I blacked out one of them said, "This is your one and only warning", or something like that.'

He looked all in and was almost asleep, so I got up and patted his shoulder very gently.

'Toby, I'm going to keep our appointment in Birmingham tomorrow. Take care.'

He was asleep but a voice from behind me might have curdled anybody's dreams. It was Inspector Drew.

'And who might you be planning to see in Birmingham, Mr Ludlow? No, don't answer, it's Mrs Newton, isn't it? Froggy's sister.'

I saw no point in lying to an already acerbic-looking policeman, and agreed that it was.

'If you are having fantasies of doing a Sherlock Holmes, or perhaps "doing a Lord Peter Wimsey" would be a more appropriate expression for you, forget it. I think that we have got every scrap of relevant information out of her. I can't stop you going to see her, but if you interfere in police business you will be in severe trouble.

'Just remember, too, that a man has already been killed and another one half killed. You found them both – an odd coincidence, don't you think?'

'What are you implying, Inspector?'

'Just warning you, Mr Ludlow, to keep your distance, because you could be next. I'll be looking at your statement later and I'll probably want to see you in the next day or so.'

I left the hospital with Drew's warning eating away at my subconscious, but I knew that I must keep faith with Toby and talk to Froggy's sister.

As I walked to my car I wondered why the heavies had pushed Toby into the cupboard. Was it the ultimate in malice – to make sure that Toby, when he came to, in appalling pain, would have to contend with the idea that he would eventually die alone in the darkness?

Or perhaps they were tidy by nature. They had tidied him away into the cupboard where nobody would see him.

In any event he would have died from his injuries within hours. If that was just a warning I didn't want to be around when they got really nasty.

# Chapter 6

We had arranged to meet Mrs Newton at her home at ten o'clock and I left my flat earlier than necessary to try to miss some of the rush hour traffic, though how you avoid a rush hour which lasts from around seven in the morning to nine o'clock at night, I do not know. But I eventually reached the motorway and headed north.

I felt I deserved a break halfway up the M1 after negotiating the usual flurry of roadworks and contraflow systems and dodging the playful lane changes of juggernauts whose sole aim seems to be to persuade drivers of cars, and especially drivers of Porsches, that motorways are too dangerous for anything but lorries.

In the motorway restaurant I asked for tea and wholemeal toast, and saw the usual look of incomprehension on the face of the girl behind the counter. Off she went 'to see' and eventually I got my two pieces of wholemeal, well more or less wholemeal, bread. I sat down with the *Financial Times* and tried to count how many people were actually smoking underneath no-smoking signs. I gave up at half a dozen, desultorily checked a few share prices and failed to read more than two paragraphs of an article on the gilt-edged market. Time to go.

I left the motorway system east of the centre of Birmingham and, with my map of the area open beside me, headed into the grey and depressing urban blight that lies to the south of the city or, rather, that lies all around the city. Do people create their own environment, or will they learn to live in any conditions? A conundrum for minds of a more philosophical cast than mine.

Thinking wrily of Inspector Drew's pointed remarks about Lord Peter Wimsey, I reckoned I'd be better off with someone like Philip Marlowe to help me.

I eventually found Mrs Newton's road, off an interminable High

Street that was crammed with small shops mostly with Asian names over their facades. As I turned into the street I felt conspicuous, to say the least, in a red Porsche and wished I was driving a ten-year-old Japanese saloon like most of those rusting away on both sides of the road. The houses ran in long terraces, built in the late nineteenth century to house the workers and their families in this thriving industrial centre. Some of the houses stood out by dint of their brightly painted front doors but mostly the only sign of decoration was the washing on the lines and hanging from windows.

I parked the car a few doors away from the Newton house, which looked neat enough behind a freshly painted fence, and ran the gauntlet of half a dozen youngsters who were all offering to mind my car. I accepted the inevitable and picked the biggest boy, a lad of about twelve who already had the looks and the embryonic physique of the typical Pathan, the North-West frontiersmen who produce fierce fighting men and, surprisingly, great squash champions – like the legendary Hashim Khan.

I gave him a pound coin and promised him another if he did his stuff and I walked over to Mrs Newton's front door. The woman who answered my knock was dressed in what seemed to be the standard uniform of the housewife: dark trousers made of some shiny synthetic material, a plain blue sweater and a flowery pinafore. Her hair was dyed black and didn't suit her lined face, which gave clear evidence of a hard life but was, however, enlivened by a pair of watchful blue eyes.

'Good morning, I'm Chris Ludlow, a friend of Toby Greenslade. He couldn't make it and asked me to come instead.'

She looked disappointed, so Toby had obviously disarmed her with his usual charm, and had probably promised some expenses, too.

'Well, come inside and have a cup of tea,' she said, and showed me into the front room of the house. It was dominated by a huge television in one corner and she pointed me towards an armchair, covered in worn corduroy, which had once been dark red. The tea came up quickly, accompanied by biscuits, and Mrs Newton perched uncertainly opposite on the edge of an armchair similar to mine.

I began. 'I knew your brother, and I'm very sorry about his death. Toby and I both think that he got himself involved in something that was too deep for him, and that is why he was killed.'

'You mean that he was a crook,' said Mrs Newton, sharply.

'No, I don't think Froggy had it in him to be a crook, it wasn't in his nature. But it's obvious that the sudden appearance of money in his pocket and his death are linked and we want to find out how. It might tell us who killed him.'

She did not look convinced, but I soldiered on. 'When was Froggy approached to caddie for Brian Harley?'

'It was a couple of months ago, just before the season began over here. Froggy was staying with me as usual, making a few bob at caddying on the nearby courses and spending it in the local pubs. Somebody got hold of him at Edgbaston Golf Club one morning and asked him if he wanted a job this season – carrying for Brian Harley. Well, he wasn't too keen, because he reckoned Harley was a no-hoper.

'But a few days later he got a letter with a train ticket down south and two hundred pounds in notes as expenses. He was to go down to the Supersight factory for some practice with Harley and was then to go with him to a couple of the Continental tournaments.'

'A bit unusual, wasn't it, Mrs Newton, to be asked to practise with a pro before the season?'

'Yes, and Froggy didn't like it. But he liked the cash and decided to go along with it. When he got back, he'd changed his tune. He said that Harley was going to be a winner and so was he. He was going to make a lot of money.

'Well, I just thought he'd been at the whisky even more than usual, and ignored him. The next morning he plonked all this money on the table, about eighteen hundred quid, and said it was mine to re-do the kitchen and the bathroom.'

'And he'd got it, presumably, as a down-payment from Harley?'

'Yes. He said that the Supersight people had put a lot of money up front, and this was his share and plenty more where that came from.'

'This is what sounds odd to us, Mrs Newton. That sort of money is rarely, if ever, given up front – even by a big star to a top caddie. Brian Harley is no superstar and Froggy, although an excellent caddie, could well have disappeared with the money to his favourite distillery for a month. So, the money must have locked Froggy in to some deal which was important to him and important to Supersight.'

Mrs Newton was looking more and more agitated, as I spoke. At last she burst out: 'That's not the only thing. When I was sorting out his clothes yesterday I found this.'

She produced a building society passbook from her pocket and passed it to me. It showed that Froggy was richer than we all imagined: to the tune of five thousand pounds.

'Have you told the police yet about this?'

'No, and I don't want to. I'm Froggy's only relation, and I reckon I deserve the money after looking after him every winter for years. Not that he was much trouble, and he always gave me what money he could.' A few tears were rolling down her worn cheeks, partly in memory of her dead brother no doubt, and partly out of self-pity and fear of the 'authorities' who might take away her unexpected and much-needed windfall.

'Don't worry,' I reassured her, 'if he came by the money legally, they can't take it away from you.'

'But what shall I do?'

'You can't do anything yet. Sit tight. I won't mention its exist- ence to anyone except Toby.'

I rose to go, reassured her yet again, and headed back to the car. The young Pathan had guarded my car zealously and got my thanks and the second half of his reward.

The journey back to London went quickly as I mulled over the strange background to Froggy Davies' death. Whoever heard of a manufacturer signing up a has-been like Brian Harley and then advancing his caddie, who was hardly noted for his reliability, in the region of £7000 for his services? It didn't make any kind of sense. I tried to put what I knew and surmised into the context of other sports. Horse racing, for instance. Jockeys have been known to prevent their horses from winning, and favourites are sometimes 'got at' to spoil their chances. But it is impossible to force a horse to win if the talent isn't there. So how could anyone hope to make Brian Harley into a winner? It just wasn't possible – and yet he was winning tournaments.

I wondered whether it could be drugs – that a caddie perhaps had to be made privy to, because the golfer had to be topped up during the round. But there was not yet a drug invented, or ever likely to be, that could cope with all the different and complex actions and

72

judgements that make up a round of tournament golf. The furious rush and release of a full-blooded hit with a driver to the Buddha-like calm required to hole a four-foot downhill putt, and everything else in between, would require a whole pharmacy. I was getting nowhere and sought relief in some music on the stereo. I eventually got off the motorway and decided to drive straight to the hospital to see Toby, and paused only to buy him some fruit and a bottle of his favourite Bollinger.

He was still looking dozy and was obviously full of painkillers, but was at least propped up on pillows and taking notice.

'Chris, my dear boy, how are you and how was Mrs Newton?' His voice wasn't its usual fulsome boom, and probably only carried down half a mile of corridor.

'Never mind me, what about you?'

'Just three ribs broken, twenty-eight stitches in my head, and two broken bones in my right hand. Obviously the opposition were lovers of literature, but I fooled them – I can type with either hand.' He grinned briefly, but it was a painful effort.

I summarised what I had learned from Froggy's sister, and the many questions in my mind.

Toby said, 'Is that Bolly cold? I think it might aid the thought processes, old boy. There are two glasses in the cupboard.' I eased the cork out of the bottle very quietly, as if I was a *maître d'* in a very posh restaurant. I guessed that the Scottish sister would prob-ably register the sound of a champagne cork on her infallible antennae from several rooms away. So far so good: and we drank to Toby's usual cry of 'up she goes'.

'There are two angles which you might look at, young Chris,' he said as I refilled his glass. 'First, is there anything suspect about that Supersight putter? To all intents and purposes it is legal – it may look ugly but so do most of the putters these days, and the design has obviously been passed by the Royal and Ancient Golf Club, which does exercise a very tight control over such matters. As you know, it's pretty easy to stay within R & A guidelines as long as any kinks in the shaft are within so many inches of the putter head and so on. So, I doubt whether the solution lies there.

'After all, even if Jefferson has perfected some magic putter which gives Harley an illegal edge on the greens, he will never be allowed to sell it to the ordinary punter, so there's no point. Remember all the hullabaloo over the golf ball with the transmitter inside it. If you hit it into the trees you tuned in your receiver and walked straight to it. A super idea for hackers like me but the R & A immediately banned it, the swines.'

Toby gestured for another glass of Bollinger and continued: 'No, the clues may perhaps lie in that contract between Supersight and Brian Harley. Try and tap up Mike Martinez' people at this week's tournament. I believe they are importing Carl Krantz at vast expense, so the clones from the Martinez agency will be swarming all over the place.'

Toby was referring to one of the great stars in the American golfing firmament whom the sponsors were said to be paying £50,000 in appearance money, much to the disgust of most of the other professionals. Predictably they said that the money should be going into the overall prize fund; and, equally predictably, the sponsors replied that the money was being paid for Krantz to head up a special promotion for the company, and anyway they wanted some extra glamour and colour which a top American golfer would provide. Krantz had won three US Opens and numerous tournaments around the world. He was tall, good-looking and fast-talking, and was said to be a first-class shit.

'You might try to tap Andrew Storey about the contract. He's Martinez' right-hand man over here and, although he's usually pretty close about his clients' deals, he's sometimes conceited enough to boast about them. You can also talk to Jack's agent. Graham Fearnley keeps his ear to the ground and you never know – he might tell us something.'

At this point, the Scottish sister entered at speed – she had probably smelt the champagne from several wards away. Her eyes glittered as she saw the bottle.

'Mr Greenslade, you know that you are not allowed any alcohol,' she began.

'Well, sister, it'll do no harm. It's a tonic, really.'

I didn't wait until she could turn the full force of her disapproval on me. I waved to Toby and went for the door. I knew he could cope.

As soon as I got home I rang Graham Fearnley and established that he would be at the Crystal International Tournament on Thursday, its opening day, and we arranged to meet after Jack Mason had played.

'I'll see you in the champagne tent at three o'clock,' Graham Fearnley said. He was quite fond of that particular drink.

'Well, as long as you're buying,' I said defensively.

'Sure, and you can give me a few tips on the leisure market.'

I wondered how much Graham Fearnley would be prepared to tell me, even if he knew anything about Harley's contract with Supersight. On the one hand he was no friend of Mike Martinez, since the latter was always a great threat to Fearnley's own business, which was based firmly on representing European, and especially top British, golfers. If a spark of success was first engendered by a British golfer and then maintained, Martinez' clones would quickly and insidiously begin the process of prising the potential star, and his potential earnings, away from Fearnley.

Although Fearnley had contracts with his players, such contracts can always be cancelled, especially if Martinez' lawyers got involved. Or the golfer in question could claim 'non-performance' by Fearnley, that his efforts to secure lucrative contracts on the golfer's behalf had not been successful enough. In the final instance the golfer could simply refuse to work with his agent, who would then be faced with the problem of whether to sue his erstwhile client – a very expensive, long-winded and unsatisfactory process. Usually an agreement to end the business relationship was reached.

So, Fearnley was under continuous threat from the two or three agencies which operated on an international basis, and especially from the most powerful, Mike Martinez. This made Fearnley very defensive about his own business, and usually happy to dish the dirt about his aggressive competitor.

On the following day I carried Jack Mason's bag in the pro-am. He got round in par figures, but was obviously playing from memory. He was even polite to all his amateur partners. Perhaps the very nature of the course on which the Crystal International was being played had had an effect on Jack's temperament. It was a newish course, just south of Birmingham and within twenty miles of Crystal's head office. Despite the efforts of the designers, who had moved mountains to landscape the course, planted tens of thousands of trees and built artificial lakes and streams throughout, the course looked bland and uninteresting, essentially because it was so obviously man-made. Give me a links course in Scotland or Lancashire, or one of the beautiful Surrey courses any day, where the natural terrain has been used to its best advantage; such courses have the great benefit of maturity. This new course didn't seem to fit; its lay-out was more suited to California than Warwickshire, and this undoubtedly affected some players, like Jack, who couldn't react to its challenges in the usual way.

On the following day Jack still seemed to be sleep-walking his way around the course and I was not surprised when he visited the water a couple of times and eventually handed in a score of two over par. Jack didn't even bother to practise but headed for his car and the drive back to his Wiltshire home.

I bought myself some fruit and wandered over to the first tee where Brian Harley was about to drive off. He had been drawn with a young Irish player and Carl Krantz, the expensive American import. In his mid thirties, he was certainly one of the most stylish players on the golf circuits of the world. Naturally, he was a client of Mike Martinez. In some ways he was a throw-back to another era when golfers swung the golf club rather than tried to hit the ball with as much power as they could command. Krantz's swing was slow and rounded, and almost metronomic in its smoothness. I watched him drive effortlessly down the middle. The young Irishman was a complete contrast with a looping and swooping swing which nevertheless propelled the ball with great power.

Harley was next and I saw with interest that he had a new caddie who was unknown to me. He was tall and skinny and obviously in his early twenties, and was most noticeable for his permed and bleached hair, an unusual stylistic departure for a caddie. Just as the rewards for European golfers have increased dramatically over the last few years with a circuit worth nearly twenty million pounds, so have they for caddies. This was tempting a different breed into the job – it could now be seen as a rewarding all-year-round career. Harley's man was perhaps one of these.

It was time to find Graham Fearnley and I headed for the champagne tent. Jack's agent was already well ensconced at a table with half a dozen people, a couple of whom I recognised as regulars on the pro-am circuit.

I went over, exchanged greetings with everyone and Graham pointed at an empty table a few yards away and said:

'Grab that table and I'll be with you. What do you prefer – Bolly or the Widow?'

I plumped for Veuve Clicquot and sat down. I watched him at the bar, a short but fairly broad-shouldered figure with fairish hair. He was dressed in sober black-and-white checked trousers, with a plain cotton golf shirt and a navy blazer, and was going through his familiar bonhomous routine with everyone within reach at the bar. He reckoned to do most of his business in the bars and hospitality tents during the tournaments, and I wondered if he could remember the details after all the champagne.

'Good health, Chris!' he said, and we drank.

'Who's Brian Harley's new caddie?' I asked.

'Apparently he's been imported from California by Martinez. You'd think there weren't enough caddies to choose from over here.'

'Yes, it seems odd, doesn't it?'

'Why? Did you fancy the job?'

'No,' I answered. 'I'm quite happy working with Jack, as you know.'

'I don't blame you. That bastard Harley dumped me after I'd looked after him for nearly ten years. I hardly made a bean from him in the last five. I had to tag him on to group deals as a make-weight – you know, like the contract I did for twelve of my players with UK Airlines. They didn't want him, but I persuaded them in the end. As for equipment I could hardly get him a free set of clubs, let alone any fees.

'And then he ditches me, gets a new contract with that shit Martinez and starts winning tournaments. I can't believe it.'

'Well, no one can believe it,' I said placatingly, 'but why do you think Martinez took him on?'

'I've no idea. But just remember that Martinez has his fingers in every pie in golf. I admit that he's a brilliant businessman, but I just wish he wasn't in my business. As soon as one of my clients looks like winning anything important, he's after him.

'All I can say, Chris, is that he took Harley on because he knew he could get him a good contract.'

He paused and refilled our glasses, looked up and waved a greeting at a couple by the bar. His smile switched on, lit up like a beacon, and was gone as suddenly.

'I still don't understand why Supersight took a gamble on Harley, either. Jefferson has been in the business a long time and is no fool, is he?'

'No fool at all,' said Fearnley, 'and just about as devious as Martinez.'

He leaned closer across the table. 'When Jefferson left Downton International a few years ago it certainly wasn't of his own free will. Apart from the fact that there was trouble with one of the other directors – apparently Jefferson was having a high old time with his wife and, to add insult to injury, charging the hotel rooms to expenses – you may recall that Downton lost two very valuable contracts with players in tennis and golf.

'Remember the famous love affair between Mary-Ann Curtis and Larry Marsh?'

Three years ago, nobody who read either the front, middle or back pages of a newspaper could have missed reading about the exploits of these two mega-stars. Mary-Ann Curtis was the best tennis player in the world, with three Wimbledon titles and a Grand Slam under her belt, while Larry Marsh looked as if he would be her equivalent in golf. He had won a US Open and a Masters title in great style, and their affair was a natural for the pages of the world's newspapers. Whenever their conflicting playing schedules allowed, these two attractive superstars of sport managed to meet in a blaze of publicity. Between the tournaments and all that smiling at the cameras, one wondered how they found the time and the energy to do all those things that the popular press said they did.

Graham Fearnley continued. 'They were, of course, both clients of Martinez, and all this free publicity was grist to his mill. They also both had long-term contracts to play Downton equipment worldwide. But the Kane Corporation in America badly wanted them both to endorse their products and generally to revive their image. They offered Martinez millions to get them out of the Downton deal and into the Kane Corporation.

'No go, however hard Martinez tried. And his lawyers combed every syllable of the contracts. But of course Downton is a huge company, too, and would have dragged everyone through the courts if necessary.'

Fearnley was by now talking so quietly that I had to lean close to hear him.

'The story is that two other clients of Martinez,' and Fearnley named two tennis players who were well-known for their skill at ladies' doubles and notorious within tennis for their lesbian activities, 'were detailed to pursue Mary-Ann. Well, they eventually got their chance, during a rest day at the Monte Carlo Open. Some rest day! They filled her full of booze and probably cocaine and eventually had their way with her.

'Remember, at that time the general public were quite unaware of their sexual preferences. The two of them were merely a couple of outstanding lady tennis players, one of whom had won Wimbledon. The Downton company had just teamed them up, with Martinez' agreement, to launch a new range of tennis clothing and equipment for the cheaper end of the market, mail order and so on. They had already put several million pounds into a launch of the products around the world.

'When the two star-crossed lovers next met, someone, it doesn't take much imagination to guess who, had made sure that Larry Marsh suspected something was wrong. Mary-Ann, who was a bit of an innocent, told all. She was more remorseful because she'd enjoyed the experience so much,' Fearnley added, maliciously. 'Of course Marsh went wild. He rang the managing director of Downton and said that if the other two players didn't have their contracts cancelled immediately he and Mary-Ann would call a Press Conference, tear up their contracts with his company, and tell the world's Press why.

'To say the least, the company were in an impossible situation. They either had to abandon a very important marketing campaign and also write off God knows how many millions of pounds already spent on it and on guarantees to their lesbian lovelies, or let Mary-Ann Curtis and Larry Marsh go.

'This was exactly what Martinez had planned, and the rumour was that he worked the whole scheme out with Derek Jefferson. He suggested to the Downton MD that they keep the two girls to their contracts, but release Curtis and Marsh. That way there would be no trouble and Martinez, who represented all the people involved, would agree to it.

'So, Martinez got exactly what he wanted. He even got the guarantees that were still left on Curtis and Marsh's contracts paid up by Downton and then negotiated huge deals with the Kane Corporation for both of them. What an operator that bloke is.' There was a rueful admiration in Fearnley's voice.

He stopped and drew a long breath and I stared at him and said: 'Are you serious?'

'Well, you don't think I made it up, do you?'

I realised that the detail and the logic of the story made it impossible not to believe Fearnley.

'Chris, that's just one of the many strokes that Martinez has pulled in his time; and he still goes laughing on his way to the bank with his twenty-five per cent commission. Jefferson resigned from Downton International shortly afterwards, and put it about that he was fed up with working with such a large company. Not so, the managing director knew that Jefferson was knocking off one of the other director's wives, but much worse than that there had been some really dirty work going on with Martinez. Unfortunately he couldn't prove anything. But it didn't take Jefferson long to find enough money to set up a factory to make golf clubs, and it doesn't take a lot of imagination to guess who provided the money.'

I asked Fearnley whether he knew any of the details of Brian Harley's contract with Supersight.

'Strangely enough, I haven't even heard a whisper about it,' he said. 'You know how word gets out in the golf business, but there's been nothing on this one. You might try to tap Andrew Storey, but he can be very tight-lipped. But be sure of one thing,' he added bitterly, 'whoever makes money out of the deal, it won't be Brian Harley.'

I thanked him and left. I was still dazed by the extraordinary story he had told me. In my innocence I had not imagined that such Machiavellian schemes could be devised, let alone carried out. I had stumbled into the fringes of a world where cynical and ruthless manipulation of other people was the norm, and where even violence and perhaps murder was used to achieve one's ends.

# Chapter 7

I walked out of the champagne tent in a dream or, rather, a nightmare and put two elderly customers, who were coming towards me and were obviously intent on a reviving glass or two, in peril as I blundered into them. I apologised and strode on and decided to seek out the man who looked after Martinez' business in Europe. I knew Andrew Storey since we had occasionally crossed swords in the Halford Hewitt Cup – an extraordinarily friendly but highly competitive event for old boys of a select group of schools. It is held at two famous courses on the Kent coast in the early spring, when the cold is invariably at its most insidious and the winds at their fiercest. He seemed an unlikely executive for someone as American as Martinez since he was the product of an elite public school, followed by an equally elite advertising agency. He was not short of that peculiarly British brand of slightly disdainful, rather loud self-confidence.

I remembered then Sally Drayton's remarks about Martinez' own special strain of snobbery – the more 'British' the better.

Since Andrew Storey was responsible for the expensive importation of Carl Krantz by the sponsors, there was obviously a good chance that he would be doing his public relations stuff in their tent. As I walked towards it, I glanced at the leader board and saw that his client was doing his stuff too – he was two under after five holes.

I nodded to the security man and asked if Mr Storey was inside. There was quite a scrum of people at the bar giving their orders for large post-prandial brandies and ports and the commissionaire waved me through. I spotted the tall figure of Andrew Storey in the far corner of the bar. There was an ice-bucket on the counter at his elbow with a familiar bottle of champagne therein, and he had assumed his favourite pose. He was looking steadily into the eyes of one of the sponsor's publicity girls and exuding enormous interest in what she was saying. He had to look into her eyes because he was so close to her that to look elsewhere would have been blatant rudeness. Andrew was on his well-trodden path to captivating and conquering yet another willing lady. I made my way slowly through the crowd of people, pausing now and again to chat briefly to people I knew.

'Andrew, so sorry to interrupt you but I wanted to say hello. When are we going to have a game again?'

'Chris, great to see you, and let me introduce the lovely Lindy. She's with the Crystal publicity people,' he said unnecessarily. 'Have a glass of fizz. How are things? Oh, Lindy, would you excuse us? I'll be with you shortly. Don't run away.'

She eased her way past Andrew Storey and into the press of sponsor's guests. He patted her neat, round bottom automatically as she went past.

'She'll do for tonight,' he said.

We passed a few minutes in the exchanges that usually pass for conversation between people who know each other slightly and have no real business connection. How's the golf? How's old Jimmy getting on? Are you still living in . . . ? I was bending my brains to think of a way of introducing Brian Harley into the conversation when the television monitor in the corner of the tent gave me the ideal opportunity. It showed the leader board and then switched to the seventh where Krantz was preparing for a long approach putt down the kidney-shaped green. He got it close and holed out and then the camera focused on Brian Harley, who had a slightly shorter putt. The camera panned back as he prepared to play. The ball went unerringly into the hole. Harley was now three under par.

'That guy's putting is uncanny,' I said with not a little feeling and not a little envy.

'Yes, it's that fabulous putter we sorted out for him.'

'And a fabulous contract too, I hear?'

'We do our best, Chris,' he said smugly.

A little bit of flattery was now in order, I thought.

'I imagine you do pretty well for Krantz. What's he worth these days? Apart from the odd fifty thousand pounds in appearance money.'

'For a start, it's nearer seventy thousand in appearance money. Let's see, from the top and grossing it up on a worldwide basis, it's roughly fifty for the visor, two hundred for shirts and sweaters, just under fifty for the golf gloves, and a hundred for the trousers.'

Andrew Storey was enjoying this and rattled off the statistics.

'Thirty thousand for socks, a hundred and fifty for shoes, and the big one – the clubs – seven hundred thousand a year. These are all annual figures. Then there's rainwear, and we have a deal on other casual clothing in the States, an arrangement with a bank, for cars, non-alcoholic beer and a breakfast food, various commercials, company days, a three-book deal with a publisher, and so on.

'You're looking, Chris, at a golfing asset which turns over around four million pounds a year.'

I nodded admiringly.

'And who's Harley's new caddie? I hear he's an import.'

'Yes, Mike sent him over. Friend of a friend of a friend, I believe. Nothing's too much trouble for Harley, at the moment.'

'How come? I thought you'd have bigger fish to fry with clients like Krantz and Marsh and so on.'

Andrew Storey looked over his shoulder, an agent's reflex action, I supposed and leaned closer.

'Mike is treating Harley like a superstar and he's never looked like winning a major. And we've been ordered to treat him likewise. Frankly, he's a pain in the arse, but Martinez pays me a handsome amount of money and provides me with a very flashy car, which impresses the likes of young Lindy over there, so who am I to argue?'

'It must be some contract with Supersight,' I said casually.

'We wouldn't know. Mike handled the whole thing. Anyway, I must circulate, Chris. Nice to see you.' Storey moved off in the general direction of young Lindy.

I moved off to the PGA caravan to have words with Sally about our tentative arrangement for dinner at her flat.

I entered the spacious caravan and was about to ask for Sally when Oliver Moreton, the tournament director, appeared at an inner doorway.

'What do you want?' he asked stiffly.

'I wanted a word with Sally.'

'Now look, Ludlow, we are all very busy and this caravan is for PGA officials and tournament professionals. You are neither, so I suggest you leave.' He advanced towards me in aggressive style.

'Mr Moreton, Sally is an old friend of mine and if I cannot speak to her I would like to leave a message.'

At this point Sally also appeared at the door and was able to intervene between the two bristling males. She grabbed my arm and pulled me to the outer door.

'What's the matter with that idiot,' I began, but she cut me short.

'Never mind about that. I'll explain later. I'll see you at my flat tonight. Is nine o'clock all right? By the time I get back and so on . . .'

'Fine, I'll see you later,' I said as she retreated briskly into the caravan.

I was still seething at the injustice of Oliver Moreton's attitude to me. I hadn't, as far as I knew, done anything to harm him, and his words rankled. I realised that I was driving far too aggressively for my own, and any other road user's, good. I made myself calm down and Miles Davis's clear tones on the stereo helped a lot.

It was early evening when I got into London's vehicular scrummage and I had plenty of time to see Toby in hospital. His face had now assumed many superb hues, a sort of fleshy palette of violets, reds and blue-blacks.

'You're looking much better, Toby,' I said encouragingly. This didn't get a good response.

'I look as though I've been on the wrong end of a Gestapo interrogation. But however I feel, dear boy, I'm leaving this particular medical establishment on Friday. It's like a very poor imitation of a boarding school, except that the discipline is much more severe and the food twice as bad. They wake you at five a.m., which is when I'm often going to bed, and you're so knackered by mid-morning that you doze all day.'

He gestured at the cupboard.

'Behind the books. You'll find a bottle of Bolly. One of the porters nips out every day at five thirty to the off-licence and gets me a cold one.'

I opened it discreetly, with only the faintest pop from the cork, and Toby asked:

'What news of the world of golf and particularly of our friend Harley and his associates? I see that he's two off the pace today, by the way.'

I took him through the events of the day and in particular Graham Fearnley's unpleasant tale of how Martinez had fixed the Curtis/Marsh contracts. As he pondered, I said:

'By the way, what's wrong with Oliver Moreton. He ripped into me just now for going into the PGA caravan.'

'A grammar school education and a captaincy in the Royal Army Pay Corps is what's fundamentally wrong with Moreton, dear boy,' said Toby magisterially. 'And he wouldn't like a privileged and good-looking young man like you, who is clearly slumming it among the ranks of the caddies, to be on his territory.'

I still could not understand what Toby was driving at.

'Moreton is obviously trying to make it with Sally Drayton, you idiot, and you are the competition. At times, Chris, your innocence astounds me.'

Today was proving to be full of revelations, major and minor, and I sipped my champagne to cover my embarrassment.

Toby continued: 'As for this Harley business, we now know that there has been a closer relationship between Martinez and Jefferson over the years than the normal one of agent and manufacturer. We know that neither is averse to some dirty work to achieve his aims. We know that there is something peculiar about Harley's contract with Supersight. But we cannot yet assume that Froggy Davies was murdered by, or on behalf of, either Martinez, Jefferson or Harley. He could have been done in by some thug who was after the money in his pockets. Someone might have heard him talking in a pub about his sudden excess of money and decided to take it off him. After all, I could have been beaten up because I hinted in the *Daily News* that there was something improper about the Harley/Supersight deal.'

'Yes, but Froggy's murder was obviously planned, as Inspector Drew pointed out. Nobody would be wandering about with the sharpened shaft of a golf club, just in case it came in handy. It was a premeditated and very nasty murder, and may well have been planned to throw suspicion on Harley or Jefferson.'

'Or, more subtly, to divert suspicion from Harley and Jefferson. Nevertheless, Chris, we are not much further forward. We still need to know what is in that contract or we need to find out whether there is anything peculiar, and I mean illegal, about Harley's putter. I agree with you that it's not feasible that Harley is on some kind of drug – even beta-blockers wouldn't help a golfer that much. And we haven't got to the science-fiction world of brainwashing – in fact Harley came across pretty well at the last press conference. He came out with some good one-liners, though I'm told that his agent employs a script-writer to cobble up these spontaneous flashes of wit.'

We finished the bottle of Bollinger and I promised to share another with Toby on Friday. I headed for home, showered and changed. It was a reasonably clear evening and since I had already had a couple of glasses of champagne I decided to cycle over to Sally's flat in Fulham. I wrapped up a bottle of Grand Moulas in a newspaper for safety, put it in one of the panniers and went on my way.

I found her flat quite easily. It was on the first floor of a late Victorian house in a road which was not too far from Craven Cottage. Her warm and wide smile greeted me at the door and I forgot for a while the riddles and innuendos which surrounded Brian Harley and hid the killer of Froggy Davies. I was in a comfortable flat with a friendly and attractive woman who was about to feed me. What more could a normal and healthy man want? Well, one other pleasure, but that might perhaps come later. Which reminded me of Oliver Moreton.

As if by telepathy, Sally referred to his strange behaviour while I opened a bottle of Sancerre in the kitchen.

'Oliver Moreton has been badgering me to have dinner since I started work for him. I've made all the usual excuses. I was nice about it at first and said that business and pleasure don't mix; and that I don't go out with married men and so on.'

'Shades of your sales manager in the USA,' I said.

'Exactly. Well, this morning he got very heavy and actually grabbed me and tried to kiss me. His hands were everywhere, so I kicked him hard in the ankle and told him exactly where to go. Of course, he knows that you and I are old friends and he transferred his anger to you. Funnily enough, he's very good at his job, very efficient, but he's been spoiled by women, I think.'

'Well, I wish he did have cause to be jealous of me,' I said, and took the opportunity to draw her towards me and fold my arms around her.

'Maybe he will, one day,' she said teasingly into my shoulder.

We kissed and held each other and kissed again.

'But not today,' she said finally, grabbed the bottle of wine and two glasses and walked back into the other room.

Dinner confirmed Sally's blend of forward planning and sheer competence; iced cucumber soup was followed by steak Bordelaise and my favourite pud of *crème brûlée*. She had remembered from our dinner the week before.

We talked continuously, ranging over many topics, and laughed a lot and I was mentally hugging myself merely for having the good luck to be with such a friendly, amusing and vital girl. No doom and gloom, resentment or woeful tales of broken romances, no poses or pontifications here. It was relaxing and reviving.

As we drank our coffee I outlined Toby's and my suspicions about Martinez and Jefferson, and I asked Sally whether she had got on well enough with Ed Grainger, who was Martinez' right-hand man in America, to ask him questions about the Harley contract.

'We got on well. He's pretty straightforward and has a nice sense of humour – almost British in fact. Of course Ed was really peeved about how Martinez handled the whole Harley business. He was cut out of it completely and he might be prepared to talk.' She looked at her watch. 'Let's see, it's about two o'clock in the afternoon in California. I'll try him now. You can listen on the extension in the bedroom.'

A few moments later, she was actually talking to Ed Grainger. It's much easier to get through to the other side of the world than to the other side of London, and the lines are much clearer too.

After exchanging pleasantries, Sally asked: 'Ed, would you be prepared to give me some information about the Harley/Supersight contract. Just an indication of the terms, and entirely in confidence. A journalist friend of mine is doing an in-depth piece for one of the Sundays on big agents in sport and what they do for their clients. Obviously Harley is news here, although it's mainly because of his caddie's death. But he was risen from the golfing dead, so to speak, and my friend is interested in what an agent can achieve for minor stars, as well as superstars.'

There was a pause and I heard Ed say in his pleasant West Coast accent: 'I shouldn't, but since it's you, Sally, and as long as my name isn't mentioned, I'll find out what I can. But Mike handled this contract himself so I'll have to dig in the files and ring you back.'

I walked back into the lounge and said, 'You clever girl' to Sally and sat close to her on the wide sofa.

A long and heart-felt kiss was interrupted by the phone and I hurried back into the bedroom and picked up the extension in time to hear Ed Grainger. Oh well, business first.

'It's a peculiar thing, Sally, but there is hardly any sort of a file on Harley and I can't find an actual signed contract. But that is explained, partly, by the fact that Mike did the negotiations himself and they were often done face to face with Jefferson. As you know he was over here in California a lot. So there were no proposals going back and forth.

'The best I can do is a heads of agreement outlining Harley's deal. It's pretty straightforward. Harley gets a guarantee of fifteen thousand pounds to play Supersight clubs, including putters, with bonuses based on that sum for wins in certain specified tournaments.

'As I say, straightforward except for one clause which commits Supersight to market a range of putters if Harley wins the British Open. If so, the guarantee will be renegotiated for a period of two years and Harley will receive a royalty on sales of two per cent.'

While Grainger was talking I had torn a page out of my diary and written on it 'Why was Jefferson in California a lot? Ask him.' But I couldn't yet leave the phone and dash into the other room and give it to Sally.

Ed Grainger continued: 'This clause about a British Open win would normally never be written into the contract of a no-hoper like Harley. I know he's won some tournaments but he is simply not Open material. It takes an extra special player, right out of the top class, to win an Open – I suppose on the eve of the Open there are no more than ten players, if that, who have the game, the will and the sheer bloody-mindedness to become the Champion. Now, Harley is not, and never will be, one of these.

'There are other peculiar things about this deal: the clause refers to putters. Why not clubs? It would be logical to put an Open Champion's name on a full set of clubs, not just putters.

'And last, Harley's royalty is already agreed and it's far too low. Mike would never agree to less than a six per cent royalty.

'But that's all I know and, Sally, you must not quote any of those specific figures, OK? I've just given them to you as background, and because you're lovely.'

I raced into the lounge and held my note under Sally's eyes.

'By the way, Ed, why was Jefferson over in California so much?'

'Oh, his latest putter was partly designed over here. He wanted to give it a space-age look so, apparently, he went to one of the companies here which specialises in metal research for NASA.'

Sally put the phone down and turned to me.

'Did all that make any sense to you?'

'Only in the limited sense that this whole Harley set up looks odder and odder. From whatever angle you look things are wrong: even if Froggy hadn't been murdered, it was unheard of that he should be given so much money up front to caddie for Harley. And then there is this long-standing relationship between Martinez and Jefferson, and the dirty work they got up to a few years ago. Now this unlikely contract, with some unusual clauses, between Harley and Supersight. As Graham Fearnley said, the one man who certainly won't come out ahead in the end will be Harley.'

Sally came up to me, kissed me firmly on the lips and said, 'It's late, Chris. You'd better sleep on the problem. I've got to be up early – I must leave here before seven. So I'll see you at the course tomorrow.'

She was right, of course; but as I cycled the short distance home I kept worrying at the problem, juggling the pieces frustratingly in my mind, and making no sense at all. But one thing I was determined to do was to get hold of a Supersight putter and see what its secret was.

I met Jack Mason, as arranged, shortly after ten o'clock and he went through his customary practice routine. There was a desultory air to the whole performance, and I knew that he was conscious of his mediocre first round, which had put him some way down the field. Since he didn't like the golf course either he was in no real frame of mind to 'spreadeagle the field', as a well-known golf pundit invariably and irritatingly puts it on television.

'Come on, Jack,' I said, as we walked towards the putting green, 'there are lots of Ryder Cup points at stake here, and lots of lovely money too.'

'I dare say, but I'd far rather be playing snooker with a few of the boys, accompanied by a few pints of beer – preferably Devil's Dram. Four pints of that and I'm anybody's. This is a bloody awful track, and I've no idea why the PGA ever schedule a tournament here. Well, I have got an idea – it's because the sponsor wants it here, and they daren't say no to him, because they're a bunch of gin-swilling, arse-kissing prats.'

Jack's voice was as loud as usual, and several heads turned. He didn't really mean it. Many of Jack's forthright and colourful opinions were expressed for effect, and he was actually being unfair to the PGA. But he was in one of those moods. I hoped nobody had heard the full sentence and hurriedly changed the subject.

'Have you managed to get a Supersight putter out of Jefferson yet?'

'As a matter of fact I have. He gave me one to try yesterday. I had a few putts with it at home, but it's not for me, Chris. You know the problem with putters, if they don't feel right as soon as you pick 'em up and swing them, you might as well forget it. I'm not very keen on the shape, and the face seems to be a bit dead. That metal compound on the head is supposed to give you more feel, but it doesn't work for me.'

'Do you mind if I borrow it?'

'You can keep it. It's in the boot of the car – remind me at the end of the round.'

I was duly surprised that the Fates had put the new putter in my hands so easily. In my desperation I had been making plans to try and sneak the putter from Harley's bag to have a surreptitious look at it – a truly dicey plan because Harley rarely let the putter out of his sight and, when he did, his caddie obviously had instructions to guard it with his life. My chances of getting my hands on it long enough to give it the once-over were minimal, and I didn't fancy trying to steal it off Harley. But Jack Mason had solved the immediate problem for me.

I continued to encourage Jack whenever I could and to try to put positive thoughts into his head, especially on the greens. After all, a round in the mid-60s might well bring him well up the field for a charge on the final two days. He woke briefly in the middle of the round with an eagle and a couple of birdies, but eventually slid back into indifference and finished with a level-par score.

'No good today, Chris,' he said, 'it's a rotten course and I've got no feel for it. Tonight I shall have a few pints, take Jenny out to dinner, probably attack a nice bottle of claret, and sleep like a stone. I'll grit my teeth and attack the course tomorrow – death or glory, nothing in between.'

He grinned amiably, and I knew he meant exactly what he said. I reminded him about the putter and took possession of it in the car park. I followed Jack's Mercedes a short way along the side roads and he then headed due south while I shot down the motorway towards home.

I couldn't wait to get to grips with the famous putter and was duly grateful that the Friday afternoon traffic was reasonably light, with fewer than usual kamikaze lorry drivers about.

As soon as I got into my flat I looked at the Supersight club with great care. Jefferson had obviously set out to design the ultimate high-tech putter and had, to a great extent, succeeded. He had used a graphite shaft which, although rather thicker than usual, was of excellent quality. This fitted flush into the centre of the putter's head a half inch or so behind the face. The head itself, with a non-reflective black surface, was larger than normal and the back of it was formed into an oval shape. It looked rather clumsy but, when I swung it, it felt quite light. To relieve the monotony of the black head, yellow sighting lines had been painted on it to enable the golfer to line up his putt on the 'sweet spot' – the dead centre of the putter head. I putted a few balls across the carpet and rather liked the satisfactory clunk which the putter made on impact.

I then proceeded to vandalise nearly a hundred pounds worth of golf club. In the spare bedroom I had a demountable work-bench with a vice and an array of small tools. Like many golfers, and professional golfers are particularly prone to this, I liked to alter my clubs occasionally – to change the lie of a wedge by a degree or so, or thicken the grip of a putter, or change the swing weight of a driver. Some professional golfers become obsessional and are forever tinkering with their clubs and ultimately it becomes a self-defeating process.

I took a hacksaw to the shaft and, starting at the top, cut it into three sections. They were all quite normal hollow pieces of graphite tube. I then severed the last piece of shaft as close as I could to the head, and again found nothing untoward. With the head secured very firmly in the vice I attacked the outer edge of it, where the top section had been joined to the side, with a chisel and hammer. Eventually I was able to lever the top section off and the mysterious internal design of the Supersight putter was revealed.

There was nothing at all mysterious about it – just an ordinary heel and toe construction, which concentrates the weight of the putter at either end of the blade. This gives a much bigger 'sweet spot' for the golfer to use and ensures that the effect of a slightly off-centre strike is minimised.

Although I had been under no real illusions that an amazing secret would suddenly be revealed, I was nevertheless disappointed that my theories had proved to be groundless. I wondered where to go from here.

# Chapter 8

Mental confusion can be assuaged in many ways, and one of the best ways for me is exercise. I gathered together the various sawn-up and wrenched-apart pieces of putter and put them in a drawer. I then got into a tracksuit, donned a newish pair of expensive running-shoes, and set off towards Wimbledon Common. Well, they were expensive if you had to buy them but they had been given to me, along with a pair of golf shoes, by the Italian company which supplied Jack. One of the perks of the job. An hour later I was back, blowing hard and running with sweat, but feeling virtuous and much more relaxed. Running is a pretty boring way of passing the time, but is nevertheless a simple and effective way of staying fit. There are even times when I enjoy it in a masochistic kind of way – those are the times when you are really running free, bouncing along in a relaxed and easy manner, with the mind and the body in tune. Some runners talk in mystical terms of a 'high', but to me it simply resembles a perfect golf swing or tennis shot when you hit straight through the ball without any thought or any inhibition, and the result is invariably perfect.

I showered and then decided to lie in a hot bath for a few minutes with a cup of tea at my elbow and the latest Kingsley Amis in front of my face. Virtue has its own reward, I thought smugly.

Despite the quirky characterisations of Mr Amis, my mind returned, albeit lazily, to Brian Harley and his omnipotent putter, but I could not see how to fit the various pieces of evidence together to form a coherent whole. I lay in the bath daydreaming of putters that never missed and that were made of priceless and perfect metals unknown to man, of millions of pounds won on the fairways of the world, and of even more millions made off the course.

The coolness of the water roused me from my reverie, and I left the bath and decided to telephone Toby Greenslade. A call to the hospital established that he had, as threatened, checked out. I ate some fruit, followed by a tuna sandwich made with solid wholemeal bread and headed for Toby's house.

He took a long time to answer the door and his painful movements towards and into his armchair explained why. He registered my look of concern.

'It's all right, Chris, I'll be as good as new in a week or so. I couldn't stand that hospital any longer, and I'm much happier here at home. There's another bottle in the fridge; would you like to open it?'

We settled down with a new bottle of champagne on the table before us, and I summarised what I had discovered about Brian Harley's contract with Supersight and what I had not discovered about his putter. Time and time again we went over the information we had and what it meant, but made no progress.

An hour later, the bottle was finished, and Toby was too. He said, in an unusually wan way, 'The crux of this business is hidden far deeper than I imagined. Froggy's murder, and even the attack on me, simply doesn't fit in with what we know of Jefferson or Harley or even Martinez. At least two of them sail very close to the wind but I wouldn't categorise them as murderers. It's beyond me at the moment, Chris, and I think we should stand back and see what happens.'

Nothing happened over the next two days except the conclusion of the Crystal International Tournament, and a win for the ever-consistent Jose Miguel by one shot from the imported American star, Carl Krantz. The latter had certainly done the sponsors proud, whatever they had paid him to appear. Of course he was the genuine article, a great champion whose pride would not allow him to give anything but his best. Some lesser American golfers, lured over by the open cheques that sponsors often have available, had in the past performed less than satisfactorily. One or two, accompanied by a wife and children, had seemed to regard the tournament as an opportunity for a free family holiday; and some had even managed to miss the halfway cut, to the great embarrassment of all concerned, except probably Mike Martinez whose twenty-five per cent commission was safe whatever happened.

Jack Mason had continued in his untroubled and uninspired vein of the first two days and had finished way down the field. Brian Harley had seemed short of inspiration too, and his putting had failed to compensate for a number of lapses in his long game. He had also fallen foul of the rules, with a controversial decision over a free drop during the final round.

He had hit a drive off line down the left side of the tenth fairway – a crucial moment, since he was then lying three shots behind the joint leaders. Harley's ball was lying a mere few inches from an out-of-bounds fence and was therefore unplayable by a right-handed golfer. The hole was designed as a dogleg to the left, and in the trees ahead of Harley was a television camera tower. He therefore claimed 'line of sight relief'. This is a local rule which is formed to take account of any obstructions caused by the camera positions – if they are in the way of a shot, the golfer may have a free drop. Harley would, in this case, have been allowed to drop his ball two clubs' lengths away from the fence, and would therefore have been able to get a full swing at the ball.

But the rules official, who was summoned by radio, decided, after much argument, that Harley's claim was not justifiable. Harley then insisted that the tournament director, who is the ultimate arbiter at professional tournaments, be summoned. He upheld his official and Harley had to play the ball as it lay. After a sideways hack, played left-handed, a poor shot into a greenside bunker and two putts, Harley had effectively played himself out of contention.

Next week's tournament was an unusual one in the golfing schedule, since it was sponsored by a number of companies and was fronted by a comedy team from television called Lumby and Titch. They seemed to have a show every week or, if not, were invariable guests on other comedians' shows or the light relief on those interminable chat shows. They always appeared in a 'special comedy show' on Christmas night – and perhaps the creaking and overfed somnolence of that evening was the best state in which to watch their predictable routines.

This was the tournament which most of the pros approached with trepidation. Each of the four rounds was played as a pro-am four-ball, with a professional, a celebrity who was usually from show business and two amateurs, who paid handsomely for the privilege. The motives were above reproach since a large sum was raised for deserving charities every year. But the four-ball format was unwieldy and led to extraordinarily long rounds of five hours or more. Nothing can test a professional's nerve and patience more than long waits between every shot. It is bad enough for the club hacker in the monthly medal, but infinitely worse for a tournament professional when there is a great deal of prize money at stake plus those vital Ryder Cup points. Another problem was that the show business element attracted a different kind of spectator. It was a deliberate policy to appeal to the family and the television audience, who came to the tournament to see their stars, not the golf stars. So there were large numbers of spectators who simply had no idea that you should be quiet when a golfer is about to hit a shot. In fact the professional golfers almost took a back seat, and it always afforded me some wry amusement when Ryder Cup golfers of repute were ignored by the spectators who were intent on getting the autograph of some star from a television soap opera.

Jack Mason was certainly far from his best in such a situation, and I was surprised that he had decided to enter. But, since he was lying twelfth on the Ryder Cup points list and the first prize was £40,000, he could hardly afford to miss out.

The whole tournament was in effect a pro-am so the usual pro-am which precedes conventional tournaments was not required. That gave me an extra day off, since Jack had decided that one practice round was enough for him. Sally Drayton also had some time off early in that week and I suggested that we spend the Tuesday together.

After some discussion, we elected to play golf at a charming course in the Cotswolds, to have lunch in a nearby town and then go browsing amongst the many antique shops.

We played our match on level terms, with Sally having the advantage of playing from the ladies' tees, which can be anything up to forty or fifty yards ahead of the men's. Her graceful swing was highly effective and her short game was deadly. I was lucky to halve the match with her, and this flattering result was mostly due to a fortuitous birdie on the last hole, where I holed a pitch and run shot from short of the green.

Soon after the match we were strolling companionably through the handsome streets of the town, past a striking collection of houses and shops built from the mellow, biscuit-coloured local stone. Even the local garage conformed to the general pattern and this was obviously one of those fortunate towns where the planners had insisted that the character of the place be preserved, and not submerged by the usual welter of national stores.

We eventually picked a hotel which looked out over the main square and settled down in the bar. After deciding on beer – a pint for me and a half for Sally – we chatted about our golf game and then Sally asked: 'How are you getting on with the Brian Harley business?'

'Quite honestly, I'm not. I feel I've come to a full stop and so does Toby. We're unsure in which direction to go next.'

Sally was looking thoughtfully out of the hotel window and at the steady procession of passers-by, a good proportion of whom were visitors, to judge by the number of cameras to be seen. She was in half profile against the bright windows, her face glowing in the background of light. She turned to face me and gave me that vivid smile that transformed her already delightful face. It was enough to captivate the hardest heart and mine took an uncomfortable, half pleasurable jump, and I knew I was lost.

'Let's book a room upstairs,' I said frivolously, if hopefully.

'Let's have some lunch,' said Sally. 'I have a suggestion for you, which may lead nowhere, but may at least be worth a try. As you know, Derek Jefferson is one of the sponsors of this week's tournament and one of his ploys to drum up a bit more publicity is to arrange a tour of his factory. It's mostly for journalists, but there are some golfers and some celebrities. You know the form: lots of booze on arrival, a tour of the factory and then a buffet lunch with lots more booze, and plugs for Supersight products should duly appear in the trade magazines and maybe some of the newspapers. Well, I suggest that Toby arranges to be on the trip and that you go with him, either as his close friend or in your professional capacity as a caddie, or a bit of both.'

'You mean that this might give me a chance to do a bit of snooping,' I said.

'Exactly. I think that the tour around the factory will be quick,

97

but you may see something that will set your mental cogs turning again. Unlikely, I agree, but worth a try.'

'Unlikely that my mental cogs can turn or unlikely that I will see anything?' I asked.

'The phone is over there, Chris, and I suggest you try to reach Toby now,' she said in her determined way.

'I hate bossy women,' I said with a smile, and headed for the telephone.

I got Toby on the second ring and explained Sally's suggestion. With a grunt Toby agreed to arrange things and hoped that I would do the driving and that Jefferson intended to provide some decent champagne.

After lunch we walked around the town and marvelled at the prices which were being asked for some of the antique furniture. Obviously this was no problem to the American buyers who were out in force and I wondered whether within fifty years all the antiques in Britain would end up in America and we would be confined to department-store replicas.

As usual I popped into the second-hand bookshops and, as usual, failed to find any old golf books of any interest. Sally, after much thought, bought a small rosewood clock for her flat and we eventually found the car and headed for home.

I dropped Sally at her flat and drove home. No sooner had I entered my front door than there was a knock on it. It was Mrs Bradshaw, smartly turned out and as well-groomed as always.

'Hello, Mrs Bradshaw . . .' I began.

'May I come in, Chris, there's something I must tell you,' she said brusquely.

I wondered what I had done wrong. Mrs Bradshaw was a kindly lady, but half a lifetime as the wife of a top civil servant at the Ministry of Defence had given her an authoritative air which at times verged on the imperious. She often made me feel vaguely guilty, as if I'd forgotten to clean my teeth or was wearing a grubby shirt.

I ushered her into my sitting room and she continued. 'I was doing my usual Tuesday clean for you, Chris, when the phone rang. Well I know that you use an answering machine, so I ignored it. A man began to leave a message. But it wasn't the sort of message you normally receive – it was a threat, and it sounded very unpleasant.'

I crossed to the machine and wound the tape back. There were a couple of messages from the office, and then a voice, which was quite featureless, apart from some obvious London vowel sounds, came on.

'You've caused me and my friends a lot of trouble and we are going to pay you back in full. Soon.' The voice stopped and I had a similar feeling to the one I had just before I found Toby trussed up in his cupboard. My skin was crawling.

'I'm sorry, Mrs Bradshaw,' I began, but she interrupted.

'Don't you worry. I picked up the phone and gave him an ear-bashing.'

'What did he say?'

'Nothing, the little squirt. He hung up on me.'

The machine had carried on recording when Mrs Bradshaw had used the phone. Ear-bashing was an understatement. Her stern and contemptuous delivery would have reduced Stalin to a jelly.

I laughed with relief. Trust Mrs Bradshaw to bring me back to reality. She had reduced the voice to something on the same level of annoyance as a heavy breather.

She looked at me searchingly.

'Are you in trouble, Chris?'

'No, of course not. It's probably something to do with the Froggy Davies business.'

I then explained to her about the attack on Toby.

'I admit that Toby has been stirring things up in his newspaper. And I've been asking questions here and there. But, if it is to do with that, someone or other must have a pretty good intelligence system to get on to me so quickly.'

'Well, I think you should tell the police,' said Mrs Bradshaw sensibly.

'I don't think it's that important. After all, why worry about a silly phone call.'

I sounded more confident than I felt and changed the subject. On her way out Mrs Bradshaw again suggested that I phone the police, and I promised to think about it in the morning.

There was no time to think about it, because I had to pick Toby up at ten o'clock – at the crack of dawn, as he put it – to drive down to the Supersight factory. It was on one of the many new indus-trial estates on the London side of Newbury, a sort of silicon corridor along the M4, where the brave new world of high technology industry was booming away. One of my father's laboratories was only a few miles distant.

We arrived on time at the factory, which was easily recognisable by the huge Supersight logo on the front of the building – one of those light industrial units, painted in bright primary colours, which litter the landscape of Britain – bright, satanic mills, I suppose you could call them.

The hubbub in the reception area was considerable among the gathering of journalists, show business people, and golfers. I spotted several club professionals, who were clearly delighted to be out for a day's entertainment at the expense of one of the manufacturers. There were one or two tournament players who were contracted to play Supersight clubs, among them Sam Ratcliffe. He was the young player who had made such an impression on me during my year on the amateur tour. He had grown quite a bit, both upwards and out-wards and, as I shook hands with him, I reflected that it would not be long before he won a professional tournament.

We were ushered into the boardroom at the back of the building and were treated to a few welcoming remarks from Derek Jefferson, in his familiar, cheerful and very effective style. He then waved us towards a table where large fluted glasses of champagne were already poured, and Toby's experienced eye reckoned that there were suffi-cient reserves of his favourite tipple to get the three dozen or so visitors totally blotto several times over.

'Let's wade in, dear boy,' he said and led the charge. 'Champagne is medicinal, you know.'

Within minutes the noise level had increased perceptibly as the champagne began to have its effect. After half an hour or so, when some of the journalists' drinking arms were a blur, Jefferson banged on the table.

'Gentlemen, and lady,' he said with a gracious nod in the direction of the only woman present, a journalist with one of the golf maga-zines, 'I don't wish to spoil your enjoyment, but I would like to give you a brief tour, and I promise it will be brief . . .' He paused while an ironic cheer went up.

As usual, Derek Jefferson did not hold back in his praise of his own products. No false modesty. This was an enthusiastic salesman at work.

'As you know, this is one of the most advanced assembly plants in golf. We use the most advanced techniques to assemble our clubs, which have the best designs in the world.

'Although we only assemble the clubs here the components are made by expert manufacturers in America, Japan and Taiwan. Our new putter, which is about to go into volume production, is a triumph of modern technology and, as Brian Harley is already proving, is the best putter in the world.'

I nudged Toby and whispered: 'This is the only chance I'm going to get. I'll try to lose myself on the way into the factory.'

I realised that once the tour of the assembly area was over and the lunch began my chances of nosing around would be minimal.

Jefferson led the way, with his production director, out of the boardroom and across the corridor to the factory door. I lingered, on the pretext of finishing half a glass of champagne. I had noticed on the way in that Jefferson's office was alongside the boardroom and, as the last visitor went through into the factory, I turned sharp left and entered his office.

It was quite a large room, though the huge wood veneered desk seemed equal to the task of filling half of it. There was the usual paraphernalia of filing cabinets and a large selection of framed photographs of Derek Jefferson with various stars of screen, golf and Parliament. I was in two minds about closing the door, but decided that it would be safer to do so; if anyone came through it unexpectedly I would have a split second to look lost and nonchalant.

I had no idea what I was looking for and certainly no intention of starting on the filing cabinets. I decided that a rapid look through the papers which were piled into two filing trays on Jefferson's desk was my best bet.

I went through the first pile, which seemed mainly to be stock orders from golf professionals around the country, and started on the next tray. This contained miscellaneous correspondence, but near the bottom of the tray the letter heading of my favourite Sunday newspaper caught my eye. I glanced at it quickly and saw that the advertising manager had written to confirm the booking of a double-page spread in the colour supplement for six successive weeks, beginning on the Sunday after the Open Golf Championship.

The implications of this astonished me. Even with my limited knowledge of the cost of advertising in a posh Sunday colour magazine, I realised that such an exercise would mop up at least twice Supersight's annual spend on promotion. Advertising in the colour magazines is so expensive that their shiny pages are usually the preserve of manufacturers of cars, watches, television, expensive perfumes and the like. I was standing motionless by the desk, and gazing vacantly at the letter, when I heard some footsteps outside the door.

I slung the letter back into the middle of the pile of correspondence and headed very quickly for the door. As I was halfway there, it opened. It was Jefferson's production director.

'What the hell are you doing in here?' he asked. There was no friendliness in his voice.

'Oh, I'm sorry, I was looking for the loo.' I said as casually as I could.

He glared at me and then walked past and had a sharp look around the office.

'Lavatories have W.C. written on the door where I come from, not Managing Director.'

'Yes, I know, but I thought there might be one off the MD's office. I'm very sorry.'

'I suggest you rejoin the visitors and stay with them. There are lavatories in the assembly area.'

He opened the door wider and followed me down the corridor to the factory door.

'Who are you, by the way?' he asked.

'Chris Ludlow, a friend of Toby Greenslade's.'

With a nod, and another terse look, he walked off down the corridor.

I wasted no time in entering the assembly area and rejoining the cheerful gang of visitors, buoyed up by the welcome infusion of champagne and looking forward to more.

Derek Jefferson had certainly whizzed them round the factory, and was already in the final assembly area. He was explaining how the finished clubs are matched for weight, and how precise this matching had to be. He used the old but very effective trick of balancing a five-pound note on a club head to demonstrate how this changed the swing-weight quite significantly.

As we went towards the final stop on the factory tour, where the clubs were diligently checked by hand, I managed to edge alongside Toby.

'How much does a double-page spread in a Sunday colour supplement cost?' I asked him.

'Oh, about thirty grand,' he said.

'Well, our friend is planning to spend over a hundred and fifty thousand pounds with just one of the Sundays.'

'God Almighty, have you gone off your head or has he? Are you sure?'

I whispered in his ear 'I saw a letter from the advertising director of the *Sunday Chronicle*. It confirms a booking of six double-page spreads, starting the weekend after the Open.'

Toby was doing his own brand of gaping by this time. It didn't last long because we were back in the boardroom by now, and he quickly got another glass of champagne into his clutches.

'Come over here,' he said, 'let's have a word with old Eric.' Eric was the editor of a monthly golf magazine for which Toby wrote occasional feature articles.

After greeting each other warmly, Toby said:

'How are Supersight doing? I hear they're spending a lot of money on promotion.'

'As far as I can tell their clubs are doing very well. As you know they're designed for the middle to high handicap player, for the person who needs a bit of extra help. Like me, but not like young Chris here.'

Eric grinned at me and I smiled back because I knew that, at well over sixty, he still played a very competitive game of golf off a handicap of ten.

'And are they spending as much on promotion as Jefferson would have us believe?' pressed Toby.

'Well, of course, Brian Harley is doing the firm a hell of a lot of good with that magic putter of his; and, yes, they have booked some extra space with us from July onwards and up to Christmas.'

Toby looked meaningfully at me and changed the subject as we moved towards the table for lunch.

The table had been laid out as a T, with Derek Jefferson at the head of the table, flanked by his production director and, as yet, an empty space on his right. As we settled ourselves, the boardroom door opened and in came the stocky figure of a man I had met, in quite different circumstances, a couple of weeks before. It was Brian Summers, the Chairman of World Wide Insurance.

I nudged Toby and asked, 'What's he doing here?'

'I don't know, dear boy. But he is a major golf sponsor, and he's known Jefferson for years. Maybe he insures Jefferson's company or something.'

Eric, who was seated opposite, caught the tail end of that remark.

'It's a little more than that, Toby. I'm told that Brian Summers put up some money to get the company started and now has quite a significant slice of the Supersight action.'

It was a pleasant and, for many of those present, a very convivial lunch. The whole occasion was organised by Derek Jefferson with some style: from the brilliant white tablecloths and silver cutlery to the excellent food and well-chosen wines. At the close, over the coffee and brandies, he thanked us all for attending, told one short and amusing joke and wished us on our way. As we left we were all presented with a small package, wrapped in gold paper which sported the Supersight emblem.

As we set off back to London, Toby opened his parcel. It was a leather-bound facsimile copy of Bobby Jones' famous autobiography, *Down the Fairway*.

'The man certainly has some style,' said Toby reflectively.

'And money,' I added.

'Yes. On the way out I had a quiet word with young Anna from the other golf magazine. She told me more or less the same story as Eric – that they are reserving double the usual amount of space for Jefferson over the second half of the year.'

'How on earth can he spend all this money? I checked them out recently when I was doing an analysis of the golf market. The company only turned over about three million pounds last year, and made profits of just over a hundred thousand. It's just not on.'

As we drove back into London and towards Toby's house we worried away at the problem, to such an extent that the issues became more, rather than less, obscure. In the end, I refused Toby's offer of a drink, and we agreed to sleep on the problem and talk again sometime during the following day.

# Chapter 9

Despite my comparative abstinence at lunch I felt sluggish; two or three glasses of wine added to a three-course meal plus some irresistible Cheddar cheese made me feel like the Michelin man. There was only one remedy – a gentle run round the Common. I certainly set off gently but gradually got into my stride along the footpaths under the arches of trees. It was a quiet and mild evening, with just a hint of rain in the air, and after a mile or so I was bowling along quite easily, and feeling excessively virtuous as the sweat eased out of my pores.

I felt renewed, both mentally and physically, when I got back to my flat. I piled into some fruit to stem my thirst and decided against a loll in the bath in favour of a more invigorating shower.

I don't suppose there are many people in the world who have not seen Alfred Hitchcock's *Psycho*. There must be countless people who have a lasting memory of the famous murder scene in the shower. Some of them, such was the insidious power of that sequence, may even feel a slight unease when they step into a shower – especially if the shower has curtains. In a strange house or a hotel room, I have occasionally caught a mental image of the raised hand, with its knife, coming through the shower curtains – only instantly to scoff at my own imaginings.

I wasn't thinking of the entertaining Mr Hitchcock, but was enjoying the cascading water and musing on what Toby and I had learned about Supersight, when the doors of the shower flew open, and I caught a blow on the shoulder which hurled me into a corner.

The rest was blackness.

Was it hours or days later that I struggled back into a misty and painful consciousness? I was lying sprawled on my side on the bathroom floor and my head was belting out its signals of hurt. I tried to sit up but abandoned the attempt immediately and was sick on the floor instead. The retching and coughing made things worse and I must have blacked out again.

It was very dark outside when I woke, so I must have been unconscious for some time. I was lying half in and half out of my own vomit, so I inched across the floor, very slowly, willing myself not to pass out again. My head was certainly no less painful. I grabbed a towel and dabbed at my face. Dried blood came away amongst liquid that I didn't want to examine too closely.

At least I hadn't been stabbed.

I got into a crawling position and managed to fold and tie a large towel around myself. The bathroom door was a problem, but I made a supreme effort as my head spun and got it ajar enough to get one hand between the edge and the door jamb.

I wished I hadn't. The lights were blazing in my bedroom, blazing on the wreckage. The pillows and mattress had been gouged open and every drawer and cupboard had been opened and their contents strewn in a heap. The mirror was smashed and a television set stoved in; and, worst of all my precious cricket paintings, originals by Gerry Wright, had been slashed in several places. Soap powder, wine and tomato sauce had been liberally scattered about.

At one point I nearly lay down and sobbed, but bitter anger got the better of me and I got to my feet, and was even able to survive the drumming of my battered head.

Was the living room of the flat in a worse state? Let's call it a draw. Suffice to say that precious little was left unbroken or untorn. On the wall was the vandals' message: 'Bastard' painted in tomato sauce.

I found the telephone thrown in a corner and, by some miracle, it was still intact. I couldn't find my watch, and for some curious reason checked the Speaking Clock first. It was only 'ten thirty-four and ten seconds'. I assumed it was still Wednesday.

I thought of ringing Toby, but reckoned he would probably be in the pub. I even toyed with the idea of ringing my mother, but could not face the extent of her concern, however loving. Leave her till everything was cleared up.

Mrs Bradshaw was the right person.

After the tenth ring I put the phone down, but then heard the main door of the house slam. I hoped it was Mrs Bradshaw on her return from one of her ruthless sorties at the bridge table. I hurried towards the door which gave on to the hall, and nearly collapsed again from the pain bouncing inside my head.

I craned my neck carefully around the door, and saw the hem of a tweed skirt going upstairs.

'Mrs Bradshaw.' It came out as a quavering croak.

'Who's that?' she asked in her sternest voice. I realised that I had probably startled her.

'It's me, Chris.' I realised, as she turned and came back down the stairs, that clothed as I was in a soiled and blood-stained towel, I would present a bizarre sight.

'My dear boy, what on earth has happened?' she said. Her first look at the wreckage of my flat confirmed her worst fears. She took charge.

'I am calling an ambulance and the police. You get into some warm clothes and I will make you a hot drink.'

'No ambulance, thanks,' I said, 'I'm all right. Just a bit of a bump.'

'We'll see. Just wait a moment while I get my first-aid box.'

Mrs Bradshaw reappeared a couple of minutes later with a bowl of disinfected warm water, a hand towel and her first-aid kit. She sat me down on a corner of a sofa and dabbed gently at my broken head.

'Well, it doesn't seem too bad,' she admitted, 'and I've put a plaster on for now. But I think you should see a doctor tomorrow. Now tell me what happened.'

I explained that I had little to tell; that I was innocently taking a shower and was knocked out by an assailant or assailants unknown.

As she phoned the local police station, Mrs Bradshaw extracted a promise from me that I would see a doctor on the next day.

'You will sleep in my spare room tonight, Chris. Now pack some pyjamas and so on while I make some tea.' These were orders, not suggestions.

I did as I was told and in record time a pot of strong tea was produced along with some aspirin to combat the headache.

'Forgive my prying, Chris, but don't you think that it's curious that little or nothing has been stolen? When I was looking for the aspirin in the bathroom I found your watch sitting in full view on the top of the basin. It's a Patek-Phillipe, rather expensive and rather elegant, and it hasn't been stolen. Your television sets and the stereo have all been smashed to bits, whereas a burglar surely would have made off with them.'

I didn't have a real inclination to check what was missing, but a look in the bathroom confirmed that my watch was untouched. I then looked around my bedroom. Although every drawer had been opened and the contents strewn around the room I eventually found my wallet with the thirty or forty pounds I usually carried still intact, as were my credit cards and cheque book. My passport was still in the corner of another drawer along with a small cache of French francs and Spanish pesetas. My little box of cufflinks, one pair in eighteen-carat gold, a twenty-first-birthday present from my parents, was also untouched.

This was certainly odd and I was about to say so to Mrs Bradshaw when a sharp rap on the door, immediately followed by the ringing of the bell, announced the arrival of the police. A sergeant and a constable stood on my front doorstep.

They looked round with their own brand of bored sympathy, were offered tea by Mrs Bradshaw and told firmly not to take too long, and cleared the preliminaries pretty quickly. The sergeant told me to expect a detective to visit in the morning to take a fuller statement, and he would bring a fingerprint expert.

'As you know, sir, we deal with umpteen burglaries every week, and unfortunately most of them go unsolved. They're mostly opportunists who see an easy way in, and go for the cash and valuables. Your weak spot was the hall window. The burglar slipped a knife or something similar under the catch, and bingo, in he came.'

Mrs Bradshaw spoke up: 'I think there was more to it than a bit of opportunistic burglary, sergeant. Chris was severely hurt.'

'Yes, madam, I understand that. But the detective will deal with all that in the morning. By the way, sir, would you please take a look around, without disturbing things too much, and make a list of what's been stolen.'

Mrs Bradshaw was looking at me meaningfully, so I explained that, on the face of it, very little seemed to have gone.

'That does seem very odd, sir. Why should anyone take the

trouble to break in, knock you over the head and then leave without any goodies? He obviously wasn't disturbed because we'd have heard about it by now.

'You aren't in any kind of bother are you, sir? You know, married women or bookies. Anyone with a grudge against you? Giving you a little warning, perhaps?'

I said no, but Mrs Bradshaw intervened with her account of the rough-looking character who had been asking after me a few days before.

'And what about that message on your answering machine, Chris?'

'Oh, that was nothing, a mistake or a joke in poor taste,' I said quickly.

But Sergeant Hobbs wasn't going to let that one go.

'I see, sir, you've been getting threatening phone calls, have you?'

Sergeant Hobbs was suddenly looking and sounding more interested.

'I think, sir, that it would be wiser to tell our plain-clothes man everything that seems relevant, don't you?' There was just the merest hint of a threat in his voice, which he alleviated with a smile.

'I hope you sleep well, sir,' he said at the door.

I did, which was a surprise to me, and awoke to a large mug of tea prepared by my ministering angel, Mrs Bradshaw. My head was still aching, but in an acceptable sort of way, and I felt remarkably well-rested in view of last night's events.

'I've run you a nice hot bath, Chris, and breakfast will be ready in fifteen minutes.'

When I reappeared Mrs Bradshaw changed the plaster on my head, tut-tutted several times and sat me down to a breakfast of fresh orange juice, grilled bacon with tomatoes, and wholemeal toast. Delicious. Grand to have a second mother, I thought.

'I've done a little bit of tidying in your flat, nothing drastic to upset the police, and I will have another go after they've left. I noticed that there is a message on your machine. Probably the police, so you ought to check soon. No hurry, finish your coffee in peace.'

I finished my coffee as instructed and tried to help Mrs Bradshaw with the washing-up. She would have none of this and shepherded me to the door.

'Don't worry about the flat, Chris, I shall be round later.'

I thanked her again, and thanked my own lucky stars that I had such a kindly and, above all, understanding neighbour. Help and support were Mrs Bradshaw's watchwords, without a hint of criticism or prying.

As I entered the flat I saw that Mrs Bradshaw had been hard at the tidying. Heaven knows what time she had started, but all the drawers and wardrobes had been tidied up and the furniture put back in its usual places. She could not, of course, do anything about the broken television and the torn paintings, but already the flat seemed habitable again. The memory of the barbaric damage which I had found when I regained consciousness last night was already receding. But I could understand how some people, after their property has been as thoroughly violated as mine had, find it difficult ever to feel at home again, and often sell up and leave. A sort of rape.

It was lucky that Jack Mason's tee-off time in the All-Stars Pro-Am Tournament was in the middle of the afternoon, so I had time to spare.

Lucky for me, but not for Jack, who would be unhappy about setting off on a long round at just before 4 p.m. It could mean his finishing in semi-darkness, if past experience of this particular tournament was anything to go by. The greens around the hole would also be badly spiked by then. But someone has to go out last.

I dressed in some cord trousers and a casual shirt and checked my answering machine.

My boss, Andrew Buccleuth, had asked me to call him, as had a couple of clients, and the last message was from Sergeant Hobbs, telling me that a plain-clothes man and a fingerprint expert would be round to see me at 10.30 a.m. I was only to ring if this was inconvenient.

I glanced at my watch. It was 10.25. On the button of 10.30 the doorbell rang. I opened my front door and there stood Inspector Drew, with another detective, a large, tweed-coated man with glasses and a bushy, reddish beard. This was obviously the fingerprint man.

Inspector Drew was as soberly dressed as ever in a dark grey suit, with another variation on his habitual club tie enlivening his white shirt. His bright blue eyes looked as inquiring as ever.

'Well, sir, I see that we've been in the wars.' Sardonic was perhaps the right word.

I asked them in and was introduced to Sergeant Dennison, the local forensic expert. He began to spread his grey powder on various surfaces while I settled the Inspector in a chair, and offered him coffee.

After this was brewed and served, Inspector Drew took me through my statement.

'It's a peculiar burglary, isn't it, where nothing appears to have been stolen? Are you absolutely sure that you've told us everything. You haven't any large sums of money under the mattress, have you, sir, or the numbers of any Swiss bank accounts hidden away?'

There was a playful tone to these remarks but there wasn't any levity to be seen in his eyes. He continued:

'I suspect, as I'm sure you do, Mr Ludlow, that you are in someone's bad books because of this Froggy Davies affair. You are known to be a good friend of Toby Greenslade, who's been making a great fuss about it in his paper, and got half-killed for his pains.

'I know that you've been to see Froggy's sister, and it wouldn't be difficult for the villains, whoever they are, to have discovered that fact for themselves.

'I also know that you've been sniffing around the Supersight factory,' he ended. He smiled at me and suppressed his air of triumph with some difficulty.

I had to take the bait, and asked him how he knew.

'Even we, the plods, have our own sources of information,' he said, ironically. 'But I hope you will take some advice. That is – do not meddle any more in this business. I should say, for your own safety. But actually I take the view that you're old enough to look after yourself, and if you get hurt, it's your own fault. But when your interference adversely affects our investigations, then I get annoyed.

'I get just as annoyed when you withhold information. That is a criminal offence, or at least we could make it one.'

Inspector Drew then asked me about the man whom Mrs Bradshaw had confronted in the garden, and about the threatening phone call. I stuck to my story that the two things were unimportant and unrelated.

I decided to ask a question.

'Have you any idea yet who killed Froggy?'

The Inspector gave me a studied look and after an uncomfortable gap said: 'Yes, we have a theory. By the way, it's not you. I discarded you as a suspect after a couple of minutes of our first interview. You were clearly not the sort of person who would be prepared to kill someone like Froggy. But I thought I'd string you along.'

'Why?'

'Because you obviously knew more about the background to all this than you were prepared to say. And I thought I would drag it out of you if I put you under pressure.'

'Thanks.'

'And I enjoyed putting you under pressure, because I hate amateurs gadding about on my patch. You may think it's a great lark doing a bit of sleuthing on the side. But remember, this is my career. And I'm serious about my career.'

He gave me another sharp look and, as I began to speak, continued: 'The problem is that none of Froggy's current associates could, according to their alibis, have killed him. I don't think, anyway, that Brian Harley or Derek Jefferson are capable of murder. But the motive is certainly hidden somewhere in the relationships between those three men and their other business connections.'

He paused and I told him of Toby's and my discovery that Brian Summers had links with Supersight.

'Yes, Summers has one-third of the company, and has had it from the start. We've also discovered that Mike Martinez put up several hundred thousand dollars to get the company going and has a twenty-five per cent holding.'

'So, Jefferson has some powerful backing,' I said lamely.

'You could call it that, or maybe you could call it something different,' Inspector Drew said.

By this time Sergeant Dennison had finished scattering his grey powder around the flat. He took my fingerprints for elimination purposes, and we then called Mrs Bradshaw down for the same purpose.

114

She consented to the exercise with a slightly peevish air; Inspector Drew then asked: 'Are you by any chance the widow of Jocelyn Bradshaw, who was at the MOD?'

'Yes, I am.'

'Well, I'm delighted to meet you because I worked with your husband, and very successfully too if I may say so, on some very tricky corruption cases at the end of the seventies. Very hush-hush, bribery from a couple of the Ministry's major suppliers. Your husband was a tower of strength.'

Mrs Bradshaw positively blossomed.

'That's very kind of you, Inspector. I remember that business, though of course Jocelyn wasn't allowed to tell me any details.'

'Quite so. Now I hope, Mrs Bradshaw, that you will keep this young man on the straight and narrow.'

He turned to me: 'As for you, Mr Ludlow, please keep me informed of anything, absolutely anything, that seems relevant to the Davies case.'

Off went the self-contained Inspector Drew, and soon afterwards I followed him, on Mrs Bradshaw's instructions. She had made me an appointment with my doctor for midday. After questioning me, peering at various parts of my head and taking my pulse, he gave me a clean bill of health and told me to take more water with it. Very humorous.

By the time I got back to my flat the remarkable Mrs Bradshaw had already tidied and cleaned the living area and was halfway through the same process for my bedroom.

She told me that Toby had phoned twice, that she had ordered me a new mattress which was being delivered that afternoon, and that there was a salad for me in the kitchen. I started to thank her again and was told brusquely that Mr Greenslade's calls seemed urgent. Getting me a new mattress was the real miracle – on the same day, too. Anything bigger than a pot of paint is always six weeks' delivery.

The retired military men whom newspapers habitually employ to act as receptionists and telephonists eventually answered my call at the *Daily News*, and put me through to Toby.

'How are you, Chris? Mrs B told me that you'd been duffed up. It wasn't a couple of burly gentlemen in jeans and black bomber jackets, by any chance?'

'Not as far as I know. I didn't see or feel a thing – until I woke up. All I remember is the shower door slamming open; I was hurled into a corner, and then, oblivion. As directed by Alfred Hitchcock.'

'What did they take?'

'As far as I know, nothing. Not even my invaluable collection of your articles from the *Daily News*, Toby.'

'Well, they obviously have no taste. Which brings me to my editor. He's told me to lay off the Froggy Davies story. I wanted to follow up with a bit more on Supersight and Brian Harley and so on, but he told me that the story's dead and to leave it to the police. I've got to concentrate on the tournaments, and particularly on the show-biz personalities at this week's ghastly affair.'

'Well, shouldn't you be there? I'm about to leave. I've got to meet Jack at a quarter to three.'

'Yes. I'm on my way. But my editor called me in specially to tell me of his momentous decision. Anyway, have you time for a sandwich before you meet Jack? If so I'll meet you in the sponsors' lounge at two o'clock.'

The course, Radley Manor Golf and Country Club as it was rather portentously called, was no more than forty minutes' drive away, so I agreed to meet Toby, ate Mrs Bradshaw's salad at speed, and got on my way.

I arrived at the sponsors' tent and my fears that it would be too public a place to discuss the ins and outs of the Froggy Davies affair were groundless. The noise from the people having lunch, or just a few drinks at the bar, was intense. Since the show-biz element was present in force, the clash of dozens of oversized egos produced a racket verging on pandemonium.

Toby was in a corner with a colleague from the *Sunday Chronicle*, with whom Derek Jefferson had agreed to spend so much of his advertising budget. Toby waved his almost empty champagne glass at me.

'Chris, dear boy, you know Peter, I'm sure. What would you like?'

I ordered my habitual mineral water, and while they both admired the bump on my head, I shook hands with Peter McGregor, who was one of the reasons for my addiction to his newspaper. He was a stylish and witty writer who had won his golf blue at Oxford just after the war. With a rich father, and an even richer wife, he did not really have to work and this had enabled him to develop his own idiosyncratic style of golf writing, which harked back to a more leisurely age and suited his newspaper well. His editor allowed him the freedom to choose the tournaments he wished to cover; and quite often he would opt to cover an obscure amateur tournament in preference to a European Tour event.

Shortly afterwards Peter McGregor left and Toby manoeuvred me into a corner of the bar, so that his back was to the hubbub.

He looked at me seriously and said: 'I'm still having nightmares over that attack. I check every corner of the house before I go to sleep at night.'

'Don't worry, Toby, I think that they've made their point. I know exactly how you feel. I'm going through the same agonies. Every time I go into the flat I will expect a bash on the head.'

Toby brightened up a bit and said: 'I've just had a quick drink with Graham Fearnley, and I was telling him how my editor had more or less warned me off the Froggy Davies story. Do you know what he told me?' asked Toby dramatically.

'No, but go on.'

'That bastard editor has apparently done some kind of deal with the all-conquering Mike Martinez for Brian Harley's life story, if he wins the Open.

'According to Fearnley, and you know as I do that the agents' grapevine is usually pretty accurate, Martinez virtually gave the story away, as long as my paper gives Harley and of course Supersight "positive publicity". In other words, don't muddy the Froggy Davies waters.'

'How did Fearnley find this out?'

'Apparently the rumour came from one of his mates on the *Star*.'

'How much is the story of the Open Champion worth to the *News*?' I asked.

'Well, if Harley does the usual birds and booze revelations which the *News* insists on, it should be worth at least thirty thousand. They paid something similar for that Billy Hardy nonsense last year.'

Toby was referring to the revelations of one of the more demented, if immensely talented, footballers of the last few years. His sudden

117

fame, from being a promising young player in the lower depths of the Scottish Second Division to becoming the superstar striker of a leading club in England, had dizzied and destroyed him in the space of five years. His sad and unnecessarily seedy story had come and gone in a three-day burst in the *Daily News* – titillating for the readers, humiliating for him – and all to pay a tax bill.

As his empty glass was refilled Toby said: 'These people obviously expect Harley to win the Open. If you had tried to place a bet on him at the start of the season I would have given you ten thousand to one for any amount of money you cared to name, and yet his agent and the Supersight people are acting as if he cannot fail. Why?'

'Because he's putting like God,' I said lamely.

'Exactly. The key to this whole business, as I keep saying, is his putter. I bet you that it's a ringer. We've got to find out why, and how. We could try and steal the putter and take it apart, but I'm told that the putter goes into the hotel safety deposit at night, and when Harley is between tournaments it goes back to the factory for safe-keeping.'

We both stared helplessly at each other, then I said:

'Why not approach it from another angle. The putter was designed in California. Why did Jefferson bother to go to such trouble and expense, when there are dozens of people in Britain who could have designed the thing just as well? The story is that he wanted an ultra-modern, *Star Wars* look to it and went to a US company with the ultimate expertise in metal technology. OK, it is an unusual compound of ceramic and metal, but nothing that couldn't have been produced here. So, let's find out more about the US company.'

'How?' asked Toby. 'Neither you nor I can swan off to California just like that and the Open begins in just over two weeks' time.'

'My father will be on the West Coast next week and he's taking my brother, Max, with him.'

'I didn't know you had a brother.'

I told Toby a little about Max's background. He was two years younger than me, and had had, if possible, an even more erratic career. He had won a scholarship in mathematics to Cambridge and had set out to enjoy his three years there to the full. He was one of those irritating people who excels at any sport. If you invented a game on Monday, he would beat you at it on Tuesday.

His hockey blues were a foregone conclusion, and he added his cricket blues in his second and third years. He just failed to get a football blue through an injury at the wrong time, but managed to run the 400 metres for the University as well. Too much sport and too little maths gave him a third-class honours degree, much to his tutor's and our father's disgust. The latter had already, in his own mind, slotted him into the family firm.

'But Max had other ideas,' I continued. 'He joined the Army on a short-service commission, was seconded to some obscure branch of Intelligence because of his mathematical knowledge, and did several spells in Northern Ireland.'

'And I suppose he's a dab hand, like you, at dealing unobtrusively with drunken Scotsmen in Fleet Street bars,' said Toby.

'Not bad. Until recently he worked in Brixton. He taught various sports at the leisure centre, and particularly martial arts. Apparently the locals were flocking in after a couple of weeks.'

'I can imagine,' said Toby drily. 'And now they're all fully-fledged Black Belts and are out there terrorising everybody over the age of fifty.'

'On the contrary, the juvenile crime rate in the area has actually declined, because the martial arts code brings its own kind of discipline.'

'Glad to hear it. Perhaps we should both apply for a bodyguard from amongst Max's pupils.'

'Maybe. Anyway, I'll be off. I must meet Jack. He reckons half an hour's practice is enough preparation for this tournament. You know how he hates it.'

'Good luck. See you later.'

# Chapter 10

I hurried off to the clubhouse in the light drizzle which had just begun to fall. Jack Mason was on the putting green, and I could tell by the desultory way in which he was tapping his putts at the hole that his mood matched the weather.

He cheered up a bit when he saw the plaster on my head.

'Don't tell me, somebody has tried to send you on your way to join Froggy Davies, but your head was too hard.'

I managed a smile, which came out thin.

'Not far out, Jack. I had an argument with a blunt instrument and lost.'

I explained briefly what had happened and then suggested that we went down to the practice ground.

Jack's performance there was as casual as it had been on the practice putting green, and I was reduced to muttering hackneyed old phrases which might get him back into a golfing mood. Keep it smooth. Release the club head. Hit through the ball. And so on.

Jack hit no more than twenty or so shots and then suggested that we had another putt. As we walked past groups of players I heard many an old refrain.

'I'm really hitting the ball great, but the putting . . .'

'That new wood of mine is going like an arrow – except when I'm under pressure.'

'And then she told me to get under the shower . . .'

'What's the definition of eternity?'

Not even Jack knew the answer to that one. He was more concerned about his three partners for the first round, and we duly met them outside the imposing clubhouse. This was a magnificently vulgar mid-Victorian country house, which reflected the supreme self-confidence of our forebears of that time. Fast Victorian money had built it, and when the money ebbed the house had seen many uses. A hospital during the First World War, it had then been empty and neglected until a group of wealthy businessmen had turned it into a sporting club in the 1920s. A few holes of golf had been laid out, and it eventually became a fully-fledged golf club in the thirties.

It was not quite smart enough in those days to receive the final accolade of regular visits by the Prince of Wales, and so never aspired to the prefix of 'Royal', but was now a very expensive country club with tennis and squash courts, a swimming pool, and a gymnasium. Within thirty miles of central London, it was firmly positioned in the stockbroker belt.

In some ways the wheel had turned a full circle, and the fast money which had built the place in the nineteenth century had returned in a modern guise. Property developers and the newly affluent members of City firms seemed to make up much of the membership, and at weekends the place was awash with Mercedes cars, the latest designer clothing and expensively acquired tans. Why worry about your golf handicap so long as you possessed the latest metal woods? Why worry about your lobs and your passing shots as long as you used the Graphite-Pro racket and dressed in Tacchini clothing?

There was quite a crowd milling about in front of the imposing Ionic columns which marked the main entrance to the clubhouse.

I realised why when I saw a tam o'shanter sitting askew the lank and sandy hair of a well-known comedian, who worked his Scottish origins to the bone on and off the stage.

I had not seen the list of players and when I had earlier asked Jack which celebrity he had drawn had not taken in the significance of his description. 'Some sodding comedian' had been shot at me through his pursed mouth. It was the sort of phrase that Jack used to describe anyone on the golf course who didn't play to a handicap of plus two.

The sodding comedian in question was Jimmy McCoy, 'the real McCoy', a forty-ish and middling comic who had become fashionable in the last few years.

He had been written up by the theatre critic of one of the posh newspapers as an alternative comedian, and had never looked back.

I had seen his act, and if alternative comedy consisted of strings of obscene and lavatorial words, coupled with simplistic jibes at the current government, all delivered at full volume in an almost indecipherable Glasgow accent, then Jimmy McCoy was an alternative comedian.

His private life was lived in public. His latest conquest was a dizzy, leggy, blonde actress who, as Toby once put it, imploded on the screen in her latest and only role as a dumb blonde.

But maybe she wasn't so dumb. Because her career had certainly taken off in the six months or so that their affair had lasted. The gutter press reported the progress of the relationship in lovingly salacious detail. It was great publicity – and especially for Christa Downes who became famous, or notorious as Mrs Bradshaw would have put it. For a time the process was self-perpetuating. Christa Downes was famous, so her photograph appeared more and more frequently in a certain type of newspaper; and so more and more offers came in to her agent for her to appear on television chat shows, to open supermarkets, and to act in this series and that series. Therefore her photograph became even more desirable for the newspapers, and so on.

Jack Mason gave the loving pair a perfunctory wave over the heads of their fans, and pointed towards the first tee.

'Let's get away from this sodding circus,' he said quietly to me, and walked on. His two other partners were waiting for him by the tee, and I was relieved to see that they were unlikely to add to the irritations which Jimmy McCoy would inevitably create for Jack. One was a middle-aged businessman who was a regular on the pro-am circuit and played a middling game of golf off a fairly high handicap, and the other was a former Test cricketer who played an excellent and stylish game off a handicap of four.

There were greetings all round; the cricketer said he hoped they could help Jack to win some money; and I reminded Jack that there was, after all, a first prize of £40,000 at stake and Ryder Cup points as well.

The group ahead of us had now driven off, and we could see and certainly hear the McCoy entourage approaching. The harsh Scottish voice of Jimmy McCoy was at full volume with a familiar repertoire of one-liners, and the cameras were clicking away like muted machineguns.

It was clear that Christa was going to accompany us for at least a part of the round – probably until her stilt-like high heels gave way under the strain.

I watched a succession of feelings flit across Jack Mason's face. First, irritation at the disruption which McCoy and his hangers-on were causing; second, an automatic appraisal of Christa Downes and obvious approval of what he saw; and then irritation again, because Jack had firm views on the place of women at a men's professional golf tournament. In short, he believed that they should stay on the spectators' side of the ropes. He was unhappy, for instance, that one or two of the younger and impoverished professionals employed their wives or girlfriends as caddies. It seemed sensible to me, but Jack argued cogently that it was bad for the player's golf, and probably for the relationship of the couple, too.

On the tee the McCoy patter continued and I knew that Jack's temperament, ever uncertain, would not necessarily survive the pressure. Nevertheless, he hit a glorious one-iron down the first fairway, and his partners followed in their different ways.

As we walked down the first hole I lingered a little in order to have a quiet word with McCoy.

'I hope you won't take this amiss, Mr McCoy, but this is an important tournament for my boss, and if you can keep it quietish, it would help.' I made a vague patting motion with my hand to reinforce my comment.

'You do your job and I'll do mine, laddie,' was his reply and he strode on up the fairway. His arm was entwined with the lovely Christa's and, to the delight of the hovering photographers, he squeezed her backside.

'Prime rump – even if it isn't Scottish.' Christa pouted and simpered, again for the benefit of the photographers.

As I walked down the fairway towards Jack's ball I reflected that I had rarely seen eyes with less humour in them than Jimmy McCoy's. Some comedian.

The round went quite well for several holes. Despite his dismissive attitude towards me, McCoy had perhaps taken some notice of my remark and got on with the game with the minimum of fuss. Jack had got to two under after seven holes and seemed to be concentrating pretty well, especially since the seven holes had taken nearly two hours. The slow pace suited Christa since she was able to teeter along in her high heels at her own speed and still stay with us.

The eighth hole is one of the longest in championship golf. It is a shade over 600 yards and is a double dogleg – first to the left and then to the right. The purists regard it as gimmicky, but lined as it is with tall trees, it is a dangerous hole.

The truth is that course designers are getting desperate. The pros are hitting the ball further each year, not because they are better players than their forebears but because their equipment is better.

After two shots, Jack was about eighty yards from the plateau green and, with his efficient short game, in with a good chance of another birdie. He was on the right side of the fairway, and Jimmy McCoy and Christa were about forty yards away on the other side amid the knots of spectators.

Just as Jack was starting his backswing, Christa trod on a pine cone, one of her high heels buckled under her and down she went with a squeal. The photographers converged and got some pictures of the star in a heap, with long legs and micro-skirt awry.

Jack could not stop his swing and did very well to hit the ball at all. It scuttled about forty yards up the slope and stopped. Instead of a possible birdie we were now hoping just to save par.

Jack set off across the fairway at speed and I raced after him. With the gentlemen of the Press out in force, I had visions of a colourful tirade from Jack, followed by a record fine and suspension by the PGA.

I grabbed him by the arm and tried to slow him down. Difficult to slow fourteen stones of angry sportsman.

'Jack, calm down, and be careful. The Press will blow whatever you say out of all proportion.'

He slowed down, certainly, and then pushed, none too gently, through the group which was surrounding the stricken Christa.

To my relief, he took her gently by the arm. 'Are you all right, my dear?' he asked, gave her a gentle pat with his other hand and said to McCoy: 'Could I have a quick word, Jimmy?'

He propelled him through the crowd and towards the middle of the fairway. I followed closely and apprehensively.

Jack put his arm round the Scottish comedian, smiled and spoke. From a distance it looked as though he was telling him a joke or perhaps offering some friendly advice about some aspect of the golf swing.

'Look, you Scotch berk, this is where I work and where I earn my living. Your bloody stupid woman has just cost me one or maybe two strokes. By Sunday afternoon that may cost me several thousand pounds.'

I saw McCoy try to pull away. But Jack, still smiling, tightened his formidable grip on McCoy's shoulder.

'Both of you behave or I'll take it out on your ugly Scottish face when the round is finished. And if you tell anyone that I threatened you, I will deny it.'

Jack stopped smiling, gave McCoy a last stony look, and went off to play his next shot.

I was thankful that Jack got up and down in two shots for his par five, and so, I thought, was Jimmy McCoy. Christa had taken refuge in the clubhouse. A solicitous official had had his moment of glory by driving her there in one of the buggies.

But Jack's concentration was certainly impaired and he dropped several shots over the next few holes. On the sixteenth fairway, during what seemed like an interminable delay while the green cleared, he delved in his golf bag and produced a bottle of Owd Billy's Best beer. I declined a taste, and within seconds the bottle was emptied.

Jack finished with a very moderate two over par score. Despite his annoyance, he joined his two amateur partners in the bar for a quick drink. McCoy had wisely kept well away from Jack but, as we prepared to leave the bar, he was holding court in a corner of the clubhouse. I was uneasily aware of the loud Glaswegian tones of McCoy, and the peals of sycophantic laughter. I was even more uneasy when Jack glanced over and registered the source of the merriment.

He thanked his two amateur partners for their support and they wished Jack well in the next round.

'I'm just going to say my farewells to my other partner,' Jack said, as we walked towards the door.

'Take it easy, Jack, it's not worth the bother.' I manoeuvred myself between him and McCoy's table, as another burst of laughter counterpointed one of the famous comedian's stories.

Jack walked round me and, short of strong-arming him out of the bar – a tactic which had a dubious chance of success – there was little I could do to stop him.

Jack loomed over McCoy and his group. In the pause which followed Jack nodded at Christa Downes.

'I hope your ankle is not damaged beyond repair, Miss Downes.' He smiled benignly as she twittered her thanks. He turned his eyes on McCoy.

'I hope, Mr McCoy, that my tournament is not damaged beyond repair. Maybe, one day, I'll turn up when you're working and we'll see how your sense of humour stands up. OK?'

To my relief Jack turned and strode from the bar. We arranged to meet at eight o'clock the next morning.

As I walked through the light drizzle towards the car park, I glanced at the main scoreboard. It confirmed that Brian Harley was three shots in the lead with a first round of 62. The magic putter was still weaving its spell.

By the time I got home, the headache had returned. I was too weary to cook, and merely made myself a tuna and lettuce sandwich and drank a bottle of Ruddles beer. The message light was glowing on my answering machine, but I didn't even bother to play the tape. Tomorrow would be soon enough.

I woke up at seven, put some carrot and apple through the juicer and ate a couple of peaches and half an avocado pear.

My answering machine only had one message, a pleasant one. It was Sally, who proposed dinner with her on Sunday night.

When I met Jack Mason outside the clubhouse I suspected that it was not going to be one of his better days. Although he would not at first admit it he was obviously in the grip of a hangover and, rather than a session on the practice ground, he steered us towards the players' lounge for a cup of coffee.

Knowledgeable as he was about the progress of hangovers, Jack had half a cup of coffee only and followed it with nearly a litre of mineral water.

'I don't know why I do it, Chris, and particularly at my age. I'm so hungover that my bloody teeth ache. But maybe that's the best way to survive this bloody awful tournament.

'Who am I playing with, by the way?'

I looked at my copy of the starting sheet and read the names to Jack. There was nobody to object to, although Jack groaned gently at the last member of the team, a former racing driver whose clothes were usually as scruffy as his golf swing.

At this point Toby Greenslade came into the room, poured himself a cup of coffee, spoke to one of the stewards and greeted us cheerfully.

'What on earth are you doing up at this ungodly hour?' asked Jack.

'Pursuing my noble profession, honestly and efficiently, as always,' said Toby. 'I'm under strict orders to follow that great British golfing hope, Brian Harley, and to report his every triumphant shot to his adoring public. He's in the group ahead of yours, Jack, and that's why I was ripped untimely from my lovely bed.'

The steward appeared at Toby's side and handed him a glass. Jack took one look at it and gave yet another groan.

'Good God, Toby, how can you?'

'Hair of the dog, old boy, and you look as though you need one, too.'

'It would take more than a large brandy to get my heart started.'

'Perhaps Christa Downes could trip it into action,' said Toby maliciously.

'Very funny. Come on, Chris, let's have a putt before this farce begins. See you later, Toby.'

'You'll see me soon, because I'll be following Harley,' he said as he tipped the remnants of his brandy into his coffee and gulped it down.

As we left the clubhouse, Jack handed me the keys to his car and asked me to fetch his clubs.

'I'll see you on the putting green. And bring the collapsible chair with you.'

I looked at him questioningly.

'These rounds take so bloody long, I'm going to take it easy between shots. Then these sodding officials will maybe realise that this slow play has got completely out of hand. Five and a half hours yesterday. Even with four people putting everything out, it shouldn't take longer than four hours. Ridiculous.'

Jack was right, of course. The curse of slow play had seeped into the game at all levels. From the time that the phenomenal Jack Nicklaus had adopted such a studied approach to the game, the professional game had got slower and slower – especially on the greens where most of the current crop of players prowled about and studied the line from every angle. It was quite often self-defeating, since doubts were sown where doubts need not have existed. For most golfers, Bobby Locke's advice on putting would be far better: 'decide what you are going to do, and go ahead and do it.' He was the best putter the game has ever seen.

It is even more ludicrous at the amateur level, where you see club hackers imitating the pros. They mark and wipe their ball, agonise over the line of the putt, and then miss easily from three feet for their three-over score. And all the time the game is slowing down.

I didn't like Jack's plan, although it was typical of him to make this kind of protest. I was surprised that he hadn't brought another chair, a table, a picnic basket and a silver service.

Not quite, although when I looked into his suspiciously heavy bag I found three bottles of Owd Bill bitter. Obedient caddie that I was, I hefted the bag on to my shoulder, grabbed the folding chair, and walked over to the putting green.

After a few putts we strolled over to the first tee and greeted the other members of the team. We were due off in five minutes and I was surprised to see that Brian Harley and his team were still on the tee. The matches were timed at eight-minute intervals and I would have expected the preceding players to be lining up their second shots.

The tournament director, my old friend Oliver Moreton, was talking earnestly to Brian Harley. I saw Toby on the fringes of the little group.

'What's up, Toby?' He pointed.

The young American caddie with the stylish haircut came through the crowd and on to the tee. He walked rather stiffly towards Harley. In those circumstances I would have been highly embarrassed, but this caddie had a curious half-smile on his face.

'Sorry, man, I overslept.'

Harley stared at him for a moment and said: 'You've cost us a penalty of two shots.'

I admired his restraint, but no doubt he would make up for it later, out of earshot of officials and spectators.

Brian Harley asked his caddie for his one-iron, threw the ball on the tee and hit a low raking shot which hooked into real trouble well to the left of the fairway. He tossed the club back to his caddie, who bent to pick it up, staggered and nearly fell. The half-grin had not left his face.

I turned to Toby and said quietly, 'He's as drunk as a judge.'

'Not drunk, I fear, but stoned. This is going to be some round.'

It certainly was and we had a good view of it as we followed Harley and his team down the fairways.

Jack's folding chair got a great deal of use, and of course caused much amusement amongst the spectators. Jack became almost jovial as he watched Harley visit many of the obscurer parts of the course. Even his magic putter couldn't save him and the red figures on the scoreboard, which signify below-par figures, changed during the course of the round to blue, which shows a player as being over par.

Harley scored eighteen shots more than his first round and went from eight under par to two over for the tournament. Jack scored a reasonable one-under-par 69 and drank three litres of Owd Bill.

While Jack was checking and signing his card, and also checking the team card carefully because there were useful team prizes to be won, I wandered in the direction of the PGA caravan in the hope of seeing Sally Drayton. She was by the entrance and was talking to Oliver Moreton. She was in three-quarter profile when I first saw her, and I felt an immediate lift in my heart – a lightening of the spirit, as when you awake from a long sleep, walk over to the window and throw the curtains open on a bright and brilliant sunny morning.

I was amused by the body language. Oliver Moreton was looking over her and towards her, and Sally was leaning backwards in an attitude that cried out, 'Help, let me out.'

She saw me, smiled, and slipped around Oliver Moreton.

'My God, Chris, what's happened to your head?'

I realised that I had not spoken to her since I had been attacked and began to explain, when she threw her arms around me and hung on tight. Over her shoulder I saw Oliver Moreton, after glaring at me with great distaste, retreat into the caravan.

'I'm OK, Sally. I just had a slight accident.' I told her about my unknown attacker and reassured her that I had suffered virtually no ill effects. I changed the subject.

'I see that Oliver Moreton's still after you, then.'

'Yes, and very boring it is, too. Are you all right for Sunday?'

'Of course – your place or mine?'

'Well, I haven't seen your flat, so why don't I pop round. Is eight-thirty OK?'

So that was agreed and we tentatively planned a quick drink on the following day. This would be the Saturday of the tournament when the crowds would increase, and so would the pressure on the players.

I was curious to learn more about Harley's disastrous round, and headed for the Press tent to find Toby.

The security man let me through the door without demur, and I saw that one of the tournament leaders was being interviewed at one end of the tent.

'And what iron did you hit into the fourteenth green?' I heard one of the journalists ask.

Toby was at the other end of the tent and was studying a television monitor with close attention. It was tuned in to the Test Match at Lord's.

'Hello, dear boy. Foster's nearly got his ton. Lovely player, wish I was there.'

He was referring to Martin Foster, one of the few England batsmen who could stand up to the battery of Australian fast bowlers.

'He was in the same Cambridge side as brother Max,' I said.

'Was he, indeed? And when is your famous brother going to do some sleuthing for us?'

'He's off to the States on Sunday for a week. I've asked him to the tournament tomorrow. Can we have a drink with him after Jack's played?'

'Fine.'

'What happened to Harley, by the way?'

Toby grinned.

'Well, he was furious as you saw, and that's no way to start a round of golf. He dropped two shots on the first and two more on the next two holes. His caddie was so stoned he could hardly stay upright, and he certainly couldn't work out the distances on his chart.

'Worst of all he was swaying about on the greens. He was hanging on to the flags for dear life, and they were rattling about like ships' masts in a force ten. Not surprisingly, it ruined Brian's putting.'

'So he's not number one in the Harley hit parade at the moment.'

'Absolutely not. If looks could have killed . . .'

I refused Toby's offer of a drink and headed for the car park. As I went through the line of hospitality tents, which are such a feature of golf tournaments now, I reflected on the capricious nature of golf.

How could an experienced player like Brian Harley, who had scored eight under par on the first day and was seemingly in prime form, collapse in such dramatic fashion?

Anger could certainly ruin a golfer. Bad decisions in the heat of the moment lead to poor shots, and then the desire to repair the damage leads to more bad shots as the player tries to force the golfing pace.

There is a subtle difference between the player who is taking positive risks to improve his position in a tournament and one who, in a mood of anger or despair, is trying to retrieve a situation which he believes is not of his own making. Harley had no doubt fallen into the latter category. The golf course is no place to vent your anger.

# *Chapter 11*

I awoke early on the Saturday morning. Jack, who surprisingly was in a reasonable position in the middle of the field, was due out at midday. I reflected that the bright sunshine would certainly bring the television fans to the tournament, and maybe even a few golf fans.

I felt a great desire to roll over and snooze for another hour, to revel in that delightful limbo, half-awake and half-asleep. But sternly I forced myself out of bed and put on a tracksuit. After a few minutes of stretching exercises I began a circuit on the weight-training machine, languidly at first, and then with more gusto as the flow of blood and the pulse rate increased. Rodrigo kept me company on the stereo.

With some feelings of unease I got into the shower, and nervously left the door ajar. It was a rapid shower, although I kept reassuring myself that the same sort of attack couldn't happen twice. I was glad to dry myself, however, and put on some clothes.

I was biting into a breakfast apple and thinking that I should ring my brother, when the doorbell pinged. The milkman, I thought, and scrabbled about for some change.

However, it was Toby Greenslade who was standing on the doorstep.

'Good morning, Chris, may I come in?'

I stood back and he headed for the kitchen.

'Any coffee on? Oh, of course you don't drink such poisonous stuff. But you may need something stronger. My editor rang me about half an hour ago and told me to hotfoot it down to Radley Manor.'

Toby looked at me and gave me the full dramatic pause.

'Harley's caddie was found dead this morning by one of the greenkeepers. Maybe we should say stoned dead.'

Toby grinned nastily. 'He had been dumped in one of the bunkers at the eighteenth. It must have been a particularly unpleasant death, because whoever killed him had in effect suffocated him. They'd tied his arms and legs up and then filled his nose with cocaine and taped his nostrils up; they then filled his mouth with sand and taped it up. It can't have taken him long to die.'

'It probably seemed long enough to him.'

I sat down in one of the kitchen chairs, but could find no words which were adequate.

'It's not very healthy to be Brian Harley's caddie, is it?' I said rather helplessly.

'No, and it almost looks as if the poor fellow was punished, a trifle severely in my opinion, for turning up late and the worse for drugs. It certainly looks bad for Harley; he's bound to be a suspect. One death is unlucky, but two looks like more than that.

'Anyway, I've got to get down there to cover the story.'

I decided to follow Toby down to Radley Manor, even though it was nearly three hours before Jack Mason's round began. I paused only to ring Max, to tell him where to pick up his ticket and where to meet us.

I trailed Toby through the Saturday morning traffic of the M25 and we eventually arrived at Radley Manor to find that the normal bustle of a Saturday at a major golf tournament had increased immeasurably, especially in the Press tent.

Telephones were being shouted into by voluble reporters, and typewriters were rattling away. Toby had a quick word with one of the Press Association reporters and told me that a Press Conference was arranged for 10.30 with Inspector Drew, who was in charge of the case.

He was on time, and sat down at the table which was normally used by golf's superstars for their post-round interviews. He had forsaken his usual dark suit and plain shirt for a sports jacket in a very subdued grey and blue check, dark grey trousers and quite a lively striped tie. Obviously it was the weekend gear, or perhaps the Inspector had dressed up, just a little, to meet the Press.

The crush of reporters in front of him immediately began to shout questions, but the Inspector raised his hand, palm outwards, and asked for silence.

134

'Gentlemen, I am going to tell you the facts, as we have so far ascertained them, and you may then ask me your questions – one at a time.'

The man had a natural and unfussy air of command and, in almost total quiet, except for telephones ringing in the background, he summarised what the police knew.

Ricky Steiner, the American caddie, had been found at approximately 6 a.m. in one of the bunkers by the eighteenth green. He had been dead for about four to six hours and had died of suffocation. Inspector Drew confirmed the horrible manner of his death.

He went on to tell us that a blood test showed that he had taken a large amount of drugs, mostly cocaine, during the last twenty-four hours. Apparently he had been seen in several local pubs during the Thursday evening, after Harley's brilliant first round of 62, and was obviously celebrating. The last sighting of him was in the bar of the main local hotel where he had been talking and drinking with several of the show-business crowd. He named a few of the latter, and my ears pricked up when he mentioned Jimmy McCoy who had been fined several times for using marijuana, and I wondered if he had graduated to cocaine. Even at eighty pounds a gram he could afford it.

Inspector Drew then told us that so far they knew nothing of Steiner's movements from then onwards.

He asked for questions and they came thick and fast. No, the police had no idea of the motive. Yes, they had already interviewed Brian Harley and he had a perfectly sound alibi. No, they had no idea who might have supplied Steiner with large quantities of cocaine. And yes, Brian Harley had apparently withdrawn from the tournament.

Toby put his arm up and, after a nod from Inspector Drew, asked: 'You have already made the obvious deduction, Inspector, that the murders of the two caddies are linked in some way. Do you think that someone is actually trying to discredit Brian Harley, to throw suspicion on him in this rather obvious way, for some reason?'

Inspector Drew said that such speculation belonged in the pages of Agatha Christie novels, and that the Press Conference was now at an end.

As he came down from the dais and headed for the door he saw me and stopped.

'Mr Ludlow, how nice to see that you are keeping tabs on these cases. In fact, I'm surprised that you didn't find the body.' He gave me a thin smile. 'I would like to go back over one or two points relating to Froggy Davies' death. How's your head, by the way?'

I thanked him for his concern and explained that, because I was meeting Max later, I could not see him until the early evening.

'Well, let's say seven o'clock in my office, then,' he said, and marched to the door before I could think of any excuses. They wouldn't have helped because his words were more in the nature of a command than a request.

I felt a tap on my shoulder. Andrew Storey, Mike Martinez's right-hand man in Britain and agent to Brian Harley, greeted me.

'Do you know any good caddies,' he asked with a wry smile, which diluted the bad taste of his remark.

'I think Brian should start carrying his own clubs, because I don't think anyone else will. It's too dangerous.'

'Well, Brian is innocent enough,' said Storey. 'We spent yesterday evening together, and we didn't see hide nor hair of Steiner.

'In fact we took a couple of popsies to dinner and, as far as I know, Brian spent the night with his.'

'As you did with yours.'

'But of course.'

It was curious how Andrew Storey reverted to fifties slang when he talked about women. Popsies, indeed. Or perhaps Etonian slang was stuck in some kind of time warp, when all cars were open-topped and all gentlemen wore cravats, and took their popsies to Brighton for a dirty weekend.

'Presumably you have told Inspector Drew all this?'

'Yes, and he's going to interview the two girls, and they will undoubtedly confirm the story. I expect it'll be in graphic detail, too. Brian Harley is quite the sexual gymnast.'

I turned away and headed for the exit before I said something really unpleasant to the one-track-minded Storey.

I still had time to see Sally before Jack arrived at the course. I found her in the PGA caravan and beckoned her outside. I was still rather cautious about being seen in there after the recent unpleasantness with Oliver Moreton.

'You've heard the news, have you?' she asked anxiously.

I admitted that I had been at Inspector Drew's Press Conference, and told her some of my conversation with Andrew Storey.

'Were you with Andrew or Brian last night?' I asked jokingly.

'Very droll,' she said with a withering look.

I changed the subject and asked her if she would like to meet Max later on, and explained that he would try to find out more about the American company which had designed the Supersight range of putters.

'Well, we must arrange for him to meet Ed Grainger as well,' was her parting remark.

'OK, we'll see you in the sponsors' tent at five o'clock.'

Jack Mason, surprised as he was to find himself only eight shots off the lead, decided to ride his luck. He attacked the course with gusto, got a few important putts in and, with the help of a rather lucky pitch and run shot which gave him an eagle halfway through the round, recorded a score of 67 which put him within five shots of the leader.

I just made it to the sponsors' tent by five o'clock. The familiar figure of Toby, in his well-practised pose with a champagne glass at the ready, was already well established, a proprietory elbow on a corner of the bar. He didn't just look at home, he looked as if he was the chairman, the managing director and most of the board of this particular sponsoring company.

Within a couple of minutes Sally joined us, and finally my brother Max came into the tent. He waved cheerfully at us. He looked as fit as ever, in fact he looked like an athlete in full training. At a shade over six feet tall, quite slim but with broad shoulders, his dark hair short and with a lightly tanned skin, he looked like most people's idea of a golfer, tennis player or middle-distance runner.

With the introductions completed, and when Toby had had his own glass refilled with champagne and had secured cold beers for the rest of us, I began to explain to Max the background to the two murders and our suspicions about the Harley set-up.

With frequent interruptions from Toby, I tried to summarise, for Max's benefit, the events of the past four weeks, and the ways in which we thought they were linked.

Max knew, of course, about Froggy Davies' murder and about the attack on the *Daily News'* doughty golf correspondent.

He turned to me and said, with some amusement:

'When I read that Toby had been attacked, at first I thought you must be the attacker, Chris. Revenge for that appalling "Upper-Crust Caddie" headline. You should be ashamed of yourself, Toby. Chris didn't even make it to Cambridge.'

Max never neglected an opportunity to tease me about opting for a provincial university rather than going all out for a place at Oxbridge.

Toby hastily disclaimed all responsibility for the headline in question: 'made up by a junior sub, dear boy,' he intoned.

Max continued: 'On that same topic, I can understand why Toby was beaten up, because he was asking some nasty, insidious questions in his paper about this business. And he was clever enough to hint at a much greater knowledge than he actually possessed. But surely the villains in question were going over the top in attacking you, Chris?

'OK, you went to see Froggy's sister in Birmingham, though there's no reason to suppose that they found this out, and you are known as a friend of Toby's, but that's hardly sufficient reason to risk a violent attack on you and your property.

'Are the Gerry Wrights OK?'

I told him that they were irreparable but that when the insurance money came through it would allow me to replace some of them with other paintings by the same artist.

'Well, that'll be in about five years' time. You know what these insurance companies are like,' Toby said.

'It strikes me that this sequence of beatings-up and murders may not necessarily hang together in the way you've described it,' Max continued thoughtfully, as Toby refilled his champagne glass and ordered more beers for us.

'At first sight you have a fairly sophisticated plan. A golf-club manufacturer and a powerful sports agent get together and decide to groom an average pro golfer, who hasn't won a tournament for years, to win the Open. We have deduced that they've provided him with a huge advantage, some sort of magic putter, which must be illegal, although we don't yet know how this magic putter works.'

Toby and I nodded our agreement, and Max continued.

'The object of the exercise is to make lots of money from Brian

Harley's name when he is the Open Champion. But how much could Martinez make out of him, Chris?'

With a questioning look at Toby, I said: 'Well, between one and two million pounds I suppose. There would be deals for clubs, Supersight of course, clothing, shoes, some TV commercials . . .'

'They surely won't allow him to advertise condoms, will they?' asked Toby nastily.

'. . . a car and an airline contract, and appearance money as well. Yes, that would be a reasonable estimate.'

'But it isn't worth it, is it?' said Max. 'Even if Martinez has some special arrangement with Harley and is taking way beyond his usual twenty-five per cent commission. Let's say fifty per cent. To a man like Martinez, even a million pounds doesn't make murder and mayhem worthwhile. His company, worldwide, must be turning over at least twenty times that amount.'

'Fair comment,' I said. 'According to Andrew Storey, Martinez is making at least a million a year from Carl Krantz.'

'Exactly, so the basic premise behind your theory looks pretty far-fetched. Nevertheless, Harley has suddenly started to win tournaments, and mainly because of his sensational putting. But, and this is a crucial but, would your suspicions about Brian Harley have surfaced if Froggy Davies was still alive and well and being his usual good friend to distillers and bookies?'

Toby began to speak, but Max held up his hand placatingly and carried on. 'You see, that's the other reason that I don't believe that these two Svengalis would have been so naive as to start knocking people off. The last thing they would want is to attract any unwelcome attention to themselves and Harley.

'Let's think about Froggy Davies for a moment, and let's assume that your theory, Chris, about the Harley putter is correct: that it is the key to the puzzle, that somehow an unfair and illegal advantage has been built into it – despite the fact that you yourself have pulled one of the self-same putters to bits and found nothing untoward.

'I wish I could have been there, by the way. You could have done the same thing to my putter – can't hole a thing with it at the moment.'

All three of us grinned sympathetically, but I knew that Max had a touch on the greens that most professionals would envy. He was probably putting even better than usual and was really offering a little propitiation to the golfing Gods in the hope that they would hear his humility and let his streak continue. You may have noticed that you rarely, if ever, hear a good golfer, and especially a professional one, claim that he is putting well. 'I'm putting nicely' or 'steadily' is the most exaggerated description you will get from him. That usually means that the golfer in question has just had a sensational round of about twenty putts. But he is aware that the sin of pride will instantly be punished.

Max continued. 'The caddie was obviously in on the conspiracy. Hence the days of training which Froggy's sister said he had to undergo. Well, perhaps Froggy got greedy and tried to blackmail more money out of Harley's associates. But, surely Martinez and Jefferson had plenty of options and murder wouldn't be one of them? They could simply have called Froggy's bluff; after all who would believe such an outlandish story from a broken-down old caddie, who was probably fantasising after too long and too close an acquaintanceship with the whisky bottle? Or they could have threatened him and perhaps roughed him up a little to show they meant it. Or even have paid him a little extra. Why worry? His fees were just small change to someone like Martinez. But to murder him seems an extreme and unlikely reaction.

'Similarly, the murder of Steiner doesn't fit. As you tell it, it seems almost like the ultimate form of punishment. He turned up stoned and was obviously unreliable, and therefore might blow the lid off the whole thing. OK, so why not give him a few thousand quid's worth of cocaine and dispatch him back to Big Sur or wherever he came from?'

Toby and I looked at each other. Under the strain of Max's critical analysis, our tower of conjecture certainly looked pretty insubstantial.

Sally spoke up: 'Are you suggesting that the murders and the attacks on Chris and Toby are unconnected with the putter business?'

'Possibly. Or even that the magic putter is a figment of your imaginations, and that Harley is just having a lucky streak. It can happen. Remember Orville Moody?'

Toby smiled and for Sally's benefit encapsulated Moody's career. 'After fourteen years in the US Army, Moody tried his hand on the

American tour and won not much more than ten thousand dollars in his first year. He didn't have a great swing and didn't like practising but entered for the US Open in 1969. He took a week's holiday before the tournament and then proceeded to win it by one shot. Rather odd.'

'Actually, I don't really think that my big brother is as daft as he looks,' continued Max. 'Maybe Jefferson and Martinez *have* hatched this extraordinary plot. But maybe they have someone on their team who doesn't acknowledge the constraints of normal behaviour. Perhaps it's someone they can't control, and he is responsible for all the mayhem.

'Of course, the quickest way to resolve the question of the putter would be to steal Harley's. After all, golf clubs are always going missing and we could take it apart and find out if there is anything dodgy about it.'

I explained the heavy security that surrounded Harley's clubs and especially his putter.

'One other question, why haven't the police latched on to this putter theory of yours yet? Surely they could simply commandeer it, take it to pieces, and resolve one of the mysteries?'

'Simply because the plods haven't thought along those lines, yet,' said Toby. 'To them, it's a couple of murders to investigate and they haven't got beyond the normal motives of revenge or greed.'

'Well, greed must be one of the motives. But why don't you or Chris tip off Inspector Drew?'

'In my case,' said Toby, 'because I don't want to spoil a great story. I want to see it unfold to the bitter end and then tell it all, from the inside, to an astonished and grateful world.'

'And you, Chris, apart from the fact that you're a stubborn and independent bugger?'

'Apart from the fact that I don't like to be pushed around by these hooligans, and don't like to see my friends half-killed, I also want to see the full story come out. I'm sure that the police will find the murderer or murderers, but they won't necessarily make the connection stick with Jefferson and Martinez. Let's say I hanker for some poetic justice. And if we can find out what's really behind all this, we might be able to arrange that poetic justice.'

'OK,' said Max, 'I'll have a quiet look at this Californian company which helped to design the putter. It's based in Tustin, you say. I know just the man to help me, Nicholas Carey. We spent a lot of time together in the army. A great snooper, a specialist in electronic surveillance. He's poacher turned gamekeeper now, and has set up as a security consultant in Los Angeles. Naturally, he specialises in the electronics industry, so he should be able to help me one way or the other.

'Look, I must go. I'm adjudicating at a karate competition at the Brixton centre in just over an hour. Then I've got to pack, because Dad and I are catching the eleven o'clock to Los Angeles.'

He shook Toby by the hand and kissed Sally lightly on the cheek.

'I'll report back as soon as I find out anything. In the meantime, keep rolling with the punches; especially you, Chris, you should know how to duck those sucker punches by now.' He had been nearly as amused as Jack Mason by the bump on my head.

He moved off easily through the crowd of drinkers, which parted amicably and immediately for him. They all thought they knew him or had seen him on television or that he was famous for something. He had that effect on people.

'Wow, what a brother,' said Sally, mischievously.

'I'm glad he's on our side,' said Toby.

I glared at both of them, saw that they were grinning at me, and relaxed into a smile.

'I now have the dubious pleasure of an interview with Inspector Drew, so I must push off,' I said. 'I'll see you both tomorrow.'

I pushed the car along the M25 pretty hard wherever I could, although the traffic was as dense as ever. Sartre got it wrong, I thought – hell is other people in other cars.

I was twenty minutes late for my interview with Inspector Drew. After the inevitable offer of a cup of tea, the Inspector, without much preamble, began.

'Mr Ludlow, I think you know more about the circumstances of these murders than you have admitted.' He smiled a brief smile. 'I am not suggesting that you are withholding information as such, but I suspect that through your special position as an upper-crust caddie you have some knowledge, or even just a theory, which would help us.' He smirked and continued.

'I am in a peculiar situation with you because of this. I could give you a hard time, threaten to detain you for questioning and so on, but I don't think that would be very productive, so I asked you here to make you aware of my thoughts.'

He paused. I said nothing, and he looked out of the windows and over the crowded police car park.

'I am asking you to help us in any way you can. These two murders have been particularly unpleasant – the work of a lunatic. On the other hand there are also, as we know, some gentlemen out there playing for high stakes.

'Poor Brian Harley seems to be a victim of this mayhem. Not an innocent victim, because he is clearly hiding something. But he's no murderer, in my opinion. And of course a young lady supplied him with a cast-iron alibi for the night when Steiner was murdered – confirmed by the manager of the hotel who had to ask Harley to keep the noise down, after the people in the next door room complained. If he is pulling a double-bluff, he would have to be the most consummate liar I have ever met.'

I spoke carefully: 'I agree with you about Harley, Inspector. But I have told you all the facts that I know.'

'Maybe all the facts, but not everything you know.'

I shrugged and Inspector Drew continued: 'Obviously we are putting men about at the next few tournaments. It's Monte Carlo next week, then the Scottish Classic and then the Open. Expect to see Sergeant Aitken, and of course I will be keeping a watching brief, too.'

I explained that Jack Mason was not playing in Monte Carlo, so I would not be making the trip either, but we would be in Scotland and then in Lancashire for the Open.

As I opened the door to leave, Inspector Drew said: 'Remember, Mr Ludlow, to tell us anything that might help. You may need a favour from us in the not-too-distant future.'

I was to remember that remark a couple of weeks later.

# Chapter 12

The final round of the All-Stars Tournament on the following day brought out hordes of fans who wanted to see their favourite television stars. The golf was incidental.

As I went with Jack Mason towards the first tee, through a crush of eager autograph hunters who ignored one of the great stalwarts of European golf to get the signature of some shooting star of the goggle-box, I had a nightmare vision of the golf tour a few years hence. The players, to a man, would be wearing clothes in the sponsoring company's colours, with the name and logo emblazoned on every piece of clothing and equipment, from sun vizor to the toes of their shoes. Maybe they would be forced to have the name temporarily tattooed on their foreheads.

As we passed the bulging hospitality tents, noisy with hearty laughter, the nightmare deepened; I envisaged the spectators being composed entirely of corporate guests, with not a genuine golf fan in sight.

Jack had one of his ordinary rounds, although I was relieved to see that he had not brought his folding chair with him, nor any litre bottles of strong beer. Nevertheless, he more or less held his position as at the end of the third round and finished in equal ninth position. He pocketed a satisfactory cheque, maintained his position in the Ryder Cup points table – he was currently lying eighth and would therefore gain an automatic selection to the team – and was looking forward to a week off.

We had a couple of drinks together in the clubhouse, and I asked Jack what he was planning to do.

'I've promised Jenny I'll do a bit of painting around the house, and apart from that I'm going to investigate one or two pubs in Dorset; I've heard there are some interesting beers down there. In between times I'm going to work on my short game – especially pitch-and-run shots. You know what these links courses are like. What about you, Chris?'

'I'm virtually committed to a full week in the office, although I think the boss wants me to have a day's golf with him at Sunningdale, probably on the Friday.'

'By the way, thanks for tipping me off a few weeks ago about Garth Enterprises. I made a decent profit. And I see that the share price has rocketed down. There was talk in one of the papers yesterday that the company is in big trouble.'

I had also read the article, which pointed out that the company had borrowed huge amounts of money to finance acquisitions and some new leisure projects on the strength of its high share price. In the jargon of the City, the company was highly geared. That's fine as long as the share price continues to climb, but if it drops, as Garth's had done, the results can be disastrous.

The loans which the company had outstanding now looked top heavy, and could not be justified in terms of the company's market capitalisation. This was more City jargon which simply meant the total value of the company: the value of each share multiplied by the number of shares which had been issued and were held by the directors of the company.

But the company had some good assets and, in particular, a strong base in property. It owned pubs, restaurants, clubs and leisure centres; it had a couple of marinas and a golf club under development.

It was a classic situation for a takeover bid by another aggressive entrepreneur. The share price was very low, and the successful bidder would pick up an excellent property portfolio at an artificially low price. The board of directors at Garth Industries would try fiercely to resist such a takeover, but the banks and institutions which had lent them money would undoubtedly force them into the sale. So would the other shareholders in the cause of recovering some of the money they had invested.

'Maybe, Jack, you should buy a few more shares in Garth and make another profit on the bid. I'll give you a call tomorrow.'

I left a contented Jack Mason in the car park. He had performed better in the All-Stars than anyone would have predicted, and was looking forward to a week off.

I was looking forward to entertaining Sally Drayton to dinner that evening, but was not so sure that my work in the office would be very diverting. Garth Enterprises were bound to be a problem.

Sally, as always, was relaxing but stimulating company and I forgot all about the ramifications of Brian Harley and his putter, and certainly about any problems I would encounter in the City during the coming week.

To my disappointment Sally left quite early since she had an eight o'clock flight to Monte Carlo for next week's tournament. She would phone me on her return and we would meet either in London or at the next event in Scotland.

At seven o'clock the radio alarm woke me from a dream. I was playing in the last round of the Open Championship. I was in a deep bunker and was trying to play the ball out with a putter. The scoreboard showed I was thirty over par. What a way to start the day.

I was on the tube by 7.30 and wended my uncomfortable way, in the crush of other travellers most of whom seemed to have a bad case of the Monday blues, towards the City.

I got to the office, a huge, upended oblong of steel, copper and glass, shortly after eight o'clock. The entrance hall had a huge glass atrium roof and all around you could see the rest of the building soaring into the sky. The bronze and glass lifts were hurtling up and down the sides of the building. The hallway was filled with plants and small trees. A twenty-first-century jungle.

I wondered anew at the follies and ineptitudes of planners and architects and the greed of property developers who had between them despoiled large stretches of London. It was now a poor imitation of downtown New York. It wasn't a question of keeping the philistines from the gates: they had built the gates and the walls around them.

With this gloomy thought I said good morning to the security guard, who congratulated me on Jack's good showing in the All-Stars, and hit the lift button for the eighteenth floor.

I walked into the main office, or dealing room, a curved space which was almost long enough to accommodate a three-quarter shot with a wedge. The rows and banks of desks stretched across the room. Each desk had its essential computer screen, which gave

147

up-to-the-second analysis of what was happening to the market and to every quoted share.

Some of the salesmen who dealt in American and Canadian shares had their overnight analyses of that market and were already trying to move some shares with their British clients. The first of many bargains were already being struck.

I was just in time for the daily briefing, when the salesmen are told by the company's analysts of any special situations in the market. There are about thirty analysts in the company who specialise in different sectors of the market, and whose job it is to sniff a complex brew of market trends, rumour, speculation, Press comment and company reports and advise the dealers accordingly. Each day they might come up with a dozen or more stories which the salesmen can use in order to persuade their clients to buy or sell shares. Action is all to stockbroking firms – if the market is quiet their turnover suffers. If the market is on the move, either up or down, there will be buyers and sellers and therefore the firm will be making its commission.

I took the usual greetings from my colleagues, dressed in their usual colourful array of striped shirts and not-always-matching striped ties and suits, with a smile and a casual wave: 'Here comes the company layabout', 'Have you any spare golf balls for me?', 'I used to know someone who looked a bit like you', etc.

I headed for the corner of the office where I shared some space and some telephones with several salesmen and found a note from my boss, Andrew Buccleuth. I was to see him at nine o'clock.

I tapped promptly on the senior partner's door at nine, entered and was greeted by Andrew Buccleuth. He was a tall man, with thinning grey hair and a rather jovial, fleshy face. His jowls gave him the appearance of an amiable bloodhound. He was in his accustomed striped grey suit, with a rather subdued blue shirt and his Old Wykehamist tie. He was standing by the window, looking out at the elongated buildings sprawling threateningly along the City horizon. He was holding a golf magazine, so at least he had his priorities right.

'Well, Jack seems to be on his game. Is he worth a bet for the Open?'

'You might go for him each way – just for fun. You should get forty to one. But Carlssen must be a good bet.' I also mentioned one or two of the American golfers, who were always prime contenders.

'First things first, Chris, are you all right for Sunningdale on Friday?'

I nodded.

'Good. You know that merchant banker friend of mine, Charles Carleton, and he's bringing the chairman of World Wide Insurance, Brian Summers. Do you know him?'

'I've met him a couple of times.'

'Fine. Now, boring business. I had a call last night from George Stevens, of Garth Enterprises. I won't tax you with the tirade of abuse I received from him. You know of course that they're in big trouble and apparently it's all our fault, and yours in particular because of your buy recommendation at what Stevens termed a critical time for the company.

'I tried to point out that you were correct in your judgement – that Garth has a liquidity problem – and of course subsequent events have proved your judgement correct.

'But he would have none of it. He told me that he would get his own back in his own way. In particular he said that you should watch your back – or some such yob-speak. He's a complete hooligan, you know.'

I knew about the Stevens brothers' background. They had come up the hard and traditional way from their origins on the borders of East London and Essex. The A13 had probably been their playground. They had dabbled in second-hand cars, had done a bit of amateur boxing and then managed – to destruction – a few pro fighters. The story was that they had been involved in protection rackets in and around the Essex clubs, and had eventually bought a broken-down pub in Grays. Transformed into a disco pub and fast food restaurant with a late licence, this had been the first step on their particular road to success and riches.

I reassured Andrew that I would be looking over my shoulder for any ill-intentioned acolytes of the brothers Stevens, and went back to my desk to call a few clients.

By lunchtime I had bought nearly 200,000 shares in Garth Enterprises for various clients and a few for my own portfolio at an average of 62p each, and sat back to see if my prediction of an imminent takeover would be fulfilled.

When the market closed on Tuesday the share price had risen to just over a pound on the expectation of a takeover bid. By midday on Thursday the price stood at 140p. Late on Thursday afternoon, a bid of 200p a share was announced by Discerama Industries, a leisure conglomerate with interests in pubs, television, records, magazines and publishing. My clients were happy, and so was I.

At just after eight o'clock on Friday morning Andrew Buccleuth arrived at my front door. My clubs and bag were ready in the hall and soon deposited in the back of his car, an elderly Bentley. No vulgarity for Andrew Buccleuth.

We charted our stately way down to Sunningdale golf club and met our opponents in the lounge. Charles Carleton, the merchant banker, was a slightly smaller version of Andrew. He came from the same background, except that he had been educated at Westminster, and they had met at Balliol and played cricket and football together.

The stocky figure of Brian Summers, the chairman of World Wide Insurance and patron of a major European golf tournament, did not quite fit. It was nothing specific, but a combination of minor details that singled him out as not quite at home in this company. Perhaps his suit was almost too well-cut, and perhaps indefinably the wrong shade.

Andrew had told me on the way down that Summers was a client of Carleton's company and was possibly planning a takeover of another company in the insurance market. But there was nothing much more to it than entertaining an important client.

'Quite frankly,' said Andrew, 'Charles would rather take him out for a day's golf with friends than be stuck on his own with him over a long lunch.'

The introductions had been made and Summers had responded to my name with the comment: 'Oh, the caddie.' To which Andrew had responded, 'In his spare time. He's here today as one of my best salesmen.'

At that point we heard one of those electronic bleeps that intrude everywhere. It came from Brian Summers' pocket and he produced the inevitable portable telephone.

'I hope you're not going to bring that thing on to the course,' said Charles Carleton.

Summers excused himself and went to a quiet corner of the lounge. No doubt to do an important deal.

'Those bloody things are a menace,' said Andrew. 'Do you know, I was at Lord's last week and they were bleeping all over the damned place.'

'Same at Henley, old boy,' said Charles. 'I would bar them from public places.'

'There's something odd about people who have to demonstrate their indispensability in public by always being on call, isn't there? Nobody is so important that they can't take a day off, in my opinion. In a way, it's an insult to all your other executives.' So said Andrew as Brian Summers returned.

At last we made it to the first tee and the stakes were agreed. It was to be a £100 Nassau, with automatic presses of fifty pounds, and ten-pound bits.

In other words Andrew and I were to play Charles and Brian Summers at match-play, off handicaps. We were betting £100 on the first nine holes, £100 on the second nine holes, and £100 on the match. If either team became two holes ahead, the press came into action. This means that a new match started over the remaining holes for a further stake of fifty pounds. The bits were paid for such things as birdies, nearest the hole in one shot at the short holes, up and down from a bunker in two shots (a 'sandy') and so on.

It could make an expensive or a rewarding day out, especially with the press coming into action. I had known one or two gamblers who would deliberately lose a couple of holes in order to get a press going. Not nice people to play with.

As the player with the lowest handicap, I had to give shots to the other golfers, seven to Andrew and Charles, and the little matter of thirteen shots to Brian Summers, who played off a handicap of twenty. If he was at all competent he would be difficult to hold on a shortish course such as Sunningdale, even given the difficulty of the approach shots into the greens.

Suffice it to say that he was competent and after the seventh hole we were two holes down, and Summers had done most of the damage. Perhaps he was having one of those good days, which all high handicap golfers occasionally have, but he looked more like a ten-handicap player than one of twenty.

Andrew won the short eighth with a two from about six feet and therefore earned us twenty pounds in bits – a birdie and nearest the hole.

It was here that I noticed that Brian Summers was a cheat. It was clear that Andrew had an excellent chance of a two, but Summers was also about eight feet from the pin in two, after visiting a bunker. He had a chance to earn ten pounds for a 'sandy' and also put some pressure on Andrew, if he holed his putt.

I was discussing Andrew's putt with him and had my back to Summers. As I turned to look at his line I saw him mark his ball. A golfer, unless he declares a different method, puts his marker behind the ball. Summers, in what seemed like a well-practised move, put his marker ahead of the ball and therefore nearer the hole; it was also well ahead of the ball, by an inch or two.

I said nothing, but watched Summers as he replaced his ball with the marker behind it. He had shortened his putt by several inches; he missed the hole, but I resolved to keep a careful eye on him for the rest of the round.

I drove the short ninth and got a birdie, and so we were all square as the second half of the round began. We had 'rolled-up' the £100 from the first half, and so were playing for £300 a man over the next nine holes.

As we walked down the tenth, I said casually to Summers:

'How is Supersight doing?'

'It's doing fine, as far as I know.'

'I was told that you are a shareholder.'

'A small shareholder.'

'Like Martinez?'

'Yes. But what's your interest?' He looked sharply at me.

'Oh, I just thought that if all these ambitious plans come to fruition, you might be candidates for a listing on the USM in a couple of years.'

The Unlisted Securities Market is the second tier of the stock market, through which smaller companies sell their shares to the general public.

'And your company would like to handle the issue of the shares, is that it?'

'We certainly would like it,' said Andrew, who had caught up with us.

152

'It's highly unlikely,' said Summers dismissively, and strode off to study his next shot.

Highly unlikely indeed, I thought, because most of the profits, if there were to be any, were probably earmarked for Martinez' and Summers' off-shore bank accounts.

Summers hit a very nasty, high, sliced shot which ended deep in the bushes short and to the right of the green.

As we walked towards the green, I said: 'You've got an awful lot riding on Brian Harley, haven't you?'

'Not really, he's just one of many pros contracted to the company.'

'But if he won something big, you would make a killing with that putter, wouldn't you?'

Summers stopped in the middle of the fairway and said: 'Look, Ludlow, I came here to play golf, not to be grilled about a company in which I have a very small minority interest. I hardly know Martinez. I merely put up some money to get Derek Jefferson going. That's it, all right?'

He veered right to look for his ball. Two lies in that little speech, I thought. Thirty per cent of the shares was hardly a small minority interest, and he knew Martinez well because for some years his golfers had been imported by Summers to play in the World Wide Tournament.

I was on the tenth green in two, and was giving a shot to Summers. I began to follow him into the bushes to help him look for his ball, when he shouted that he'd found it. There was a swish and the ball popped out and on to the green. I went over to look at it. I knew that he was playing a Titleist, number three. It was a Titleist three all right, but the colour of the numbering on the ball had changed from black to red. Summers had either deliberately or mistakenly played the wrong ball.

As he prepared to putt, I asked, 'You're playing a Titleist red three, are you, Brian?'

'That's it,' he said.

We halved the hole and I said nothing about the change of ball. But I did warn Andrew of Summers' general disregard for the rules, and especially of his insidious way of stealing a few inches' advantage on the greens.

As we stood on the eighteenth tee, we were level in both the match and the only press. I was giving a shot to Brian Summers but not to Andrew or Charles Carleton. They both played the hole badly and eventually Andrew hacked his way on to the green in four shots; Charles had thinned his ball way through the back of the green and had gone to look for it. I was on in two, and Summers was short and left of the green in two shots.

He played an excellent shot to within five feet of the pin.

I deliberately asked Andrew to look at the line of my putt, and as we walked away from Summers we both saw him quickly use his same trick of putting his marker in front of the ball.

I lined my putt up, stroked it nicely, but it ended an inch the wrong side of the hole.

Summers put his ball down on the putting surface – ahead of the marker. He had again stolen a few vital, and psychologically important, inches. He turned to Charles and said:

'This to win three hundred and fifty pounds then, partner.'

To a cry of 'lovely putt' from Charles Carleton he rolled the ball into the back of the hole.

I nodded at Andrew and spoke up: 'A lovely putt but from the wrong spot, I'm afraid. You replaced your ball nearer the hole. We have to claim the hole and the match. Very sorry, but – the rules of golf, and all that.'

Summers slammed his putter into the green and snarled, 'I didn't know we were playing by professional rules.'

'Just by the rules of golf, which are the same for everyone,' I said.

Charles Carleton silently repaired the damage which his partner's putter had caused to the green.

'Let's have lunch,' suggested Andrew.

'Not for me,' said Summers through tight lips, 'I'm off back to my office.'

We went in silence back to the clubhouse, and changed without a word.

As he prepared to leave, Summers said nastily: 'I'll pay the pro, shall I?' He reached into his pocket and produced a formidable clip of notes.

'Here's three hundred and fifty pounds, Ludlow,' he said.

'Well, actually it's four hundred with the bits,' I said quietly.

He virtually threw another fifty-pound note at me. 'Enjoy it if you can,' was his parting shot.

The three of us looked at each other, and Andrew broke the tension: 'It's nice to have a friendly round of golf, isn't it?

'Look Charles, I'm terribly sorry about all that. I hope we haven't lost you a valuable client and masses of commission.'

'I'm sure you haven't, Andrew, and anyway you couldn't possibly stand by and allow the bugger to cheat like that. If you have to cheat to win, it's simply not worth playing the game. The subject's closed. Well played, Chris, you struck the ball well. Let's have lunch.'

Andrew and I paid for an excellent lunch.

# Chapter 13

Saturday was a chance for me to catch up on my reading, and I spent most of the morning ploughing through the financial journals and magazines, and several of the stock market tip sheets. Some of these are better than others, as in most things, but I never cease to be amazed at some of the arcane theories which surface and which are claimed to predict the movement of share prices. Astrological forecasting had had quite a vogue recently, and one weird and wonderful gentleman on Wall Street had even claimed to be able to forecast share prices by analysing the relative heights of new buildings. He spent a lot of time in the planning offices of New York City and came to the amazing conclusion that taller buildings denote optimism (a buy phase) and less tall buildings pessimism (a hold or sell phase). As one of the television commentators remarks with monotonous regularity, 'they're not all locked up, are they?' On the other hand, it was probably as good a system as any other for making money, or rather not losing it, on the Stock Exchange.

I played in the monthly medal at my golf club during the afternoon. I partnered an old friend who was stuck in a job as a senior editor at a publishing company, which had been taken over several times and was now part of an American-owned conglomerate.

Roger described how every decision was taken by committee.

'We don't commission books any more; we acquire product. We don't sell books to readers any more; we go for market penetration.'

In between sympathising with Roger's problems I had a round which I decided to forget, and which every golfer has to suffer now and again. It was a day when putts were well-struck but stayed inexorably out of the hole; when a slightly mis-hit shot found the very top lip of the green-side bunker and then ricocheted back to nestle in an unplayable lie under the back lip; when a drive, just a few yards off line, firmly deposited the ball behind a tree; and so on.

All golfers must learn to put up with the frustration and injustice of it all. I am, after all, just an amateur who plays for fun; but you can imagine how such a sequence can destroy the temperament of a professional who is playing in an important tournament: playing for his status in the game and, above all, for his living.

But at least I managed to scramble a two on one of the short holes, and so win a few golf balls in the 'twos club'.

After a couple of pints of Bass with Roger, I spent a quiet evening at home. I soothed my mind by re-reading some of P G Wodehouse's golfing stories. I marvelled as ever at his sublime command of the language.

Sunday dawned bright and clear and I welcomed an early telephone call from Roger to make up a four-ball at the club. In contrast to the day before, every putt seemed to hit the hole and stay in; I missed every bunker; and duly received my winnings of five pounds with a smile. The round of Pimms cost rather more, but who was counting? We sat on the verandah for an hour or so and talked in a relaxed way about those things that were being discussed in similar situations up and down the land. It was peaceful and wholly delightful.

I had been half-expecting a call from Max, and he had indeed left a message on my machine. He was arriving at Heathrow at seven o'clock and would I meet him? He had some interesting news for me.

I was there on time and, more surprisingly, so was the aircraft.

Max came swinging through the arrivals' gate in his usual unhurried but springy manner. He looked, if anything, fitter than when I last saw him; or perhaps it was just the contrast to the wan look of the other passengers, who had undergone a long, boring and no doubt tiresome flight. Max looked as if he had just popped over from the Isle of Wight for the day.

'How was it, Max?'

'Oh, the flight was fine. I got upgraded to Club Class, so it was bearable. The food was just the right side of plastic and I had a couple of lovely glasses of Cabernet. Stag's Leap eighty-one. Smashing.'

'Sounds good. Where's Dad?'

'He's staying for a few more days. Just to finalise this deal we're working on. It's quite a big one. It looks as though we'll both have to go back and forth quite often.'

We threaded our way through the massed ranks of worried-looking travellers. I don't blame them. Airports and everything to do with them seem to impose unwonted stress on human beings. You pay large sums of money to the airways to shunt you around the globe, and they respond by organising everything to suit themselves – not their customers. Perhaps it's time for a new CAMRA – the campaign for real airways.

I eventually found the car and, as we waited in the fume-laden queue to get out of the car park, Max handed me a small package.

'A present from Dad,' he said.

I had plenty of time to open it before we got to the exit. It was a video-cassette of Bobby Jones playing golf, a record of the most beautiful swing which has been seen in golfing history.

'My God, what came over the old man?'

'Well, we were browsing in the golf shop at Riviera, one of Dad's business contacts is a member there. Dad saw the cassette, remembered that you're always banging on about Jones's swing, so he bought it.'

We were now crawling down the M4 towards London in the usual bumper-to-bumper maelstrom which always afflicts Sunday evenings, as the weekenders return to base.

'What about our little project, Max? How did your investigations go? You said on the tape that you had something interesting for us.'

'Yes. It wasn't quite as difficult as I'd anticipated. My old chum, Nicholas Carey, is very well ensconced among the electronics and defence firms which litter the Californian landscape. Silicon Valley and all that.

'As you know, industrial espionage is absolutely rife, and several companies employ Nick to try and limit it. So he runs checks on all their employees, or all those with access to sensitive information, regularly sweeps their offices for listening devices, and generally vets their security systems.'

'Sounds interesting – and rewarding, no doubt.'

'Very, especially if Nick accepted the bribes that are continually offered. Apparently, he is approached regularly by shady gentlemen, who prefer to remain anonymous of course but have access to large amounts of cash if he will give them an idea of how they can breach the security of this or that company.'

'And he's not tempted?'

'Not at all. For the obvious and practical reason that if he helped someone, however subtly, to penetrate one of his client companies his contract would sooner or later be terminated. It would be like burgling your own house. The even more important reason is that he is as straight as it's possible to be in that business – incorruptible, or as near as damnit.

'Of course, the Americans can't believe it. But they're prepared to suspend their disbelief, especially for someone like Nick with his impeccable background.'

By now we had reached the approach to the Chiswick flyover and were at a standstill as three lanes of traffic, manned mostly by tired and aggressive drivers, tried to squeeze into two lanes. Several hired vans and souped-up small cars flew down the last stretch of the outside lane and rudely inserted themselves into the queue, to the squeal of brakes and threatening gestures of drivers who were near to breaking point.

'Anyway,' Max continued, 'Nick knew a bit about this company which Supersight used. In fact there were several people at Stellar Products whom he had vetted in the past. By some devious means he got a list of all their employees from some contact of his, and discovered that the company has quite wide interests.

'Their main business certainly is rare and sophisticated metals and ceramics and so on, but they also have quite a substantial interest in electronics.

'Well, this is where we struck gold, because Nick saw a name on the research staff of one of Stellar's subsidiaries that rang a very loud and persistent bell. A cracked bell, you might say.

'He saw the name Dennis Quilter, which is in fact a pseudonym for someone who was once the head of research for one of the major companies in the American electronics industry.

'Dennis Quilter was, up to five years ago, one of the key men in a highly secret defence project. He's a genius, and like so many of them, he is flawed. It was discovered that, despite his apparently

160

happy marriage, with two wonderful children'— Max did an excellent imitation of a mainstream American accent—'he actually preferred boys, and the younger the better.'

Max paused for effect, as we moved another couple of feet towards central London.

'The Pentagon moved quickly. Not out of any considerations of morality, but simply because this made him a very bad security risk – an easy mark for blackmail by a hostile power.

'Quilter and his wonderful family were simply taken out of circulation. For three years they kept them under wraps somewhere in New England. This was long enough for the project to progress to the point where Quilter's knowledge of its early development would be irrelevant. Scientific research at this level moves so fast that you can lose track in a couple of months, let alone three years.

'So then they gave him and his family a new identity, on the understanding that he would remain under surveillance for a few more years. They even helped to find him a low-level research job at Stellar.'

'How did Nick find out that Mr Quilter wasn't what he seemed?'

'That was relatively simple. He already knew the gist of the story and, after a few calls to some contacts of his in Washington, he'd confirmed that Quilter was the man he thought he was. There's a huge and very effective "old boy network" among all these security agencies and Nick, of course, was very well-connected only a few years ago.

'Suffice it to say that within a couple of days Nick had, with some sort of informal blessing from the Pentagon, managed to contact Quilter. He arranged for us to meet him in a restaurant in Hollywood – I expect you know Mario and Frank's.'

I nodded, and Max continued.

'Well, Quilter turned up with a sort of minder from one of the US government agencies. He was there to make sure that we only talked specifically about his activities at Stellar. The minder could have stepped straight out of a fifties B-movie, by the way, and he gave me some very old-fashioned looks, until Nick explained that we had worked together in Ireland.

'It was a treat to watch Nick at work again. He's the most subtle and sensitive interrogator I've ever seen. He has a sort of insidious, avuncular manner, which used to work with a lot of those Irish hard-nuts we used to question. By the time he'd finished with them they used to be pleading to tell him more; they ended up wanting to please him.

'It was the same with Quilter. Nick implied that he more or less knew everything about the Supersight project, and just wanted to cross a few t's and so on. Quilter, like so many of these brilliant scientists, is a comparative innocent. Once he was convinced that the information would not get him into trouble, he was delighted to talk.

'It was fascinating to listen to him as he described how he set about solving what, to him, was a very simple scientific problem, and coming up with a workable solution.'

We had by now inched our way into Hammersmith, and Max began to summarise what the problem and the solution had been.

For once I forgot all about the traffic which noisily surrounded us and drove on autopilot towards Putney. I was enthralled by the story, and also realised that the last few pieces of the puzzle had fallen into place.

The problem which remained was how to use that knowledge to thwart the scheme in the most public way possible.

We drew up outside my flat in the half light of a fading summer evening. As we strolled round the house towards the front door, Max and I decided not to go out for a late meal but to have a sandwich at home.

'Anything as long as there's no meat in it,' said Max. 'I must have eaten several cows in my week over there, and I'm not used to it.'

I flicked the light on in the hallway and Max dropped his small bag on the carpeted floor.

I opened the door to the living room, reached for the light and at the same time half-turned to Max to say something like: 'Make yourself at home, I'll see what's in the fridge.'

My half-turn saved me. As the light went on I was hit very hard in the meat of the right thigh – no prizes for guessing where the blow would have landed if I had walked straight into the room in the usual way.

I staggered back across the hall with my attacker upon me. We clattered into my golf clubs near the front door. He went for my eyes with his thumbs, but I turned my head and also managed to grab one of his arms. He was a strong and wiry man, and I also registered, in a moment of clarity amid the furious grappling and straining, that he badly needed a bath.

I also wondered what Max was up to, and why he wasn't helping. A heavy thud a few yards away in the hall was followed by a scream and a sort of sobbing moan. The weight of my assailant was then suddenly removed from me as Max grabbed him around the throat and one arm and pulled. He slammed him into the far wall, luckily missed a rather nice print of young Tom Morris, and said:

'Keep still, or I'll break your arm.'

My assailant kept still, and his team-mate was still groaning and cursing on the floor.

Max took charge.

'Chris. Hold this bloke. You know what to do if he starts anything.'

'You,' he said to the man on the floor, 'get up and into that room.'

The man didn't move.

'Get up, or I'll help you up. There's nothing broken – yet.'

A thousand B-films had obviously given Max a good turn of phrase for these situations, and the chastened heavy moved quickly into the living room.

Max grabbed the other man none too gently and spun him round.

'Bloody hell,' said Max, 'Dave Carter. What the hell are you up to? In there, you stupid bastard.'

He propelled Dave Carter into the room and pushed him roughly into one of the chairs.

'Christ,' said Carter, 'if I'd known it was you . . .'

I was feeling a bit out of it by now. I had been attacked, for the second time, in my own flat, and my brother knew at least one of my attackers.

Max pointed at Carter.

'Up to about a year ago, he used to come to my martial arts classes. But I had to warn him off because he was causing fights in some of the local pubs. In other words, misusing what he was being taught.'

'Yeah, you knocked seven bells out of me first, though, didn't you?' said Carter resentfully.

163

'I obviously didn't knock enough out of you, did I, Dave? But I'll start again, if you don't tell me why you're intent on duffing up my brother here. Or were you just doing a little bit of house-breaking?'

There was a knock on the door. I guessed it was Mrs Bradshaw. It was indeed my neighbour, and she was wearing a dressing gown. Not that it impaired her dignity.

'Chris, is everything all right? I heard some banging and thumping while I was having a bath. I had visions of another attack on you.'

I was thinking of various white lies to explain the noise, when the other pseudo-heavy made his own contribution to the conversation with a groan.

'Shut up, Tel,' snapped Dave and Mrs Bradshaw stepped into the flat.

'What's the matter with that young man?' she asked. Max decided to take the initiative.

'You must be Mrs Bradshaw,' he said. 'I'm Chris's brother, Max, and yes, we have had a spot of bother. Well, more a case of mistaken identity, I think.

'These lads mistook Chris for someone they had a grudge against, but it's all sorted out now.'

Mrs Bradshaw was obviously not convinced.

'This is the second time he's been attacked. That doesn't suggest mistaken identity to me. I think we should call the police. That nice Inspector Drew will deal with this, I'm sure.'

It was time for Max to turn on the charm, because the last thing he wanted was the police to turn up and arrest our two assailants before we found out why they had been lying in wait. Dave and particularly Tel had turned even paler at the thought of an imminent meeting with the boys in blue.

'Mrs Bradshaw, you are absolutely right. But these lads have done us no real harm, and I actually know Dave over there, and I believe his story. He's no Brain of Britain, but he is reasonably honest and I believe him when he says that it was a mistake.'

Max smiled his generous smile, all white teeth and openness, at Mrs Bradshaw, who nevertheless was not going to give up so easily.

'Very well – as long as Chris agrees.'

I nodded my reassurances at her, and her final words were: 'And

I would like a proper explanation from you both in the near future.'

'You shall have it, as soon as we know it, Mrs Bradshaw,' said Max, and he showed her to the door.

'Christ, she's not going to phone the cops, is she?' asked Dave.

'No. But I will, if you don't tell me what's what,' said Max.

'It was just a job. A geezer we know in the local asked us if we'd like to earn a ton each. Just to duff up some smart-arse in Putney. Nothing heavy, just knock him about a bit, break a rib or two or his nose, that's all. They'd had one go, and made a bollocks of it, so they wanted the job done properly.

'And we could keep any cash or watches or anything we found – make it look like a robbery. You know.'

'Why,' asked Max.

'Honest, I don't know.'

'Who does the geezer in the local work for?'

'Don't know. But he's big mates with the guv'nor.'

'Right, let's go,' said Max. 'It's ten o'clock, we've got time to get to the pub. The Seven Stars is your local, I suppose?'

Dave nodded, and Max went on.

'Sunday night's a big night. So your geezer is bound to be there, and the guv'nor. Chris and I want words with both of them.

'By the way, Dave, if you cooperate, no police, OK? If you mess about, plenty police. And you'll go down for breaking and entering, robbery with violence, and whatever else they can dream up. Let's go.'

We crammed Dave and Tel into the back seats of the Porsche, which was good security in itself, and headed for the Seven Stars.

It turned out to be a huge pub on the fringes of Clapham Common, and it was really heaving with people. They had spread into the garden, and were lolling about with their pints of lager, and Southern Comfort and cokes.

The inside was jam-packed, too – a huge fake-Victorian emporium with a square bar in the middle, red plush seats, chandeliers, stained-glass interior windows, prints of Olde London on the walls, and all the other accoutrements that the designers could dream up. It had obviously been a real Victorian pub, had been modernised in the sixties – in other words ripped apart – and then, when the nostalgia boom had hit the eighties, the owners had converted it back to the Victorian style. That's progress.

The noise was tremendous, mainly because all the customers had to shout in order to be heard above the rock music which was thudding out of the speakers at a level way above the threshold of pain.

As Dave piloted us past a corner of the bar I picked up a menu and glanced at it. It was all fast food with fanciful names, and the usual array of potent and very expensive cocktails with even more outlandish names.

On the front of the menu the name of the Seven Stars was emblazoned, with the subtitle 'A High Summer Tavern'.

I grabbed hold of Max's arm.

'Max, this is a High Summer Tavern.'

'It looks more like a low dive to me.'

'Do you know who owns High Summer Taverns?' I asked rhetorically, and to Max's annoyance. He hates rhetorical questions, and he was also being tugged one way by Dave and held back by me.

'No, of course I don't.'

'Garth Enterprises.'

'So . . .'

'Max, I've been totally on the wrong track.'

It had suddenly become clear to me, in the familiar and figurative blinding flash of light, that George and Mike Stevens, the owners of Garth Enterprises, had been behind both attacks on me. One of their minions had probably made his hooligan mark on my car, too.

They had blamed my firm's activities in the stock market, and me in particular, for the decline in their share price, and therefore for the demise of their various takeover plans. They had sworn to get even with me, and this was their predictable way of doing so.

I explained this rapidly to Max, but he still insisted on confronting the men who had sent Dave and Tel out on their 'search and destroy' mission.

A group of four men and three women were seated around a table in a corner of the bar. There was a scattering of bottles of designer lager on the table, and several empty cocktail glasses with cocktail sticks with those silly paper umbrellas.

One of the men was holding court, and was obviously the landlord. He was calling for more drinks from the bar, with much waving and snapping of fingers, and only a landlord can get away with that in a crowded pub on a Sunday night.

He was in his mid-thirties, and was dressed in the clothing which landlords of busy London pubs assume at weekends: a dark suit, a plainish shirt, and a tie in an indeterminate Paisley pattern. The sovereign rings were in place, and so was a gold identity bracelet. He had a square and fleshy face, and his shirt collar was overlapped by his thick neck. His suit seemed a little tight around the shoulders. He looked like a boxer slowly going to seed. Since he worked for the Stevens brothers that was probably what he was.

' 'Allo, Dave,' he said, 'who's your mates?'

Dave was hanging back, but Max wasn't.

'I believe you're the landlord of this shed. I'd like to have a word with you, in private.'

'This is private enough for you, sonny.'

'OK,' said Max. 'These two lads were sent by you, or George and Mike Stevens, it doesn't matter which, to duff up my brother, Chris here. Well, they're not very good at their job and got just slightly duffed up themselves.'

The landlord, red with anger, half rose from his seat and snarled: 'Look, ponce, I'll do the sodding job myself, now.'

Unfit though he obviously was, a man of his size is still dangerous. Especially so when he has friends around him, and has a reputation as a hard man. And, even more so, when he's got some booze inside him.

Despite my ability to defend myself, and Max's undoubted talents in that direction, I looked around for the nearest door. I noticed that Dave and his chum, Tel, were already edging away towards it.

Max did not move an inch. With an insouciance which I admired, but which also put the wind up me, he held up his hand in an authoritative enough way to make the landlord pause.

'Before you do anything stupid,' said Max, 'I'll remind you that these lads will be done for robbery with violence, if we choose to shop them. And you'll go down with them, as an accessory. I'm sure Inspector Drew, whom I expect you know, can arrange that – or even better . . .'

At this point Max leaned over the table and said something, which nobody else but the landlord could hear. He sat down abruptly and just muttered: 'OK, OK, but now you can sod off.'

'Sure we'll sod off,' said Max, 'but make sure you pass on the message to your friends, the Stevens.'

As he turned away, Max's hand knocked over a full pint which was on the edge of the table. It cascaded over the guv'nor's trousers.

'You stupid bastard,' was the predictable cry, as he jumped up.

Max just stood in front of him and stared at the blustering landlord, who, after a few seconds, sat down again.

'Come on, Chris.' We took the nearest door out of the pub, to the relative quiet of the car park. I imagined that the hapless Dave and Tel were now getting the rough end of the landlord's anger.

'You really wanted to have a go at that bloke, didn't you? And you knocked that glass over on purpose.'

'Yes. I was just making a point. I bet they won't bother you again. Anyway, I knew he'd back off. All gaiters and no breakfast, as Dylan Thomas put it.'

'Good God, Max, talk about putting your head in the lion's mouth. What on earth did you say to him at the end?'

'I just mentioned a superintendent I used to know. He ran a squad of plain-clothes men. He used them to infiltrate IRA sympathisers in and around London. Needless to say, they spent a lot of time in pubs, and a by-product of their work on the Irish problem was that they latched on to a lot of other crime, petty and not so petty, via the pubs.

'It was a long shot. But I reckoned that if he had worked for the Stevens' for any length of time, he would know who I meant.'

'Thank God he did. I still think we could have been in real trouble there.'

Max smiled. 'Not really. Anyway I hate bullies.'

'Well, at least it solves one problem. I thought that the attacks were to do with the Supersight business. At least I can take a shower with an easier mind.'

# Chapter 14

Max and I got back to the flat and were discussing the relative merits of an Australian Cabernet Sauvignon and of a Shiraz. A pretty sterile discussion since the wine would merely accompany a ham and cheese sandwich. However, within a few minutes of our return the phone rang. It was Mrs Bradshaw, who invited us to her place 'for a little supper'.

We were soon sitting in her roomy kitchen, which was a model of good organisation. It seemed that within seconds a bottle of Chardonnay was put in front of us, and a plateful of casseroled chicken. There was a hint of lemon in the sauce. Mrs Bradshaw let us eat our meal in peace and it was only when the cheese was on the table that she asked us about our encounter with Dave and Tel.

'Now what were you boys up to earlier on? And what's happened to the other two?'

'Well, as we told you, Mrs Bradshaw,' Max began, 'the two lads in question mistook Chris for someone else whom they had some sort of grudge against and were lying in wait to inflict some bodily harm. But it's all sorted out now.'

'Nonsense,' said Mrs Bradshaw, 'I am not a fool. There have been odd-looking men asking after Chris, and threatening phone calls. He has been beaten up once, and now it seems more threats of violence. This is not just mistaken identity, and I would like the courtesy of an explanation. Your mother would be worried stiff if she knew what was going on.'

I looked at Max, who shrugged his agreement that the insistent Mrs Bradshaw, good friend and good neighbour, should have her explanations.

I began. 'I was very puzzled myself about these various incidents. I thought at first that it was all connected with the Froggy Davies business. Because I had found the body and was known to be a good friend of Toby's someone was warning me off, just as they had attempted, rather violently, to warn him off.'

I paused and cut myself a piece of crumbly Cheshire cheese.

'Originally I didn't really connect the man who was asking for me here and the gouges on my car, for example.'

'Those could easily be envy scratches,' Max said. 'Someone getting back at you yuppies.' He grinned, but Mrs Bradshaw glared at him, and he covered his slight embarrassment by concentrating on the cheese board. Max was realising how fiercely protective Mrs Bradshaw was.

'I think that the threatening phone call convinced me that there was a pattern to it all. Mainly because Toby had also had a nasty phone call. So, whoever it was was following the same routine with me. And then of course they knocked me on the head and I assumed that it was the same bunch who had nobbled our latter-day Henry Longhurst.'

'And is it?' asked Mrs Bradshaw, a shade impatiently.

'Well, no. This is what fooled me for a while. It's all to do with Garth Enterprises and the two brothers who run the company, Harry and George Stevens.'

I explained the background briefly to Mrs Bradshaw; that they obviously blamed me for the decline in their share price, the collapse of their takeover plans, and their consequent vulnerability to a takeover themselves.

'And to think that I had shares in their business,' said Mrs Bradshaw. 'Such people shouldn't be allowed to run a company.'

'Agreed,' said Max, 'and assuming that the takeover by Discerama goes through they won't be running that particular company any more. The first thing the new owners will do is show the Stevens boys the door. And they will trip gaily down to the bank to count their millions.'

'And probably start another company,' said Mrs Bradshaw.

'Probably. After they've made nuisances of themselves on the Costa del Sol, or wherever they've got their villas.'

'Actually, Max, they've got a huge place at Quinta.'

'Well that's a place to avoid then – especially for you, Chris. A pity, it's a great golf course.'

170

Mrs Bradshaw intervened. 'But what are you going to do about these two hooligans?'

'There's not a lot we can do. The police could give Dave and Tel a hard time, and that unpleasant publican, but it would be difficult to prove the connection with the Stevens boys. And, anyway, we promised Dave and Tel that we would let them off the hook. They did take us to the pub, and we made our point there.'

'I'd love to have five minutes alone with that publican, preferably in a locked room,' Max said. 'But that's by the by, and would be sheer self-indulgence. I could, of course, have a quiet word with my old pal the superintendent about the Stevens brothers and their activities. Nothing he can do directly, but he might be able to pass the information on. Grist to someone else's mill, perhaps.'

'What about Inspector Drew?' asked Mrs Bradshaw.

'I think we'll keep him out of it,' I said quickly. 'He's got enough on his plate with the Froggy Davies case and the other murder.'

We both refused coffee, thanked Mrs Bradshaw who seemed at last to be satisfied with the story we had told her, and sought our beds. Even Max, with his stamina, needed some sleep. Because of the time change from Los Angeles, his body was telling him that he should have been in bed six hours ago. If he didn't get off to sleep quickly his body would soon be telling him that it was time to get up.

The BBC time signal woke me at seven o'clock the next morning, followed by the voices of the *Today* programme. I shuffled into the kitchen to make a cup of tea and found Max already there. He handed me a mug.

'How did you sleep?'

'Not bad, considering. I woke up – really wide-awake, too – at about six. I've been trying to work out how we should scupper Harley and his merry men, and I think it's fairly simple in one way. The technicalities are easy. The biggest problem is to get one of us close enough to Harley at the Open to foul up his system.'

'I've thought of various ways. Using Toby, for instance. He would have every excuse to follow Harley, but even the gentlemen of the Press don't get close enough to the action. So I thought we might nobble the marker or the scorer. But if we told them our story and what we wanted them to do they would probably ring for the police.'

'Or more likely for the men in the white coats from the local funny farm,' I said.

'We could, of course, simply tell Inspector Drew about our theories and let him collar Harley and the rest of them.'

I knew Max didn't really mean it, but I reacted as he would have wished.

'No, Max. The whole point is to let those crooks believe that they're going to pull the whole disgusting coup off. They'll be mentally counting up their ill-gotten gains, when we dash the cup from their lips.'

'You're mixing your metaphors.'

'I normally do at seven in the morning.'

'Anyway,' I continued, 'we don't want to give them the slightest chance of disposing of that putter, and of aborting the whole plan. At the slightest whiff of danger that could happen. We would then be left with a mass of circumstantial evidence. Pretty tough to prove. No doubt the boys in blue will find the murderers of Froggy Davies and the other caddie, but they wouldn't necessarily catch the real culprits – the masterminds behind the whole scheme. Martinez and co.'

'So, you want to spring the trap on the last day of the Open – a grand finale which they certainly won't be anticipating.'

'Exactly.'

'That brings me to the main problem. To achieve this dramatic climax, you must take over as Harley's caddie for the last day.'

'And how on earth am I expected to do that?'

'That's for you to work out.'

'Thanks, Max.'

Twenty minutes later I was on my way out of the door to go to the office, and Max's last words were that he would phone his superintendant and tell him about the nefarious Stevens brothers.

I hardly noticed the discomforts of the journey to the City; I was concentrating so hard on the problem that Max had given me to solve. The fact that we were crushed together like cattle hardly impinged. Not like cattle, I thought wrily, because there are stringent regulations about the amount of space which an animal must have when in transit, whereas London Transport can cram us all in with impunity and charge us heavily for the privilege. Even the thump and hiss of the various personal stereos – what a misnomer that is – hardly bothered me. How could I substitute myself as Harley's caddie for the crucial final round of the Open? On the journey I didn't get beyond vague thoughts of nobbling his current bag-carrier, whoever that might be. I would not be too popular with Jack Mason either, especially if he was in line for a good prize. If he was up with the leaders, God help me.

The first hour in the office passed by me in a hazy succession of 'Good mornings' and 'How's your golf' and 'Who should I back for the Open?' I hardly heard a word of the analyst's sales briefing, and gazed uncomprehendingly at the summary of the special situations which we salesmen were supposed to use to part our clients from their money.

Shortly before ten o'clock my internal phone rang and it was Andrew Buccleuth. Would I kindly join him in his office? I imagined that he wanted to fix up another game of golf. As long as Brian Summers wasn't one of the four, I didn't mind.

I went into his office and saw that Andrew already had a visitor. He rose from his chair as I entered, and I assumed that this was yet another City golfing chum of Andrew's. He was a tall fair-haired man; in his mid-thirties, I guessed; and had all the usual trappings of a regular City gent.

I nodded at him, and Andrew said, 'Chris, may I introduce Chief Inspector Franklin.'

We greeted each other, and I shook the hand which he offered. I wondered what a chief inspector was doing in the office, and especially one who looked totally at home in this environment. I once heard a politician criticise the police for not attracting enough people of real intellectual calibre, for not getting enough graduates, for example, on to its strength. He developed the argument by criticising the police obsession with training every recruit by making them walk the beat and deal with all the essential routine of the work. His theory was that they needed an officer class, as in the armed forces. Inspector Franklin was clearly one of the officer class.

Andrew was looking at me in a very concerned way. He looked more like a bloodhound than ever. A harassed one.

'Inspector Franklin has some questions about Garth Enterprises.'

'Fine. Fire away.'

'I'm from the City Fraud Squad,' he said with a smile. 'I want to ask you about your dealings in Garth shares, because we have received allegations of insider dealing in those shares and specifically by you.'

No wonder Andrew Buccleuth was looking worried, because anyone guilty of insider dealing was for the high jump these days: huge fines and a long time in prison. The problem with the whole question of insider dealing was one of interpretation. For generations, stockbrokers had used their own special knowledge to make profits for their clients and, of course, to line their own pockets. It was, after all, their business to ferret out what was happening in the market and to capitalise on it.

But privileged information could not be used for financial gain. A very fine line exists between the two concepts, and the trouble really began when this particular rule had to be closely and formally defined. It used to be an unwritten rule in the City, and there was therefore some flexibility in its interpretation. Some of the wider boys in the City stretched this flexibility to breaking point, and some of their counterparts on the New York Stock Exchange are now doing very long stretches in prison.

Inspector Franklin took me at length through my dealings in Garth Enterprises shares, and the trading slips were examined and summarised.

'Mr Ludlow, you seem to have foreseen exactly what would happen to Garth Enterprises, with a degree of accuracy that is very unusual. One might say uncanny.'

Once again I explained my reasons for making a buy recommendation on the shares.

'So you're really saying, Mr Ludlow, that you were slightly concerned that the Garth shares had gone too far too fast, but the clincher was George and Harry Stevens' behaviour at the presentation.'

'Yes.'

'If I may say so, that seems a very flimsy basis on which to downgrade some shares so vigorously.'

'Well, it's the truth. It was a bit of intuition, and my intuition was right.'

'Did you not know that George and Harry Stevens were about to face a charge of fraud in relation to their takeover, three years ago, of the Happy Pizza chain?'

'No, I didn't.'

'The Stevens brothers say that you did. And that you knew this would cause a dramatic decline in the Garth share price. And that you used this inside knowledge, which was not available to anyone else, for your own financial gain.'

'That's untrue.'

Inspector Franklin looked at me steadily. I felt pale, and hoped that I didn't actually look it, under his calculating gaze. Thank goodness I was well tanned from walking the golf courses of Britain during the last few weeks.

He began again. 'The Stevens' story makes more sense than your claim of some infallible kind of intuition. I am not disputing the part which it can play. A "gut feeling" can often back up a considered judgement. We policemen often get it, but would be literally laughed out of court if we ever mentioned it in evidence. And rightly so. But your intuition,' and the Inspector stressed the word lightly, 'is a little too convenient to believe.'

'Inspector, this is the first I've heard of any fraud. It doesn't surprise me in the slightest, though. Why don't you talk to Peter Hobbs? He's the leisure industry analyst with whom I went through all the arguments for and against Garth Enterprises. He'll tell you that on balance we decided that they were a sell, and my experience of the Stevens at that presentation tipped the balance markedly against them.'

Andrew was nodding encouragement. Inspector Franklin took a couple of notes without any sign of interest and said: 'I'll need to talk to you again, after I've done some more digging. Thank you, Mr Buccleuth. Good day to you.'

I began to speak, but Andrew stopped me.

'You don't have to say it, Chris. I know it's utter nonsense. Don't worry about it. You know how sensitive the City is at the moment about any hint of insider dealing. He has to go through the motions, but the Stevens brothers hardly carry much credibility, do they?'

He changed the subject.

'To more serious matters. Do you think I should have a punt on Brian Harley for the Open?'

'No, he can't possibly win. Put your money on Carlssen or even Krantz, but not Harley.'

'All right, Chris, and I shall have a tenner each way on Jack, of course.'

'Just a thought, Andrew, at the risk of being accused of using inside information.' I grinned and Andrew laughed a bit nervously. 'You might back Harley to be in the lead, or at least in the first three, after three rounds.'

Andrew made a note of this, and said he'd find out what the odds were, and confirmed that he'd be at the Open for the final two days as a guest of one of the clearing banks. He told me that their lunches were easily the best. Didn't I say he had his priorities right?

During my interview with the smooth Inspector Franklin, my brother had phoned and so had Sally Drayton. I spoke briefly to her and we confirmed where we each would be during the Scottish Classic, which was being played at a public course near Edinburgh. Unlike many of the public or municipal courses in England, it is a superb golf course. The public links in Scotland tend to be of a high standard because golf is very much the people's game up there and good facilities have always been available. St Andrews, for instance, is a public course.

I reached Max in his office and he outlined exactly how we could upset Brian Harley's grand design.

'The equipment you need isn't a problem,' he said. 'The only problem is to get you in place as his caddie on the Sunday. But I'll be there to help. I've negotiated an extra week's holiday with Dad. And what a palaver that was. You'd think I'd asked for a year's sabbatical.'

The Scottish Classic fulfils several needs in the week before the Open. It is, first of all, the last chance for many golfers to try to qualify straight into the Open, without having to endure the minor hell of the final pre-qualifying tournament, which takes place over thirty-six holes on the Sunday and Monday before the Open starts. If a player who has not yet qualified for the Open finishes in the top twenty in the Scottish Classic he wins a place in the Open. It is a great incentive for players to turn up for what might otherwise be an unpopular event. Many leading players prefer to rest and practise in the week before the Open. Jack Mason was not one of these. He had decided to miss the Monte Carlo Open and then tune up in the Scottish Classic, which is usually played on an uncompromising links course which is often similar in character to the Open course. Ideal preparation for the main event.

Although the Classic was being played inland near Edinburgh, a tough course had been chosen with many of the characteristics of a links, including narrow and undulating fairways and fierce rough mostly comprised of heather. I knew that Jack would relish its traditional challenges and would be looking forward to sharpening up his short game for the ultimate test which the Open presents. In particular he would be honing his chip-and-run shots, an essential weapon to have in your armoury on these fast-running and exposed courses.

I had one more task to perform before I left on my annual holiday, for that is what Andrew called it, at the Scottish Classic and the Open Championship. I had been summoned to Inspector Drew's office and agreed to meet him on the Tuesday morning before I drove north. I reflected that I was seeing far too many policemen at present, and would be happy never to see another close up again. I loaded my car with everything I needed for the trip, set my answering machine, said my goodbyes to Mrs Bradshaw, and set off for Richmond Police Station.

I took what was now a familiar route to Inspector Drew's office, accepted, for once, the offer of a cup of tea, and sat down opposite the Inspector.

He gave me a friendly smile and I wondered if he was planning to put me behind bars. He began.

'How are you getting on with Inspector Franklin?' He paused for effect, and smiled again at me. Sweet as a razor, as the poet put it.

'He's an old friend of mine. In fact we were on a course together in Zurich a couple of years ago. A very bright man. Very shrewd.

'Anyway, to get to the point, I realise that you are off to pursue your other career for a couple of weeks and I wanted a quick word.'

The way he said 'other career' made it sound particularly unsavoury, as if I were a part-time child-molester.

'Yes, Inspector, and I was planning to be in Scotland by lunchtime; it is now nine o'clock.'

'Well I'm sure that your speedy German car will get you there on time,' he said jovially.

'We reckon,' he continued, 'that this whole business could come to a climax at the Open. We don't anticipate any more murder or mayhem. Unless they try to knock you off once and for all.' He grinned nastily at me.

'We don't foresee any problems this week, although I have had words with my colleagues in Edinburgh and my sergeant will be in attendance. It's a pity, really, that he doesn't play golf. Prefers snooker. But we will be at the Open in force.

'I realise that you will be concentrating on guiding Jack Mason to a good prize, but if you hear or see anything which we should know about, then contact us. We will have a special line at the police office on the course.'

He gave me a card with a phone number written on the back.

'You can ring that number at any time. Twenty-four hours a day from next Sunday onwards.'

I thought quickly about our plans, such as they were, for the final day of the Open. I knew that we couldn't expect to spring the trap successfully on all the suspects, without the help of the police. We could foil the plot, which would be satisfaction in itself, but the real success would be in seeing all the villains caught. A hint was necessary.

'I am sure you're right, Inspector, and I would take a guess that the last day of the Open will see the denouement.'

'Tell me more.'

'No more to tell. Just intuition, I suppose.'

'Oh yes, the famous Ludlow intuition.'

I don't know why I bothered about a hint. The Inspector seemed to know plenty, including all the details of my unpleasant interview with his colleague, Franklin.

He rose and said: 'I'll see you at the Open. Drive carefully. I suppose that's good advice for Jack Mason, too.'

I smiled politely at his pun and headed at speed for my car.

I drove north and even the cramped and dangerous conditions of the motorways did not depress my spirits. Despite the accusation of insider dealing, and despite the problems and possible dangers of thwarting Harley and his associates, I felt light of heart. I was about to re-enter the golfing environment, in which I felt most at ease. The culmination was to be the Open, the greatest golf tournament in the world: the best organised, the most prestigious and the most international event in the golfing calendar. Even though it was every professional golfer's ambition to win the major events, and especially the US Masters and the US Open, this was the Holy Grail, the ultimate tournament to win. No golfer could be considered great unless he had held aloft, in triumph and humility, the famous old claret jug. Could it possibly be Jack Mason's year? I doubted it, even though I would tax every nerve and muscle on his behalf. I knew that it would be the greatest day of my life so far if he did win, even if I was not to be at his side. It was unlikely, though, in a field which included so many superb players and so many great champions.

Jack possessed great skills and real personal courage, but I wondered whether he had the final piece in the weird jigsaw that is a champion. That final piece is almost indefinable: it's courage, of course, extreme determination and belief in yourself, selfishness too, and a bloody-mindedness that verges on mania. The winner was more likely to be an American like Carl Krantz, or Bjorn Carlssen or one of the tough contingent of Australians or maybe one of the younger British or Spanish players who, after several Ryder Cup successes, no longer felt inferior to their American rivals.

The one man who wouldn't win was Brian Harley. Over my dead body.

It might well be over my dead body, I thought, as I braked hard to avoid a lorry which pulled out in front of me without any warning at all. I had nowhere to go with a Mercedes coming up fast in the outside lane. This juggernaut driver was in a particularly playful mood this morning as he swung in and out of the middle lane, with just a cursory wink of the indicator light.

He obviously had a different view of the use of indicators: 'Oh, look, I'm confirming that I've just pulled out in front of you.'

The motorway gets much less crowded after the Preston junction, and the traffic became bearable. Soon I was cruising through the gorgeous Cumbrian countryside of eccentric streams and dramatic fells, which suddenly give way to gentle rolling fields. No wonder

Wordsworth fell in love with the place. I bowled along to the luscious voices of Bjorling and Los Angeles in *La Bohème*, and thought of my other reason for my current high spirits: Sally Drayton. I would be seeing her soon.

I had arranged to meet Jack at Montford Golf Club at three o'clock for a practice round. The tournament began on the Wednesday, a day earlier than usual, to leave the Sunday free for those golfers who would have to play in the Open qualifying rounds.

I had time for a quick lunch and stopped at one of those excellent craft centres which can be found along the main roads in Scotland. Apart from trying to sell you all manner of clothes, especially woollens and tartans (I refrained from starting a search for the MacLudlow tartan), and displaying a vast range of malt whiskies, they usually have a café which serves fresh food at fair prices. This one was no exception and I had a plateful of salad, a slab of passable venison paté and some chunky wholemeal bread.

Jack was waiting for me on the putting green at Montford. He looked as commanding a figure as ever, but perhaps not quite as solid. He confirmed that he'd lost some weight.

'I stopped the alcohol last Sunday morning. Shocking hangover. My local had a guest beer in from Shropshire of all places. Lovely stuff, and I went overboard, I'm afraid. Anyway, I'm allowing myself only two glasses of wine a day until the Open finishes.'

As we wandered over to the first tee Jack showed me two new clubs which he had acquired, a wedge and a sand wedge. He had practised for several hours each day with them last week, and was enthusiastic about their properties.

'These beryllium copper heads are much softer. You can feel the ball off the club much better. I really feel I can place the ball more accurately. The only trouble I've had is that I was pitching the ball too short with them. Because they give you a softer shot, you've actually got to hit the ball a bit harder to get it close to the flag. They're ideal for these sort of courses.'

It all sounded a bit Irish to me, but if Jack believed he could play better shots with these clubs he probably would.

We watched a threesome of young hopefuls drive down the first fairway. Jack had arranged to play with young Sam Ratcliffe, who had signed up with Jack's agent, Graham Fearnley. As the round progressed I realised what a wise decision it had been not to try to compete with the likes of Sam Ratcliffe on a professional level. He hit the ball vast distances but his great length was not even the most impressive feature of his game. It was his great dexterity around the greens. He seemed to know the basic grammar of the game so well – what sort of shot to play and when. Not surprising when you knew that he had been brought up on a golf course and his father was a professional. But very impressive.

On the way round, in between pacing the course and checking the measurements between various landmarks, I was wondering when I ought to broach the subject with Jack of my probable defection to Brian Harley. This was obviously not the time or the place, because I would need to take him into my confidence to a certain extent, and the later this was done the better.

Jack must be able to read minds because he suddenly said: 'Harley's got yet another new caddie. I hope he's paying him danger money. Though from what I remember of him he can look after himself. He's a nasty piece of work.'

To my inquiring look he said: 'Jake Baxter. Son of Jimmy.' He grinned. 'Not the footballer. You won't remember Jimmy but he was a great character, and a typical Scottish caddie. Knew the game backwards and forwards, and wouldn't have any nonsense with his golfers. You know the form; when his man had a good round he'd say, "We shot a sixty-six today, and we played well." When it was a lousy round he'd say, "He had a seventy-four today, and he played like a clown."

'I saw him carrying for an American at the Open in the sixties. It was Ed Bowring, who was no ordinary golfer. He'd won about thirty tournaments over there including the PGA. Anyway, he put his drive into the heather at one hole. I was right by the ball. About a hundred and fifty yards to go. He pulled something like a seven-iron out of the bag. Jimmy just grabbed it out of his hands, said, "You'll leave it there with that, sir" and handed him the wedge. Well, he got it out on to the fairway, pitched close and saved his par. Old Jimmy was right.'

'But Jack, I've never heard of his son, Jake.'

'No, you wouldn't have. Because he was warned off about ten years ago. There was some talk that he was trying to organise a little betting coup with some of the other caddies. He approached the ones who were carrying for the leading players and suggested that they got together to influence the results of tournaments. Before the last round they'd decide who was likely to win, put their wages on him, and then the other caddies wouldn't quite do their best for their pros. You know, select the wrong club for a shot, or misread the line of a putt, and so on.

'A crazy idea, but he's reckoned to have a screw loose anyway. The PGA couldn't prove anything but they told him not to show his face again.'

'But he's popped up again,' I said. 'Why have they let him back?'

'It's so long ago, I suppose. The guys who run the pro tour now have probably never heard of him and it is, after all, ten years ago, so the bloke has served his time, so to speak.'

The round ended with Sam, having got round in roughly six under par, taking some money off Jack.

'You know, Chris, he'll win the Open one day, that lad. Not this year, and probably not next, but one day soon. I suppose you're going to this thrash tonight, are you?'

Jack was referring to the sponsors' reception, which was always held in one of the large Edinburgh hotels in Princes Street. I confirmed that I would be there, but didn't tell Jack that I was only going there to see Sally. We arranged to meet at ten o'clock on the morrow.

Time was short, so I raced into Edinburgh and parked outside the flat which Andrew Buccleuth had arranged for me to borrow. It belonged to one of his many Scottish cousins, and was just a *pied-à-terre* in the capital city. Some *pied-à-terre*, with three bedrooms and a huge living room with a balcony and a lovely view of the garden square in which it was located. A note told me that the cupboards and fridge were full, and that the wine and beer was in the kitchen.

No time for a drink. I had a very rapid shower, with hardly a tremor, changed into a suit and took the five-minute walk to the reception. The Scottish Classic was sponsored by several companies, including an airline and naturally a whisky manufacturer. Their hospitality was legendary and, if you had work to do the next day, it was wise to confine your time there to less than an hour. Even a half-empty glass was seen as an affront to a guest, and an army of kilted young women ensured that glasses were full at all times.

Toby Greenslade was the perfect guest for these sponsors, and I soon spotted him in the thick of things. His champagne glass was firmly held by the stem, and was describing a steady and graceful arc from waist level to lips, and down again.

I went across and nudged him. 'Enjoying yourself, Toby?'

'Just entering into the spirit of things.'

'We ought to get together. A few things have happened in the last few days and you ought to know about them.'

'Max has returned bearing news, I imagine, from the Americas.'

'Exactly. But I will need a little of your time to explain.'

'Fine. We'll meet tomorrow evening, shall we? Dinner? Or are you planning to monopolise the fair Sally? But I should be quick – Brian Harley was chatting her up a few minutes ago.'

I looked around the room sharply, and Toby smiled at my reaction.

'You're quite smitten, aren't you? She's over in that corner, talking to one of the sponsors. Off you go.'

I set off through the crush, and resisted several offers of more champagne from the determined and charming waitresses. Sally was actually pinned in one corner by the massive figure of a Scotsman. I could tell he was a Scotsman because he was dressed in the full traditional Scottish outfit of tartan kilt, sporran, short tweed jacket and all the other accoutrements. I'm no fool.

My only reason for being at the reception was to see Sally, and my face lit up. So did hers. In what seemed like a desperate move she ducked under the huge and protective arm of the attendant Scot and said brightly:

'Chris Ludlow. I've been searching for you all day. I must talk to you about starting times tomorrow. There's been some sort of mix-up. Excuse me, Mr Maclean, I'll catch up with you later.'

Sally pulled me away into the crush and said: 'That's Maclean's Whisky, one of the sponsors. I'd been trapped in that corner for nearly half an hour. I think he was just about to ask for my phone number in London. A nice man, but . . . Everybody at parties ought to have a little placard that they can surreptitiously display in those situations. With "Help" on it, I suppose.'

'I hear you've been chatted up by Brian Harley, too.'

'Yes. He's quite an attractive man, in a heavy sort of way.'

I frowned, and Sally smiled. 'But of course he fancies himself like mad and, as we both know, he's not to be trusted.'

She squeezed my hand and said: 'Tell me over dinner. Let's slip away now. I've done my duty by the sponsors and the PGA.'

Within a few minutes we were sitting in the corner of a busy Italian restaurant off Princes Street. The noise of the diners, with a multitude of accents and languages, was considerable enough to drown any confidences we were about to share. We settled for salads, pastas and a bottle of Barolo. In between diversions, while the waiter laid the table, brought the bread, a bottle of mineral water and the first course, I told Sally what Max had discovered during his trip to Los Angeles.

'So you've got to lure this caddie somewhere quiet on the morning of the final day of the Open and knock him on the head, or tie him up in the woodshed, or something like that. And then you've got to persuade Martinez and his merry men that you're just the man to caddie for Harley.'

'Yes.'

'Well it sounds outlandish to me. They're bound to smell a rat, surely. Their man's caddie disappears and you are suddenly on hand to step in and help Harley out. Too convenient, surely?'

'Not necessarily. Remember that they're supremely arrogant. They won't believe that anyone can have worked out what they're up to, and they certainly won't believe that anyone can have worked out how to stop them.'

'Chris, I wonder if I could lure Harley's caddie somewhere quiet for you.'

'Absolutely not. You're not to get involved. Max and I will work something out, maybe with Toby.'

'Well, we'll see. The offer's there. In the meantime I wouldn't mind being lured back to your flat for coffee.'

I settled the bill in very quick time and we walked hand in hand through streets that were relatively peaceful compared to London's, towards my borrowed flat. I made some coffee and we actually sat out on the narrow balcony in the gentle night air and looked out at the city spread around us. There was little movement in the square below us, just the occasional car passing and an infrequent walker, usually accompanied by a dog.

After a few minutes we both rose and I started to clear away our cups. Sally stopped me, put her arms around me and clung on hard.

'Leave those till morning, Chris,' she said. 'I think the time has come to get to know each other a little better, don't you?'

It was a lot of fun getting to know Sally Drayton a little better.

When I woke up the next morning I mentally hugged myself as well as my adorable Sally. What a beautiful girl. What fun. Wasn't I lucky?

Sally for once didn't have to be at the course at her usual indecently early hour, and I was able to make some tea and toast and lay out some fresh fruit. We sat by the window and looked at the bright and awakening city, never brighter than when two new lovers awake together for the first time. We smiled a lot and said some of the foolish things which lovers say the world over. It was smashing.

# Chapter 15

We giggled like fools in the shower together, and I dropped Sally back at her hotel and waited while she changed her clothes for the working day ahead. I drove her to the course and we parted in the car park. I went in search of Jack and hoped nobody thought I had lost my mind. I had an irresistible urge to smile at everything and everybody.

Jack didn't notice. He was concentrating too hard on his practice. This was the beginning for him of a long build-up to the most important tournament of his life. However many times he had played in it, each year the Open was the most important tournament of his life. Not that Jack was going about his task grim-faced. He was as expansive as ever and had a word for everyone, especially some of the younger players whom he hardly knew. He knew that many of them were on the rack and were hoping that they would squeeze into the Open by finishing high in this tournament. But I sensed that he was trying to put himself on a higher than usual plane of concentration.

By the time Jack teed off just after eleven o'clock the early morning sunshine had been replaced by bursts of rain from clouds which were scudding by in the driving wind.

They were desperately hard conditions for golf. The gusting winds made it difficult enough to control the ball through the air. If a shot was hit marginally off line the hard and bouncy fairways would not hold it and the golfers had to contend with the punitive rough, with its tough and wiry heather. The greens had been cut close and were lightning fast. It was too severe an examination for many of the players. The tournament director, having received a favourable weather forecast of sunshine and light breezes, had set the course up for the predicted easy conditions. Even the positions of the holes on the greens were difficult.

After the first hole I saw Jack grit his teeth. If it were possible I would have said that he gritted his whole body to try and secure a reasonable score. Into the wind he concentrated on hitting the ball as low as he dared, and his one-iron did him proud. His hours of practising his chip-and-run shots also paid off, and his new wedges had obviously given him a new confidence and accuracy for those shots from fifty to a hundred yards from the flag. He only had one real disaster, ironically at a hole where the wind was behind the players. Despite hitting a three-wood for safety his ball careered on into the heather and he dropped two shots. That's the trouble with playing in a high wind: it's very difficult to play the holes against the wind, and almost as hard to judge distances when the wind is helping you. A golfer who is 200 yards from the green with the wind in his favour simply does not believe that he can get there with a seven or eight-iron, when he knows that he would normally hit a four-iron.

Jack played superbly to record a score of two under par. But Brian Harley, who had started quite early, was six under for the day. In contrast there were many scores in the high 70s and in the 80s. A couple of poor souls hadn't even broken 90. No Open Championship for them this year.

'I should've saved that round for the Open,' Jack said.

'Plenty more where that came from,' I said encouragingly.

'No point in practising in this. Let's hope the weather relents tomorrow. Wet and windy in the morning, and then just as I step on the tee the sun comes out and the wind drops,' Jack fantasised.

'See you tomorrow. Say, one thirty?'

'Fine.'

I went off in search of Toby to make arrangements for that evening, but my footsteps took me unerringly towards the PGA caravan to see if I could find Sally. I approached the open door cautiously, since I was mindful of Oliver Moreton's antipathy towards me. I couldn't see Sally, but Moreton came around the corner of the caravan and saw me. I turned away, anxious to avoid any further unpleasantness.

'Hello, Chris, how are you?' I was slightly taken aback by his affable greeting. 'You're looking for Sally, no doubt. She's just gone for a quick drink with one of the sponsors, Iain Maclean. She seemed reluctant to go, so I'm sure she wouldn't mind if you rescued her. The sponsors' tent, I would imagine.'

He smiled again and turned into the caravan. 'Must get on. See you later, Chris.'

I wondered what had come over him.

I walked to the sponsors' hospitality tent, which was fairly quiet. This wasn't really one of the major tournaments, although reasonable prize money was offered. No big stars had been imported from the USA, although several second-rank American and Australian players, who hadn't qualified for the Open, were here to try and secure a high finish and a place in the Open.

I caught a glimpse of Sally, pinned yet again by the burly Scottish whisky-maker in a corner of the bar. He did a very good pin. Very practised. I guessed that he had been a rugby player, by the width of him probably a front row forward.

I took the easiest way out. I waved at Sally, walked over and said: 'Excuse me, Mr Maclean, but Sally is needed back at the caravan. A minor crisis, according to Oliver Moreton.'

He smiled benignly at us both, and patted Sally on the arm. 'Off you go, my dear. I expect Oliver wants a cup of tea, or something.'

If sexual equality had yet reached Scotland, it certainly hadn't penetrated the whisky industry.

'Will you join me for a dram, young man?'

He held up his glass, which looked pretty small in his mechanical shovel of a fist, but probably contained about half a pint of Maclean's Old Tartan Whisky.

I made the excuse of having to join Jack for some putting practice, and made my escape with Sally. He patted her playfully on the bottom as she went by.

'You've made a real hit there, Sally. Now there's a man who could set you up in a nice little flat in London. And he wouldn't bother you much – he's probably only in town once or twice a month.'

'I already have a nice little flat.'

It was time to change the subject, and I asked Sally why Oliver Moreton had suddenly become friendly.

'Easy. He's found a new love. You know Lucy Bennington, I expect. She's suddenly the light of his life. I'm no longer of any interest to him, thank goodness, and your role as his deadly rival has obviously finished.'

I explained that I had arranged to have dinner with Toby to cover the latest developments in the Harley affair and left to find the dedicated journalist in the Press tent, where he was watching the racing from Ayr.

That evening we strolled down the road to a bistro and Toby ordered a bottle of house red. It tasted as if Esso had gone into the wine business, but it didn't seem to worry Toby as I summarised for him, as I had done for Sally twenty-four hours ago, what Max and I had found out about the Harley plot.

I also explained how the Stevens brothers' unpleasant activities had been coincidental to what Harley and his friends were plotting.

'So the Stevens boys just muddied the waters, so to speak,' mused Toby. 'It makes me think that I am quite lucky to survive that beating I got.'

'Why do you say that?'

'Well, these people who are manipulating Harley – and manipulation is the right word because Brian may be a fool, and he may have bent the rules of golf in the past but he's not a killer – might well have decided that I knew more than I really did and decided to cut me off in my prime. What a loss to golf. I haven't even won Sports Writer of the Year yet.'

'And you're unlikely to if we drink any more of this rubbish.' Toby emptied the carafe into his glass and drank most of it down.

'Chateau Gorbals, I would say.'

'Quite frankly, Toby, I think it was only a warning. At that stage, Martinez or Jefferson or whoever is running this scheme would certainly not have wanted to draw even more attention to themselves by knocking off a fearless and dedicated member of the British Press.'

'I'll drink to that.'

'Enough damage had already been done by Froggy Davies' murder. I suspect that there are two factions behind this Harley scam. Originally it was dreamt up as a way to make a lot of money. Fraud, in other words. But one of the backers got out of control. Froggy was murdered for trying to blackmail them for more money when they could just as easily have bought him off, and the next caddie was eliminated because he was too dangerous to have around. Someone with a heavy coke habit is liable to blow the gaff on the whole scheme. Even then Ricky could have been shipped back to the States with enough coke to keep him happy until Harley had won the Open.

'But there is obviously a joker in the pack. Unstable enough to use murder to achieve his aims. But you, Toby, were lucky enough to be lined up for a spot of discipline by the more reasonable members of the gang.'

Toby had gone a little pale, but recovered sufficiently to order a bottle of Rioja to go with the main course.

'So how do we sprag these bastards?' he asked.

'Well, a vital piece of the plan is to get rid of Jake Baxter for the last day, and I will be carrying Harley's bag instead.'

'Just like that, Chris. "With one bound, Jack was free" – is that what you mean? Look, Baxter is a hard-nosed bugger for a start. If Harley is in with a chance of winning after three rounds, and from what we know and surmise he will be, wild horses wouldn't drag Jake away. For a start, he'll be looking at a fee of nearly ten thousand pounds plus whatever extra these villains are paying him.

'A big bribe might work. But you'd probably have to come up with twenty grand. And even then I'm not so sure. If he has a heart, which is debatable, even Jake Baxter's would go pit-a-pat at the thought of bringing in the Open Champion.'

We looked into our respective glasses of rather thin Rioja and I said: 'We'll have to nobble Jake on the Saturday night, ring Harley the next morning and tell him he's ill or been arrested or something, and then I'll have to offer to stand in.'

Toby stared at me. 'I think you're losing your marbles, Chris. First, why should Harley necessarily accept you as a last-minute caddie? Second, what the hell is Jack Mason going to say, when his faithful bag-carrier ups and leaves him on the morning of the last day of the Open? I wouldn't like to be within a mile of him, by the way. And third, how do you spirit Jake Baxter away? You still haven't told me that. Oh, kidnapping someone is still a crime in this country, by the way.'

'Sally has offered to sort of, er, lure Jake away on the Saturday night,' I said with great embarrassment, 'and Max will be there to clobber him and keep him quiet for twenty-four hours or so.'

Toby looked at me pityingly. 'This isn't a John Buchan novel, Chris. Jake Baxter wasn't born yesterday and he wouldn't necessarily believe that a classy piece like Sally Drayton would be after him. There's a slight chance, I agree, that he believes that well-brought-up gals with plums in their mouths "like a bit of rough". He probably reads the *Sun*, so you have a very slight chance. But he's unlikely to trot off somewhere at her request. A quick tumble behind a hedge is Jake's style and then back to the boys in the pub to tell them about it.

'I have a better idea, and it won't endanger your girlfriend's virtue. I'll ask him for an interview. You know the spiel. An exclusive with the Open Champion's caddie. What does he talk about during a round? Does he have Weetabix for breakfast? What's he like to work for? And so on. I'll have to pay him, and he'll probably want cash up front, but the paper will pick up the tab. Now, he *will* fall for that. Nobody can resist the thought of their name in the papers.

'But your other problems remain,' continued Toby. 'I know Max can handle himself, but Baxter is a really vicious bugger. Not like his dear old Dad at all. You know he did time for GBH, do you?'

'No, but I'll be there, too, and of course you will be there to back us up, Toby.'

'You leave me out of it. Physical violence is not my *métier*. I will deliver him and trip lightly out of the spotlight, thanks. And another thing, where are we going to do the deed? We can hardly lock him up in a room at the local Hilton, can we?'

I reassured him that Max and I would secure the formidable Baxter in Jack's house.

'It's got plenty of rooms and is detached. It costs a fortune but this is one week when Jack really does things in style. He says you can't be a champion unless you think like a champion.'

'Hence his abhorrence of these young players who carry their own clubs, or have their wives or girlfriends as caddies.'

'Exactly. He says it costs them at least three shots a round.'

'Chris, instead of these elaborate schemes why don't you simply get hold of Inspector Drew and his merry band of law enforcers and get him to arrest Baxter on some phony charge?'

'Because he wouldn't play ball or, rather, not that limited kind of ball. He'd want to arrest the whole lot of them: Harley, Jefferson, Martinez and whoever else is involved. He'd want to solve the case with the minimum of fuss, whereas we want to thwart them and we want them to realise that they are being thwarted. Sweet revenge with the maximum publicity. And don't forget your part in this, Toby. You've got an inside track. It'll be one of the biggest stories in sport, and you'll have exclusives coming out of your ears. Not only now, but during the trial.'

'Yes, it'll be sheer delight to monopolise the space that my conniving little editor has allocated to the Brian Harley story. And then there are the magazine articles, especially in America. And a book probably,' Toby grinned expansively. 'You can be my co-author, if you like, Chris.'

'Perhaps we ought to write it as a novel.' I said.

'One last question, though. You still haven't told me how you're going to insinuate yourself as Harley's caddie. Even assuming that this fanciful scheme has the slightest hope of working.'

By this stage Toby was toying halfheartedly with a piece of very tired Stilton, and wholeheartedly pouring a large port down his ever-receptive throat. 'I didn't know they made port in Scotland,' he said, but down it went. I was drinking Badoit.

I told Toby about the charges of insider dealing that had been made against me.

'I think I could use this, and the other assumption that Inspector Drew made about me that I had lost a lot of money in that mini-crash on the market last year. Put the two together and you can draw a convincing picture of a man with an expensive lifestyle without the money to sustain it.'

'Champagne tastes and lemonade money.'

'Yes. Now we need a white knight, as they put it in the City, to help us on the last morning. Someone who will be one of the first to know about Baxter's disappearance. I thought that Oliver Moreton might fit the bill. He was actually quite friendly towards me today.'

'I wouldn't be fooled by that, Chris. You're still on his list of least favourite people. It's only because he's got luscious Lucy of *Golf News* on the go that he's temporarily forgotten about his designs on Sally.' The gossip drums beat as insistently in golf as in any other relatively small society.

'Oh, you'd already worked that out, had you?'

'Child's play. But you are probably right. Oliver Moreton is the man to set it up, preferably unwittingly too, because the less he knows the better.

'I think I could set the ball rolling. On Sunday morning I'll ring Moreton and tell him that Baxter has gone. That late the night before when I was toiling away on the interview he had a message to tell him that his father was desperately ill, and that he set out for Dornoch, or somewhere like that up in the Highlands. It's where all Scottish caddies go to die, they say.

'I will then feed him the story. You're desperate for cash, and for a decent fee from Harley you'll desert Jack Mason and go on as the last minute substitute.

'Now, Moreton is not a subtle man. In general, his feelings rule him, despite the fact that he's a good administrator. He'll be delighted to hear that you're in financial trouble, and he'll want to believe that you're a big enough bastard to desert Jack for the sake of some easy money.

'I'll ask him to ring Harley and suggest the deal, and tell him that you'll be calling him in about half an hour. Then it's up to you.'

I was duly impressed by Toby's very lucid plan, especially when I totted up the amount of alcohol he'd got through that evening; and some of it could easily have passed itself off as paint stripper.

'OK, I think that has a chance. And it means that we don't have to tell Moreton any of the real details, because I agree that that could be dangerous. Even if he believed our story he might act oddly enough to make Harley – or rather Martinez – suspicious.'

'One last point, Chris. What are you going to tell Jack, and when? Because I'd like to be there to assess the decibel count.' Toby gave me a wide grin.

'I'll have to tell him the truth, as late as possible. Sometime on Saturday before you lurch into the house with Jake Baxter. But I've lined up Max as my replacement.'

'You've got a chance of staying alive, then.'

Jack Mason's wishes came true on the following day. It dawned bleak, windy and rainy, but by lunchtime seemed to relent, when the sun came out and the wind dropped appreciably. With every-thing in his favour, in comparison with the day before, Jack didn't improve on his first round score. He came in with another two under par round. It's a funny old game, as the television commentators say with relentless monotony.

Nevertheless, Jack was well up the field, since so many had stumbled badly during the difficult first round. Brian Harley maintained his progress, with another superb round which put him in the lead at ten under par.

I bumped into a rather liverish Toby, who blamed it all on the port. 'At my age I shouldn't go near a glass of port not even a vintage one, let alone one made in Glasgow.' I sympathised, and he passed on another morsel of information.

'My sources tell me that Harley has been quite heavily backed to win the Open. The odd thing is that this isn't a question of mugpunters backing the Great British Hope, but a series of serious bets have gone on in London. Maybe all from the same source. If I knew who it was I'd tell him to cover himself with a few quid on Krantz or Miguel or even Larry Marsh. I see that he won a tournament a couple of weeks ago in the States.'

'Maybe you wouldn't tell him to cover himself. That is, if I'm right in suspecting who it is.'

I'd had a flash of inspiration but before I could pass it on to Toby he jogged me in the arm and said: 'There's Harley's new caddie, the lovely Jake Baxter.'

He walked past, no more than ten yards away and I saw why Toby didn't fancy tangling with him in any way, let alone physically. He was well over six feet tall and looked a rather gangling figure, all angles, until you spotted the breadth of his shoulders. He was carrying a tournament bag, Harley's presumably, at the trail in one hand. No mean feat, but the size of the hand gripping the handle made the huge bag look flimsy. His clothes all looked the wrong size on his awkward frame, which was topped by a long and expressionless face with thick, lank, black hair, worn long enough to cover the back of his collar. A thin cigarette, obviously a roll-up, smouldered in his lips.

'What a charmer,' I said. 'Does Clint Eastwood know about him?'

The next two nights and days flew by. Sally and I got to know each other better and better in the borrowed flat in Edinburgh, and Jack Mason made a solid and unruffled attempt to catch Brian Harley and to win the Scottish Classic. He kept his temperament firmly under control and in fact made it work for him. Controlled aggression was the order of the day, and I'd never seen him putt more consistently. The rain on the first and second days hadn't affected the pace of the greens, which demanded the most delicate of touches. Sam Snead once described the greens at the US Masters at Augusta as so fast that it was like 'putting down a marble staircase'. Well, they weren't that quick, but quick enough to give all but the very best putters the shakes.

They didn't worry Brian Harley who picked up the first prize of £30,000. He claimed at the post-tournament Press Conference that he had averaged an astonishing twenty-four putts per round.

Jack couldn't catch him but finished in second place and received a very satisfactory prize of £20,000. A confidence-booster for the Open. But, mindful of the spiteful outlook of the golfing Fates, he grumbled that he'd left a lot of his best shots out there on the Montfort course and should have saved them for the Open.

I knew that Jack was really in good heart, and so was I. Not even the thought of what had to be faced during the next week, and the thought of Jake Baxter was bad enough by itself, could spoil the thrill of anticipation. The Open.

# Chapter 16

On the following morning I lingered in bed until after nine o'clock. What are Sundays for, after all? I strolled out and got some newspapers and scanned their pages over tea and toast. The headlines on the sports pages were mostly about the Third Test at Old Trafford. England had been rattled out in their first innings for under 200 runs by the Aussies and were following on. Brian Harley had monopolised the golf headlines: 'BRIAN BLOOMS IN PRE-OPEN EVENT', 'HARLEY A HOT TIP FOR OPEN VICTORY', 'HARLEY WINS HIS FOURTH' and so on.

By the middle of the morning I had packed, and tidied up the flat. I took one last look around and one last look through the windows to the elegant Edinburgh square below, very quiet in its sober Sunday best. I thought fondly of how Sally and I had sat together in this very spot. I would be seeing her soon, but she had driven straight down to Lancashire after the finish of yesterday's event.

I set off through the relatively traffic-free streets and headed south towards Lancashire where the Royal Prestwood Golf Club, the venue for the Open Golf Championship, awaited. The Open is only played on links courses, and this is one of the severest tests on the championship circuit. When you first look across the links it seems a desolate stretch of land. The narrow and undulating strips of fairway seem very small amid the surrounding scrub and sand dunes. The course stretches away into the distance to a featureless but rough landscape which resembles a military training area more than a golf course. Apart from the dangers of the rough, the course is littered with bunkers, and most of them are pretty deep – and very intimidating, since the faces of the bunkers are lined with old railway sleepers. The course is laid out in the traditional way: you go out for the first nine holes, and then come back to the clubhouse for the second nine holes. The course is difficult enough, but when the wind blows off the sea, as it usually does, it becomes a tiger. Prevailing winds usually help you on the way out and you may well compile a flattering first half score, but then the real fun begins on the way back, especially over the final few holes which represent one of the toughest finishes in golf. I remember listening to a leading American golfer a few years ago after he had only just broken ninety on a windy day at Prestwood. He was almost in tears and kept repeating: 'I can play golf. I can draw the ball and fade the ball; I can hit high shots and low shots; I've got a good short game and I can putt. But I can't play this course. I can't understand it. I can play the game.' And so on. I don't think he ever bothered to play in Britain again.

I had now left the motorway and was driving due west towards the coast through a series of small suburban villages. Prestwood had been a somewhat genteel seaside town since Victorian times, when it had become a favourite spot for successful Lancashire industrialists to build their second homes. The professional middle classes had followed them there between the wars and a rash of bungalows and chalets had appeared. Whatever charms it had shown in the past looked faded now. It had neither the raucous and lively appeal of a real seaside resort like Newquay or Blackpool, nor the style of Brighton or Le Touquet. But it did have one of the best golf courses in the world.

Jack Mason was renting a rather grand double-fronted Victorian house a few hundred yards from the course. With its pillared front entrance it was almost grandiose and I hated to think how much it was costing Jack in rent, but his second place finish in Scotland had boosted his bank balance enough to soothe any worries.

I rang the bell and Jack appeared almost immediately. He showed me to my bedroom, which looked out over a huge and immaculate back garden with a swimming pool. He gave me a quick tour of the house and I found out that there were more than enough bedrooms for the two of us, for Max, whenever he arrived and for Jack's wife. I asked him when Jenny would arrive.

'She isn't. I suggested that she watched on TV. I've found that she puts me off. I look for her in the crowd, especially if I've just hit a lousy shot. For sympathy, I suppose. And it ruins my concentration.

Jenny doesn't mind. The crowds are so huge now that it's no fun to try and follow a match all the way round.

'This may sound fanciful, Chris, but I thought I'd be a bit more like the old time boxers, who used to isolate themselves in the Catskill Mountains to prepare themselves for the big fight ahead. Or perhaps a better parallel is the Italian football teams who go away from the comforts and distractions of their families for a couple of days before their next match. It's worth a try, anyway.'

Jack really was taking it seriously, and I was duly impressed. I was even more wretched about the thought of breaking the news to him that I wouldn't be carrying his bag on Sunday.

We decided to have a walk in the sunshine of the late afternoon and our steps inevitably turned towards Prestwood Golf Club. We walked down a long street towards the sea. It looked very suburban, with a series of squat bungalows huddled together, each with their own neat patch of garden. You wouldn't guess that this was the setting for the world's foremost golf tournament.

At the gate to the course Jack showed his player's badge to the security guard and we strolled along the edge of the first fairway. The stands behind each green were empty and skeletal. We noticed how many security men were on duty – twenty-four hours a day – to guard against any damage being done to the course; just in case any publicity-hungry pressure groups decided that this was the time and the place to make a protest.

The breeze was very gentle off the sea. As if reading my mind, Jack said: 'Sod's law decrees that the wind is now negligible, so it'll be about force eight on Thursday.'

'Well, after last week you should be able to cope better than most.'

Jack grunted. We walked a few more holes and turned for home. Jack helped me cook a modest meal of roast chicken, and kept to his resolution not to exceed two glasses of wine. We went to bed early, and Jack told me that our first practice round was to be with Larry Marsh at eleven o'clock in the morning.

I had never met the dashing Larry Marsh, although he was a familiar figure to me from the television, the newspapers and the golf magazines. Since the end of his affair with Mary-Ann Curtis his game had gone into a steep decline but, as Toby had pointed out,

199

he was perhaps on the way back after a recent victory on the American tour.

He looked every inch the sporting superstar, with his fair hair swept straight back from a tanned face. There was a squarish look to his face, with grey-blue eyes and perfect white teeth. Doesn't every American have perfect white teeth? There was the air of the young Bobby Jones about him, and he was the perfect size and weight for a golfer, just an inch or two under six feet tall with a middleweight boxer's build. A nice package. The advertisers had certainly liked it, because he was a walking gold mine, with every conceivable endorsement and promotional deal already done for him by his agent, Mike Martinez.

Sam Ratcliffe and another young English player called Stephen Moore joined us. It was just another small example of Jack's concern for the up and coming players that he should arrange a practice game for them with a star like Larry Marsh. Some small bets were struck – Jack and Sam against Larry and Stephen – and off we went.

These practice rounds take a long time, mainly because the players often hit two or more balls into the greens, especially on the short holes. They will also throw several balls down into the bunkers and other trouble spots near the greens. Add to this the players' urge to practise their putts from various points around the green, and it all makes for a lengthy sojourn on the links. With eight people on each green and several golf balls whizzing about, no doubt it all looked pretty chaotic to the spectators. In addition, we caddies were checking our distances carefully, so that we could tell our pros the exact distance they were from the flag wherever they might be on the course.

Marsh's caddie had taken this measurement of distance yet a stage further. He had a pedometer which he trailed behind him. Like the mileometer on a bicycle wheel, it told him the precise distance of every hole. In particular he used it to measure the length and breadth of every green. I suppose that in the near future caddies will also start carrying a wind-speed indicator and a small computer, and human judgement will almost be eliminated. Fortunately such artificial aids are banned from competitive play.

As we waited on the twelfth tee for the green to clear, Jack pulled a wedge out of Marsh's bag. He mimed a few shots with it and said: 'A beautiful club, Larry. They don't make 'em like that any more.'

'That's right, Jack. An old Wilson wedge. I found it in the pro's shop years ago at Spyglass. It's a real old persuader.'

'But I see you've got Greenright on your bag.'

'Yeah. I'm supposed to be playing Greenright clubs in Europe. Martinez fixed me up with a deal but there's no way I'm going to change my clubs when I'm over here. I'd be several shots a round worse off. So the advertisements say that I play Greenright, but all it means is that I plaster their name over my bag when I'm over here. They're launching the new range tomorrow at the Links Hotel. Want to come?'

I interrupted. 'Do you mind if I come, Mr Marsh?'

'Call me Larry. Yes. Feel free. It's at noon.'

I guessed that Mike Martinez would be there, and I wanted to see him close up.

Larry Marsh continued the conversation as we walked towards the green: 'I should be concentrating totally on the goddam Open, not messing about with the launch of some new clubs which I don't even use. OK, it's money, good money, in the bank, but I don't really need it. I sometimes think I'm running so hard just to fuel Martinez' own business. He shunts me all over the place, this promotion and that company day. And what for? I don't need any more money. My basic endorsements and my earnings on the tour bring in about three million dollars a year.'

The two young professionals looked awed at the mention of such riches.

As we waited on the next tee, Jack said: 'This endorsement business is a bit of a farce, isn't it? You say that you're contracted to play Greenright in Europe, but you never touch the clubs. That negates the whole point of an endorsement, doesn't it?'

'Yeah. But Greenright know the score. They just wanted my ugly mug on their advertisements. It goes on all the time. Mary-Ann won Wimbledon playing a certain brand of racket, or so the ads said, and the sales of that racket went through the roof. In fact she couldn't get on with the rackets at all, and had the rackets she really liked painted up to look like the others.

'You see Martinez doesn't give a damn as long as the money is there. He's obsessed with earning more and more. To hell with the players, as long as his company's bank balance increases.'

Larry Marsh hit a glorious two-iron into the heart of the green and Sam Ratcliffe, twenty yards further on with his drive, followed him with a slightly shorter iron.

'That boy can play, can't he?' said Marsh to Jack. 'Another trick of Martinez' is to invest your money in schemes for his own benefit. He bought an apartment building in Bel Air a couple of years ago. He was only able to finance it by using his clients' money. Me and Carl Krantz and Mary-Ann and so on. But naturally he ends up with the majority share of the building, and of course he has the gall to charge us an extra percentage for his investment advice. I also heard that he screwed the estate agent for some commission. None of it came back to us, of course.'

'Why don't you move to another agent?' Jack asked.

'I would. But his contract is so tight that I can't do a thing until it ends next year. And even then he'll still have a piece of most of my endorsement deals until they come up for renegotiation. And of course he has a three-year option on our management contract.'

'So he'll make it tough for you to leave.'

'Tough. You don't know the half of it. He's one of the really unpleasant people I've met in my life. I know that when I try to terminate the contract, he'll use every possible kind of pressure.'

I interrupted. 'Violence, as well?'

Larry Marsh looked long and hard at me. 'I wouldn't put it past him. I've heard that he has some shady connections, though of course he's only ever seen in public with company presidents and owners of television stations.

'His first move will be through his lawyers, and I know that I'll have to spend a million or two on my own lawyers. And I'm reconciled to the fact that I'll probably have to pay him off in the end. It'll drag on for a year or two and then I'll pay him a million dollars or so, and that'll be that.'

'Which agency will you go to?' asked Jack.

'I'd like Ed Grainger to set up on his own and look after me. He's a civilised guy and honest, too. God knows what he's doing working for Martinez. He'll be at this launch, by the way.'

Jack and Sam Ratcliffe took the money on the bets by a whisker;

a birdie at the daunting last hole from Sam did the trick. We all went down to the practice ground, Larry Marsh to work on his long iron shots, and Jack to get to grips with his wedges. After about an hour Toby Greenslade made his way through the crowd which, even on the first practice day, was sizeable. The stand at the back of the practice ground was about half full, and many of the fans had binoculars trained on their favourite players. I noticed that many of them seemed to be focusing on Larry Marsh. And rightly so, since he had a most impressive swing; a shade fast for the purist, perhaps, but powerful and well-balanced. For handicap golfers, watching the top golfers on the practice ground is an excellent way to get a picture of a good swing. Far better than reading any amount of books or magazine articles. Monkey see, monkey do.

As Toby walked over to us, Jack looked at him in mock astonishment: 'Good Lord, it's Mr Greenslade of the *News*, isn't it? Toby, this is a golf club, and those are golf balls, and this is my caddie.'

'Yes, yes, very droll, Jack. How's your game? Should I have a flutter on you?'

'Save your money. Put it all on Harley, or Larry Marsh, over there.'

I interrupted to ask if Toby was going to the Greenright launch on the following day.

'Do I have to?' he asked.

'Well, I thought I'd take a look, because Martinez will probably be there and I've always wondered what he's like.' The penny dropped and we arranged to meet at the Links Hotel just before midday.

The next day was similar to the first, but in reverse. A couple of hours practice in the morning and a practice round planned for three o'clock. Jack released me at 11.30 so that I could go to the Greenright launch.

One of the conference rooms in the hotel had been hired for the occasion and we were handed badges with our names on as we entered. Four men were lined up to meet us as we entered the room. First in line was the superstar himself, Larry Marsh, who had a cheerful word for everyone. Next to him was the managing director of Greenright, a thin and rather nervous man with a slightly clammy handshake. There was then a gap and two other men stood together to greet the guests of Greenright. The first was a tall and fit-looking man, with a small beard and glasses. He had a tanned face which seemed to have a naturally humorous and good-tempered look. It was Ed Grainger and, as he wished me good-morning, I recognised his voice from his telephone conversation with Sally. It seemed a long time ago.

Next to him was Mike Martinez, and I recognised him because I had seen his photograph so often. He was in the newspapers more often than his clients. If I were one of them, I would be asking why.

Martinez was tall and broad-shouldered and wearing an elegantly cut light grey suit. He seemed to have a slightly larger than normal head, and his dark hair was lightly flecked with grey. His eyes were especially noticeable, a very light brown, almost verging on yellow. I noticed with interest that he had a slight nervous tic in his left eye.

'Thank you for coming, Mr Ludlow,' he said in a flat American tone. Those eyes looked at me briefly. No expression. Just a look. Dismissive.

'Thank you for coming, Mr Greenslade. I was talking to your editor this morning.' The same sort of tone, with slightly more expression because Toby was from the Press.

We were handed a glass of wine and asked to take a seat. The attendance was thin, although I spotted one or two journalists from the down-market papers. I reckoned that they would get short shrift, probably from Martinez, if they asked any questions about Mary-Ann Curtis.

The managing director of Greenright gave a competent and mercifully short run-down on the new clubs, and Larry Marsh made a polished and amusing speech and then asked for questions. We had the usual queries from the trade press. Why are the clubs different? How long is Marsh's contract? How much is he being paid? A journalist from one of the tabloids asked Larry Marsh if he was planning to marry anyone in the near future, and Marsh replied that he wasn't but would invite that particular reporter to the wedding if it ever happened.

Toby stood up and asked: 'In view of Brian Harley's success with the Supersight putter, and Mr Martinez' financial interest in the company, do you have any plans, Mr Marsh, to use the putter in the future? Perhaps even at the Open?'

Not surprisingly, Larry Marsh looked puzzled and turned to Mike Martinez. Jokingly he said, 'If there's an infallible putter around, I want it in my bag. If my agent's holding out on me . . .'

Amid the amused chatter, Martinez held up his hand for silence. 'We are here, ladies and gentlemen, to talk about Greenright products, not Supersight. One of my other clients happens to use Supersight, and that is the extent of my interest. Mr Greenslade was misinformed.'

This was accompanied by a cold and malevolent look from those yellowy-brown eyes. They lasered across the room, and made it absolutely plain that any more questions on that theme would be unwelcome.

The presentation was quickly concluded by the managing director, and Larry Marsh made his way out of the conference room. Martinez paused in his wake and walked over to Toby. Those eyes were still pumping out messages of disdain and danger, and I could sense the discomfort that even a hardened journalist like Toby felt.

'Mr Greenslade, your question was irresponsible. I'll be speaking to your editor directly about you.'

I felt that Toby needed my moral support, so I said: 'But we heard that you helped to set Supersight up with Derek Jefferson.'

I got the full Martinez glare, and it was an unnerving moment.

'Young man, I suggest you stay away from things you don't understand.'

One last look at Toby and he turned and walked away.

'Well, he's a bundle of fun, isn't he?' said Toby. 'He's turned my wine cloudy.'

'He's nastier than Jake Baxter.'

'Much. And much cleverer. And much richer.'

'And more powerful.'

Jack's practice round that afternoon went pretty well in the serene and sunny conditions, which took many of the terrors out of the course. But the forecast was for unsettled conditions in the latter part of the week, and the various experts who give their opinions on radio and television and in the newspapers were predicting that, if the wind blew, a score of four under par would win the Open.

I talked to Sally briefly and we arranged that she would have a meal at the house that evening. Before she arrived I went for a long run along the Prestwood seashore.

We passed a companionable evening; Jack was in a relaxed and expansive mood and told us some tales of the pro tour that neither of us had heard before. Like demure lovers of another age we parted chastely at the front door before eleven o'clock and went to our separate beds.

Both Jack and I were looking forward to getting the final day of preparation out of the way and joining the real battle. In my case I was also relishing the imminent arrival of Max. I felt in need of both his mental support and his physical presence for the other battles to come.

Much to my surprise Max arrived bright and early on the Wednesday morning. It had only just gone eight o'clock when he tapped on the front door. I discovered that he'd been working in Manchester on the previous day. Before Jack made his morning appearance Max reassured me that he 'had everything we need' to deal with Brian Harley.

'I hope you've got everything we need to deal with Jake Baxter,' I said and explained how we intended to remove the dangerous looking caddie from the scene on Saturday night.

'No problem, Chris, you can attack him from the front and I'll nobble him from the rear.'

'Thanks a million. You obviously haven't seen the size of the bugger yet.'

'The bigger they come . . .' said Max cheerfully.

The large and sleepy looking figure of Jack Mason came into the kitchen, and he greeted Max enthusiastically.

'Do you know, I've never slept so well. Cutting the booze down obviously agrees with me.'

After a quick breakfast – fruit for me and Max and bacon and eggs for Jack – we headed for the course. Jack had arranged his last practice round for just after eleven o'clock because that was his starting time for the first round of the Open on the following day. A good time to start. Nobody really relishes an early morning time, when it can be cold and unwelcoming on a links like Prestwood. And a late start means that the greens are inevitably less true, because of the spike marks of the preceding players – especially around the hole. Jack was to play with Larry Marsh and the current British amateur champion, a young and very talented player from Wales called Owen Edwards.

Max, as planned, invited himself to walk round with us. I had already coached him thoroughly in a caddie's duties, even though he had a good working knowledge, but he wanted to observe for himself what had to be done. I wondered how he would cope in the highly-charged atmosphere of the final day. Especially if Jack was in contention. A caddie's error could be fatal. Not that Jack was a difficult man to work for, unlike a certain American golfer who employed a well-known and experienced English caddie for a few months. They parted company after the final round of the US Masters, when the American looked likely to win. There was a difference of opinion over the club to use at one of the vital holes around Amen Corner. The caddie counselled a three-wood to ensure that the ball carried over the stream and onto the green. The American superstar insisted that it was a two-iron. Even with the adrenaline pumping through the golfer's body the caddie knew that he'd never reach the green with a two-iron. He was right. The ball ended in the water, and that particular golfer's dreams of victory were deluged at the same time. The caddie wasn't stupid enough to say, 'I told you so', and didn't get a chance anyway. In a fury the golfer told the caddie it was his fault— 'for putting negative thoughts in my head'. The caddie resigned his job on the eighteenth green. It is inevitable that the caddie becomes the fall guy; if something goes wrong it is the caddie's fault, never the pro's.

The crowds were considerable as we began our final practice round in company with Jose Miguel and two other Ryder Cup golfers. There was a tenser atmosphere than on the other two days, partly because of the larger gatherings of spectators, and partly because the golfers knew it was their last chance to assess the course. Tomorrow was for real. There wasn't too much levity, just earnest concentration. Jack played very solidly, and I noticed that Miguel didn't miss a fairway; a dark horse for the title perhaps. Max noticed his form, too, and said he'd probably put a tenner on him. A good each-way bet at twenty-five to one.

Jack decided to have one last session on the practice ground, but said that he didn't need my services.

207

'Take Max for a look around. I'll see you both later at the house.'

It was invigorating just to walk around the course and casually absorb the unique atmosphere. There was an air of expectation which seemed to touch everyone. Players and officials, stewards and caddies, the equipment manufacturers in the huge Exhibition tent, the journalists, the teams of scorers, even the teams of schoolboys and girls who were ready to deal with the tons of rubbish which had to be moved every day, seemed to be waiting impatiently for the great event to begin.

I couldn't resist a quick detour past the PGA caravan for a word with Sally. Much to Max's amusement, since he seemed to have an unending supply of bright and attractive girls with whom he never got seriously involved. We spoke briefly and agreed to meet on Friday evening for a final council of war.

We sought Toby out in the Press tent and found him penning his Open preview for the next day's edition of the *News*. I looked over his shoulder. 'Brian Harley, who two years ago was a washed-up golfer with a drink problem and no prospects, can this week become a superstar. He is tipped to become only the fifth British player this century to win the Open, the most important golf event in the world.'

'Are you sure about that, Toby.'

'I have to give the public what they want, dear boy. But I'm going to hedge my bets, in true journalistic style, by telling my faithful readers that he'll be chased all the way home by Marsh, Krantz, Carlssen and even Jack Mason.'

'And don't forget Jose Miguel,' Max said.

'No. Good point.' Toby drew us a little closer, and said in a quiet voice, 'My editor has got double-page spreads reserved all next week for Brian Harley's life story. Amusing, don't you think? Is everything set for Saturday night, by the way? Max knows what he's got to do, etc? Harley is out on the course, by the way, playing with Krantz and Marsh.' He consulted a list, and made a quick calculation. 'They should be on the sixteenth by now. Why don't you show the enemy, Jake Baxter I mean, to Max?'

I wondered whether that was a good idea, but Max was already striding out of the tent. With a wave to Toby, I followed him towards the sixteenth hole.

As we reached the sixteenth green Brian Harley was playing out of a bunker. He popped the ball up and it settled a foot away from the hole. He threw a couple more balls down and played those out, with equal success. The three players had attracted quite a crowd who watched them each trying putts from various points on the green.

Max nudged me. 'I think I've spotted our friend, Jake Baxter.'

He nodded at the untidy and gangling figure who was grasping the flag in his over-sized fist.

'An ugly looking brute, isn't he?'

'He makes that flag-stick look like a toothpick, doesn't he?'

Max grinned. 'I think we'll have to hit him hard where it hurts.'

# Chapter 17

On the first day of the Open my alarm clock woke me at 6 a.m. Jack was due on the first tee at just after eleven o'clock, and I was determined to follow my usual routine of walking the course to make my final checks. It was mainly superstition, like the footballer who always likes to leave the players' tunnel last or the cricketer who ties the straps on his pads in a certain way.

I dressed quickly, and went downstairs and out of the front door quietly. In the shelter of the house I looked out at the day, which was reasonably bright, but with clumps of clouds the colour of wholemeal dough moving rapidly across the sky. I checked the tops of the trees and saw that they were already waving briskly back and forth. It was going to be one of those days in which the Open specialises. Difficult. The windy conditions would make this classic links course even tougher than usual.

The security guard on the main gate looked at me as if I was deranged, but my caddie's badge got me onto the course. I walked down the semi-rough which edged the narrow fairways. I was going almost at a trot, but admired yet again the challenge that the course presented. Every shot had to be planned and executed with accuracy and finesse. It would ensure that only a true champion would hold the old claret jug aloft on Sunday evening, and even he would need an extra measure of luck.

I was round the course in less than an hour, and the place was stirring into life as I left. The first players were due on the tee at 7.30, and their alarm clocks would have sounded even earlier than mine. I knew that the honour of hitting the first shot in the Open had fallen to an amateur golfer whom I knew slightly. It was his first appearance in the Open. I saw him on the putting green alongside the clubhouse and strolled over to wish him luck. He said he was terrified and his main ambition was to make the cut for the final two rounds. The field in the Open, as in most tournaments, is reduced after the second round.

I decided to hang on for twenty minutes or so to watch the opening drives and went off in search of a cup of tea. After scrounging one from one of the many caterers who were preparing themselves for the first of four big days, I watched the various hopefuls on the practice ground for a few minutes, and then went back to the first tee. The starter announced the first match. 'On the tee, Mr Jonathan Dyas.'

The 'Mr' signified that the player was an amateur and to everyone's relief, especially his own, he hit a sweetly timed drive down the centre of the fairway. He grinned at me behind the ropes and gave the thumbs-up. His two partners drove off, and away he went on the round he would remember all his life.

I returned to the house and found Jack already sitting in the kitchen. He had a pot of coffee at his side, and a pile of newspapers in front of him.

'Morning, Chris. How's the course looking?'

'Superb, as always.'

'Good. The papers are mostly tipping Krantz and Harley, with Marsh and Carlssen getting a few mentions, too. I fancy Marsh. He really looks the part, doesn't he?'

'Well, we'll soon know. We've got the first two rounds with him.'

An hour later we were on our way to the course and Jack went through his familiar routine on the practice ground. Gentle pitch shots, then a few fuller swings, some punch shots with the medium irons, and full shots. Next the long irons and, in view of the strong wind, Jack hit a series of low raking shots which bored challengingly through the air. As always I admired his technique, and as always wondered whether the technique would master the occasion, or the occasion would overawe the technique. He hit some shots with his three-wood and then went back to his battery of short shots: pitches, cut-up shots, chip-and-run. He knew that he would need all the variations on this course.

We spent half an hour on the putting green and then it was time to head for the first tee. We walked through the crowds which were already gathering in considerable numbers. Although this was the first morning of the Open Jack was playing with a popular American golfer who was tipped as a possible winner. Jack received a number of 'good lucks' from the fans, which he acknowledged with smiles and thank-yous. The players drove off in alphabetical order: the Amateur Champion, Owen Edwards, first. A good one. Larry Marsh next, safely down the right side of the fairway with a one-iron.

'On the tee, Jack Mason.' Warm applause, and I wondered what was going through his mind. All the usual memos no doubt: take the club away slowly; swing smoothly; release the club head; swing down the line. A great moment for any golfer, and a frightening one. Like your first ball in a Test Match, or the first pass you receive in a Cup Final at Wembley. Don't let it bobble up and hit me on the knee, you pray.

Jack did all the right things, and followed Larry Marsh's ball safely down the fairway. As he handed me his three-wood he grinned and said, 'Glad the first one's over.'

The strong and blustery wind was more or less helpful over the first half of the course, and by the turn Jack was two under par with Larry Marsh one better. They both gave those shots back to the course over the second nine and Jack finished at level par, and Marsh one under.

It was a very creditable performance in difficult conditions, but Jack was unhappy with his long irons and we headed for the practice ground. After nearly two hours, which was interrupted at frequent intervals by conversations with old friends and rivals, Jack decided that he'd done enough and headed for the house. He'd decided to have a cup of tea and a late afternoon nap.

'You may not realise it, young Chris, but I'm knackered.'

His eyes certainly showed it. The nervous tension and surging adrenaline during the round had certainly taken their toll.

I had arranged to meet Max at five o'clock at the Bollinger tent, and was a few minutes late. We had a bottle together and then decided to walk around the huge exhibition tent which is a focus of attention every year. The tent gets bigger and bigger each year as more and more manufacturers cram into it. A noticeable feature of the exhibition this time was the number of time-share agencies, all selling villas and apartments on golf courses in the sun. And they were there to sell. We were accosted within the space of a few yards by several different young ladies selling their wares. Attractive, but pushy. Max gave his standard reply: 'I've already got a villa in Estoril.' We headed away from the small stands on the periphery towards the big displays in the centre of the tent. We admired the arrays of cashmere sweaters and tried to dodge the flying elbows of the Americans and the Japanese as they reached for their gold credit cards – or maybe platinum, judging by the piles of cashmere that they were taking away.

We looked with amazement at some Japanese golf clubs which were priced at £3000 a set, and finally had a look at the Supersight stand. This was as big as any of the major companies, and was dominated by photographs of Brian Harley. Most of them pictured him holing out with his magic putter, and there were piles of the same model for sale. The latest scores came up on the television monitor and I saw that Harley was two under par for the first round. He was tied for third place, with twenty or so scores yet to come in.

Max picked up one of the putters and swung it a couple of times. He grimaced slightly.

'Rubbish, isn't it?' he asked.

'Probably.'

'I'm going to buy one. As a memento. Is Derek Jefferson here? I want to buy it off him, if possible.'

I could hear Jefferson booming away on the other side of the stand and pointed him out to Max, who insisted that I introduced him. I interrupted Jefferson's sales patter, excellent and confident as it always was, and Max said: 'I believe that this is the putter that will win the Open, and I want to buy one from the man who designed it.'

Jefferson beamed his approval at Max. 'Absolutely. The best putter ever made. It's made Brian Harley into a great player, and we're going to sweep the world with this when he wins on Sunday.'

'Absolutely,' said Max, and with a smile turned towards the counter to pay his eighty-five pounds.

The second day of the Open brought similar weather to the first. But the wind was blowing much harder. The clouds were really scurrying across the pale blue sky, and the tops of the trees were bending and sighing as if in protest.

The three of us had a late breakfast together, since Jack was scheduled to tee off at shortly after three o'clock. The newspapers were full of praise for Brian Harley, who had remained in a group of players tied in third position and with nobody of any particular golfing note ahead of him. – "BATTLING BRIAN ON COURSE,' 'HARLEY'S CONFIDENT START' 'OPEN VICTORY IN HARLEY'S GRASP' read the headline in Toby's paper, the *News*. A bit premature, with players like Marsh and Krantz in the field, and Toby's account of the day's play was much more sober than the headline indicated.

But alongside Toby's column, in heavy type and with 'World Exclusive' emblazoned at its head, was Brian Harley's own account of his round. The ground was already being prepared for The Brian Harley Story, which would be another News Exclusive next week. But maybe not in the way that Harley and Martinez had planned.

Jack Mason went off to meet a potential sponsor with his agent, Graham Fearnley; an ideal way to fill in his time, rather than sit fidgeting in the house and worrying about the round to come. Max and I went down to the local leisure centre, had a work-out in their superbly equipped gym, and then had a long swim. However Jack felt, I felt tuned to the last inch for the round to come.

If yesterday had been difficult, the second round was a factor worse. The wind was strong enough to make even brilliant golfers like Larry Marsh waver – literally, because sudden gusts threw his club head out of line, and even affected his balance as he lined up for his shots. Down the first hole both Jack and Larry hit three-irons off the tee in order to stay short of a tongue of rough which stuck out mischievously into the fairway on the right. When they both sailed into it, I knew that we were in for a tough round, especially when we turned for home and met the full fury of the wind.

After nine holes Jack had actually improved his overall position and was two under par. He would need those and more, I thought, as we stood on the tenth tee. It was a daunting moment, as we felt the strength of the wind and looked down a fairway that totally lacked definition. We knew it was there because we had walked

215

down it yesterday, but from the tee it was just a wilderness of humps and small hillocks. The line was on a far-distant church tower, and you had to believe in that against the apparent evidence of your eyes. Larry Marsh was in a much worse state than Jack, since he had dropped three shots to par on the outward nine, and the course and the conditions would not yield any favours to him from now on.

But they did because Marsh gave one of those performances in adversity of which only true golfing geniuses are capable. He went up several gears in skill and you felt you could reach out and touch his determination. He wrung three successive birdies out of the course from the tenth hole onwards, and birdied the sixteenth with an exquisite pitch-and-run shot straight into the back of the hole. He had a real champion's finish at the last hole. After rolls of applause had greeted his iron shot into the heart of the green, he obliged his fans with a putt for a birdie. He was now three under for the Championship.

We all shook hands on the final green, and I shook Jack's in genuine admiration. His game might have looked dim alongside such brilliance as Marsh's, but he had clung on with great spirit to finish on level par.

Many of the golfers had gone way over par, and Jack was now well placed in the top dozen or so. Brian Harley was now in the lead on his own at four under par. Marsh and Miguel were one behind, and Krantz one further back. I noticed that my friend from amateur days, Jonathan Dyas, was going to make the cut, and if he kept going might be in line for the gold medal which is awarded to the top amateur. Good for him.

'Well done, Jack. A super round,' I said.

'I hung on, didn't I? But you'll be lucky to see a better nine holes than Larry's. He's a genius.'

We went back to the house, and Jack allowed himself the luxury of one glass of beer. I returned to the course in search of Toby, and the Bollinger tent seemed to be the obvious place to look. He was there with several other journalists and pressed a glass of champagne into my hand without delay. The place was really humming, with corks popping at a giddy rate.

I managed to lead Toby a few feet away from his cronies and asked him whether he'd made any progress with Jake Baxter.

216

'No problem, old boy,' he boomed at me. 'He's an odious man, but I promised him a monkey up front in cash for an exclusive. I even cleared it all with that twerp of an editor of mine. I'm going to meet him at some disgusting pub at eight o'clock tomorrow night and then we're going to do the interview, as planned, at your house.'

'Jack's house.'

'Yes, and have you warned Jack yet?'

'No. I'll leave it till after tomorrow's round. Don't want him brooding, especially tomorrow. All the rounds of the Open are vital, but they get more vital, don't they? And if Jack can get himself close to the lead . . . well, who knows?'

'Indeed. But just make sure, young Chris, that you and your brother are waiting with bloody big sticks. Or even better, a bear trap, because that's what you'll need for Jake Baxter.'

On Saturdays, the really big crowds begin to turn up for the Open. There is almost a festive air on that day. It doesn't have the final air of tension which infects the last day, and the spectators seem to be there to enjoy and appreciate the golf rather than just to follow the progress of the champion. The third round is also the really unpredictable day; when a golfer may come hurtling out of the pack and take the lead, or when a favourite can drop back. In contrast, it is usually obvious on the final day that the champion will be one of the leading group of half a dozen or so players. It's nail-biting and dramatic, but not so unpredictable.

The wind, to everyone's relief, had lessened to become a gentle breeze. It was dull and overcast, but rain seemed unlikely. Jack was out at lunchtime and revelled in the easier conditions. He got round in four under par, but that was not good enough to make any impression on Brian Harley's lead. He had moved to ten under with a superlative round and was now three strokes ahead of Marsh and Krantz. Miguel was one back, and Bjorn Carlssen had shot out of the chasing pack, in traditional Saturday-of-the-Open style, to move to six under par.

Back at the house, Jack Mason was quietly enthusiastic about the next day's round. I had rarely seen him so confident. Over tea and crumpets he talked at length of how and where he would attack the course.

'If I can get to eight or nine under, you never know. Harley ought to win, but he's never had anything like the pressure he'll feel tomorrow. Especially with Marsh and Krantz breathing down his neck. It might overwhelm him, destroy him. They've been there, you see. They're champions, and until you've stared a major championship in the face you don't know whether you can win one or not. The Ryder Cup is bad enough, but you can't comprehend what it's like to stand on the tee with three or four holes to go and think to yourself, "I just need par or better to win the Open." Tomorrow, Harley will find out a lot about himself.'

I was wondering how on earth I could break the news that I would not be there as usual as his caddie – his familiar and trusted helper; there to encourage and cajole and inform.

While I was still hesitating and trying to choose a moment, Max said: 'Jack, how would you feel if I carried your clubs tomorrow?'

'Oh, you fancy a nice walk, do you, Max?' said Jack sarcastically.

'No, he's serious, Jack. There's a problem and only I can solve it.'

'Now look, Chris, if this is a joke, it's in very poor taste. I need you tomorrow. Only you will do. Not Max. You.'

I asked Jack to give me five minutes, without interruptions, to explain. Off I went and tried to condense everything we knew and suspected into a coherent story. Jack heard me out, agreed with our reasons for not telling all to the police, and then said:

'If I didn't know you both better I would have said that you'd been sniffing large amounts of exotic substances and watching too many fantasy films. That you're both off your trolleys, in fact.

'But if you're right, that Harley is a miserable cheat, he deserves all the ill that's coming to him. No one should prostitute our beautiful game and get away with it. OK Max, you're on, and if you need any help with Jake Baxter, I'll be there.'

'No, you keep well away from it all,' I said. 'Just make sure that when the questions start tomorrow about your unprincipled defector of a caddie you have a few choice phrases ready.'

'No problem,' Jack said and smiled grimly.

The plan was that Toby would get Jake Baxter to the house sometime between eight and nine o'clock. Even with the prospect of earning an easy £500 in cash, Baxter had apparently been suspicious.

Why couldn't Toby do the interview on the Sunday morning? Because he would be too busy in the Press tent. Why not after the Open then, on the Sunday night? Because Toby had to file his copy for the Monday morning edition of the *News* and, anyway, Jake would no doubt be too busy celebrating his boss's win to bother with an interview. And so on, until Jake agreed to the deal.

We had time to kill until Jake arrived and Max and I decided that it would be safer if Jack was out of the way for the night. We knew that he got on famously with Larry Marsh, who had rented an enormous house just up the road. After a long argument with Jack he finally agreed to ring Larry and ask for a bed for the night, with the excuse that a lot of his family had turned up unexpectedly. No problem. Larry was delighted, and Jack departed shortly afterwards.

At nine o'clock there was no sign of Toby and we were slightly anxious. Half an hour later we were very worried indeed, and were sitting silently, waiting for something to happen. Just before ten o'clock the phone rang. We both jumped at the harsh sound and I grabbed the extension in the lounge.

'Chris, it's me, Toby. I can't get the bastard out of the pub. He wants to go on to some damned club in Blackpool now.'

Max's voice came over the main phone in the hallway. 'Give him one more drink and then get him out to the car park. We'll have to nobble him there and bring him back to the house. OK?'

'OK.' Toby told us where the pub was, and we raced out of the house.

We were in the car park within a few minutes. It was a large and dreary, brick-built building at the wrong end of Prestwood. There were no more than half a dozen cars parked there and I saw Toby's near the side entrance to the pub.

After ten minutes or so which seemed interminable, the side door opened and Toby appeared. Jake Baxter, lurching slightly, made straight for Toby's car, and lent on the passenger side. Toby was looking around for us, desperately, and we needed to get Baxter away from Toby's car which was parked in a pool of light, albeit dingy, from the pub entrance.

'Come on, Tobe, let's away to the club and get hold of some tarts. I'm still thirsty and I want some action.'

Toby muttered some indeterminate reply.

I decided to take the initiative, to act as a fall guy for Max, who had more chance of disabling Baxter than I had. I walked to within ten yards of him and said, 'Hello, you Scottish poof.'

Baxter straightened up and looked towards me as I stepped towards him into the light. For a big man, with a belly full of beer and whisky, he moved fast. He covered the ground between us in a couple of long strides, and threw his first haymaker of a punch at my head. I saw it coming, ducked under it and hit him as hard as I could in the ribs. It was like hitting a side of frozen beef. Wary that he might grab me and fall on me, I moved away. I felt rather than saw the kick coming and was only able to turn my body to take it on the thigh. The force of it put me down, and all the feeling went out of my leg. I rolled instinctively away from him, as I hit the ground, but he was after me fast. I was trying to get up as I saw his foot draw back ready to put me out of the battle for good.

The kick didn't land. There was a dull whump as Max's fist hit Baxter in the stomach. He doubled over and, as Max moved in, suddenly straightened and caught him with a two-handed, lunging uppercut. Max staggered but didn't go down, and then showed Baxter some fancy footwork of his own. He ducked under the next punch, and I'm sure I heard it hum as it went over Max's head, and anticipated the next kick. Baxter was badly off-balance as Max kicked him sickeningly hard under the knee and chopped him viciously on the side of the neck. Jake Baxter crumpled and fell.

This whole sequence couldn't have taken more than a few seconds, but enough noise had been made to bring a couple of customers to the door. Nothing like a Saturday night punch-up to enliven one's routine.

'What's going on?'

'Just a disagreement,' said Max. 'Nothing serious. We're taking our mate home. He's had a bit too much.'

This seemed to satisfy them, and by this time I had struggled to my feet. I had a severe case of dead leg, and thanked my lucky stars that Baxter's kick had not reached its intended target. I even wondered whether I would be fit to carry Harley's bag on the following day.

Max was already dragging Baxter's inert body towards his car, hindered rather than helped by Toby. I grabbed a spare leg and we bundled him into the car.

220

We bundled him out of the car in similarly untidy style back at the house and levered him into a kitchen chair. As he began to stir into life again, Max tied him quickly and efficiently to the chair.

'He should have stayed out longer than this,' Max said. ' "If I've fought tougher men, I can't remember when," to quote the old song.'

Jake Baxter came to, shook his head a couple of times and then launched into a venomous tirade of only half comprehensible threats and insults. He looked dangerous even when tied to a chair, and I noticed that Toby retreated to a far corner of the kitchen.

Max waited until he drew breath and said:

'If you carry on like that I'll put you out again.'

He advanced on Baxter with his hand raised and Baxter spat copiously in his direction.

Max continued: 'We know what's going on with Harley's putter, so with your record you'll go to jail for quite a while as an accessory to fraud. We'll offer you a way out. You'll take a nice sea trip from Liverpool to Belfast with some friends of mine. A few hours in that lovely city, and then you'll be on the ocean wave again to Fishguard. The sea air will do you good. The boat leaves at midnight, and you'll be on it. What you do after that is up to you. Is it a deal?'

A grunt was followed by another array of obscenities.

'I take it that means yes,' Max said. 'We'll have a quick drink on it.'

He left the room to get a bottle of whisky and, after a few moments during which Jake Baxter entertained us with some more predictions of what he would do to us, our boyfriends and mothers, Max reappeared with four generous glasses of whisky and the half-empty bottle of whisky. Toby grabbed his and drained most of it in one.

With a warning to Baxter, Max untied his left arm and handed him a glass. No true Scot can resist a free glass of his native booze, and down it went in one. Max topped his glass up from the bottle and half of it disappeared. Within a few seconds, Jake Baxter's glass fell on the floor and his head drooped on his chest.

I looked inquiringly at Max as Toby said, 'I'll have a pint of what he's drinking.'

'Yes, I doctored his drink. I didn't fancy the drive to Liverpool, short as it is, with him conscious and thinking evil thoughts. I wouldn't trust the bugger, even tied up in the back seat.'

'Who's taking him on this nice sea voyage?' I asked.

'Presumably not Sealink Ferries,' said Toby sarcastically.

Max grinned. 'You must admit that it would be dodgy to leave him tied up here for twenty-four hours or so. He could escape and cause trouble. And it's not very humanitarian, either. So I rang some chums in Belfast and asked whether they had any boats doing the crossing – Saturday night is a favourite time, by the way – and struck lucky. The captain is a friend of a friend. He'll put Mr Baxter to rest in a cabin and he'll wake up tomorrow with a monumental hangover. The skipper has detailed one of his lads to look after him. They'll unload a few items in the morning and then it's off to Fishguard in West Wales. So Jake will be well out of the way.

'Come on. Into the car with him. I've got less than an hour.'

Toby agreed to stay the night with us, since he had a vital role to play the next morning: a call to Oliver Moreton to tell him of Jake Baxter's departure to the bedside of his sick father.

# Chapter 18

The next morning I was awakened by Max at just before eight o'clock. He threw the curtains back on a bright and sunny day.

He grinned at me. 'A lovely day for golf, Chris.'

In other circumstances, it would indeed have been that. I would have been playing a small but significant part in the finale of one of the greatest of all sporting events. There aren't many of those: The FA Cup Final; England v. Australia at Lord's; the Derby and the Grand National; the Heavyweight Championship of the World; England v. Wales at Twickenham; the 100 metres at the Olympics; the Men's Singles Final at Wimbledon. The blue ribbands of sport. I had a strange and unwelcome part to play in the Open today, but a part which might at least ensure that its integrity was preserved.

'I've given Toby a cup of tea. He's not a pretty sight in the morning. Complaining of a hangover. Keeps saying he doesn't deserve it, because it was in the line of duty.'

'Did you get rid of our friend OK?'

'No problem. His guardian was even bigger and uglier than Jake, if you can believe that. He made Mike Tyson look effete. He carried him on board as if he was a child.'

A few minutes later we gathered in the lounge. My leg was stiff from Baxter's kick and I was limping badly. But I hoped that some exercise would relieve the problem. Toby put a call through to Oliver Moreton's hotel while Max and I shared the other phone in the hallway. We heard Moreton's brisk tones.

'You've just caught me on the way out. I should be at the course by now.'

'Well I've got some bad news for you. I'm sorry to tell you that Jake Baxter has gone. He caught a late train up to the wilds of Scotland somewhere. His old dad is seriously ill and like a dutiful son'

(Toby could not totally suppress a note of sarcasm in his voice at this point) 'he's gone to his bedside.'

'I don't believe it. Harley can win the Open, for God's sake. He'll go berserk.'

'I have a suggestion to make, Oliver. Young Chris Ludlow is willing to substitute. As you must admit, he's one of the best there is, and he won't let Harley down.'

'And what is Jack Mason going to do? He's in with a chance, too. He'll go even more berserk than Harley.'

'Well, that can't be helped. Just between you and me, Chris is in big financial trouble. He's taken a bashing with his shares recently and he's being investigated for insider dealing. A good fee from Harley and a bonus if he wins will bring him running.'

'And bugger Jack Mason, you mean.'

'Well, yes.'

'My God, what a miserable bastard he is. I always thought he was too good to be true – with his flash car and his high and mighty attitude.'

Max dug me in the ribs at this point and grinned.

Toby continued. 'Well look, Oliver, we can solve the problem, if you want. I promised Baxter I'd do the best I could for Harley. You can provide Harley with a good caddie and also ensure that Chris earns some good money. Will you phone Harley and then phone me back?'

A few minutes later the phone rang and we heard Oliver Moreton say: 'I've fixed it with Harley. He'll pay Ludlow his thirty pieces of silver. But he wants to see him at his house at ten o'clock sharp. To settle the fee and so on. My God, if this ever gets out . . .'

'It won't get out from me, Oliver.'

'Nor me, Greenslade.' You could hear the bristle in Oliver Moreton's voice. Nothing like a bit of moral self-righteousness to set a man like Moreton up for the day.

'And what about Jack Mason?'

'Oh, I've sorted a caddie out for him. I'll need a badge and so on.'

With one more remark about 'jumped-up, unprincipled shysters', Moreton put the phone down.

'He won't be able to resist telling someone about all this,' Toby said, 'and the first recipient will probably be juicy Lucy, who's probably still curled up in his bed.'

Max had another surprise in store for me. As I prepared to walk round to meet Harley, he told me that he would drive me round. He then gave me a small box, about the size and shape of a matchbox.

'Put that in your pocket. It's a transmitter/receiver. Voice activated. Whatever passes between you and Harley will be picked up and recorded on a tape machine in my car. Who knows? They may incriminate themselves.'

'Is this what I'm going to use this afternoon?'

'No. I've got a really special box of tricks for you.'

I rang the bell of Harley's rented house at ten o'clock sharp as ordered. I wasn't surprised when Derek Jefferson opened the door. There was no hint of his usual joviality as he pointed the way to the lounge.

I was surprised, however, at the group of people waiting to greet me. Apart from Harley there was Mike Martinez and Brian Summers. He was, as I'd half suspected, a part of the plot after all.

I wasn't offered a seat. Martinez was clearly in charge and he locked his extraordinary yellowish eyes on mine. 'Wolf-like' would best describe them. I noticed with interest that the tic by his left eye was working hard.

Summers broke the silence. 'So you want to make some extra money do you, Ludlow? Not earning enough at Sunningdale.' He sneered theatrically at me.

Martinez spoke. 'Quiet, Brian. This is the deal, Ludlow. You'll get five thousand to do this job for Harley. You'll keep your mouth shut or you'll end up dead. Harley can't lose, so we can afford to pay a bum like you more than you're worth.'

I nodded my agreement and Martinez outlined what I was required to do. As if he knew that I was carrying a bug in my pocket, he gave me the bare minimum of information. He made it clear that Harley would be using a doctored putter, but in words with enough ambiguity to be rendered meaningless to an outsider.

'Right. On your way. Meet Brian at twelve fifteen at the practice ground.'

I was shown out by Derek Jefferson, who hadn't said a word.

Neither had Brian Harley. At the front door I said provocatively to Jefferson: 'So this is when you all clean up is it, Derek?'

'That's our business.'

I was glad to walk around the corner and rejoin Max.

'Not very conclusive, was it?' I said, as I climbed a little painfully into the car.

'No. But at least Martinez threatened you. Although in court he'll claim that it was just a figure of speech. But it doesn't matter. We'll ruin their little scheme and you'll see them crack up then.'

'Maybe.'

It was time to ring Inspector Drew. Back at the house I dialled the number he had given me and got straight through to him at the police centre on the course. My objective was to warn him that, in theory, the whole affair would come to its conclusion that afternoon. But I did not want to alarm him into taking premature action against Harley and co. I merely wanted him to be in the vicinity of the eighteenth green and the clubhouse at approximately 6.30 when Brian Harley finished his round. And to be there with a few of his cavalry.

I began.

'Inspector, I've arranged to carry Brian Harley's bag this afternoon. His original caddie has been called away suddenly.'

'Oh really? I hope Harley's paying you danger money. Are you sure that Jake Baxter is still alive?'

'Yes, he's OK as far as I know. But I think you might find it interesting to follow Harley over the last few holes. And perhaps to have some men watching Jefferson, Martinez and even Brian Summers.'

'You're confident of a grand finale, are you?'

'I think everything should drop into place, yes.'

'Mr Ludlow, it only happens like that in mystery stories, not in real life. But I'll be there. Good luck.'

In the next hour or so Max and I yet again went through the various things we had to remember. We also answered several phone calls. One was from Andrew Buccleuth who had won a sizeable bet on Brian Harley to lead the Open after three rounds and promised me a case of Bollinger. Another from our father, who confirmed that he was a guest of IBM and would meet us that evening. He was duly astonished that Max was to caddie for Jack Mason and complained querulously that 'both my sons are now damned caddies.' Finally, Sally: to wish us both luck.

I walked down to the course with Max, since Jack was scheduled to start four matches ahead of Brian Harley, about three quarters of an hour's difference.

The pavements were thronged with spectators of all ages, hurrying with anticipation towards the course; excitement in their eyes and in their bearing. Young and old they seemed to be leaning forwards, eager to take their places in the final golfing drama.

I gave Max yet another final check of his duties. I was more nervous for him and for Jack than I was for myself. He bore my fussing with good humour. He understood.

He went off to meet Jack and in the twenty minutes or so I had left I decided to walk over to the PGA caravan to get a sight of Sally. For luck. It was a battle through the heavy crowd, which was moving purposefully to its various chosen vantage points.

The caravan was not far from the practice ground, and I had no intention of entering it. I had no wish to have an embarrassing encounter with Oliver Moreton. I just hoped to catch a comforting glimpse of Sally. As I walked past the side of the trailer and peered through the window I nearly ran into Moreton. To my discomfort he was talking to Jack Mason.

We were all taken aback, but Oliver Moreton seized the initiative.

'I hope, Ludlow, that this is the last time I ever see you at a golf tournament.' Righteous indignation, indeed.

'And so say all of us,' said Jack, and walked away. It was said with real venom and I forgot for a moment that we were both playing a part. I was shaken, and later reflected that Jack might have a future in films. As a heavy, of course.

'If you're looking for Sally, I don't suppose that she's too keen on speaking to you.' Moreton called through the door, and Sally came to the top of the steps.

'I wondered if we could meet later?' I said, hopefully.

'No. I'm rather busy,' Sally said. She turned her back dismissively and went back into the caravan.

Moreton enjoyed his smirk of triumph, and I didn't have to try too hard to put a slump in my shoulders as I trudged off. Another budding actress. Such was the finality in her voice that I almost believed her.

I walked along the practice ground towards Brian Harley and Derek Jefferson, who had just arrived. I registered that Max was already in place alongside Jack. A couple of caddies spat on the ground as I passed and sent some choice phrases my way. I could feel the hostility beaming out at me. In this closed sporting society all sorts of sins could be forgiven, but not such a blatant act of disloyalty.

Harley looked surprisingly relaxed and began his practice routine, similar to Jack's and to most of the professionals. The idea is just to rediscover or confirm their rhythm and timing. Sometimes it's there from the start. Sometimes it has to be found. Perhaps a mental trigger is needed, or the player has to concentrate on one specific action which locks the whole swing into place. Brian Harley was swinging well and further down the line I reckoned that Jack's swing looked as solid as it ever had. Was fate about to play a monumental joke? What if Jack won the Open, and I wasn't at his side to share the excitement and the glory?

Harley spent quite a time in the practice bunker and finally headed for the putting green. He didn't seem too interested, and his putting was pretty desultory. Of course that was the one aspect of his game that he didn't need to practise.

We were due off the first tee at 2.30 p.m. As always in golf tournaments, the leader or leaders go out last. Harley was partnered by Larry Marsh, and just ahead were Carl Krantz and Bjorn Carlssen.

There was a great cheer from the crowd when Brian Harley's name was announced, and many cries of 'Good luck, Brian.' The ultimate test for any golfer was about to begin. I wondered how these players could even lift their clubs up and make a swing. I know that I would be paralysed with fright, which was why I was a caddie. I would be hoping merely not to make a fool of myself, whereas Larry Marsh would be planning how to birdie every hole.

He had already hit a booming drive down the first hole, and Harley followed with an efficient and utilitarian drive into a good position on the right of the fairway. Relieved applause greeted his shot, and the game was on.

In the bright sunshine the crowds were immense, as they surged down the paths alongside the ropes. There was a warm and generous atmosphere. They were prepared to applaud anything and everything in their anticipation of a rare British victory in the Open.

Detached as I was, one of half a dozen people who knew roughly what might happen and who certainly knew what couldn't happen, I was caught up in the highly-charged atmosphere. I even made a determined effort to enjoy it, because I wasn't going to make my move against Harley until late in his round.

Like the true champion he was, Marsh had wrenched four birdies from the course by the turn, but had dropped a shot at the difficult ninth hole when his ball settled under the lip of a bunker. It took two shots to get it out, but a solid single putt from about eight feet prevented real disaster.

But he had made little impression on Harley whose workaday swing stayed very solid. His approach shots were aimed at the middle of the greens and his putting was so accurate that he was never in trouble. His pitch shots when he failed to hit the green were confident, not surprisingly since he knew that he was unlikely to miss a putt. It certainly takes the worry out of those delicate little shots over bunkers or to tight flag positions. He also had three birdies and remained three shots ahead of Marsh.

It is a well-worn cliché, and therefore pronounced by the commentators at every major tournament as if the tablets of stone have been newly carved and handed down to them by the golfing Gods, that the real competition begins over the last nine holes.

As I had suspected, Harley's putting went up a gear over the next five holes. He birdied the tenth after putting his second shot within twenty feet of the hole; eagled the eleventh hole which is a par five with a putt from well off the green; and had two further birdies at the thirteenth and fourteenth holes.

Standing on the fifteenth tee it was all over bar the popping of the champagne corks. He was six shots ahead of Larry Marsh with four holes to play.

The fifteenth is one of the hardest holes in championship golf. The landing area for the drive is tiny, if you are to stay out of the bunkers and the heavy rough. The hole measures a shade under 470 yards, and you are faced with a second shot across more rough and a line of four pot bunkers about fifty yards from the front of the green. They are there to prevent you from bumbling your second shot up to the front edge; you must hit a precise shot right on to the green.

Larry Marsh did. Harley played two iron shots very conservatively and pitched on to the green from about 100 yards. He knew he could get his four that way. The green is tricky, large but with lots of humps and hollows. The pin was on the right and near the back and had been cut on an undulating stretch of turf, which ran away on both sides. Unfriendly – as always on the last day of the Open, when the true champion is sought. Marsh holed out for another birdie.

It was time to act. As I went towards the flag to hold it while Harley prepared for his putt, I switched on Max's box of tricks. I prayed that it would work as he had predicted. Otherwise all our planning and effort would be in vain.

After his normal three practice swings, Harley settled confidently over his putt, as well he might, and set the ball off towards the hole. The line was extremely difficult to read, and Harley obviously hadn't read it. The ball was wide to the left and finished about ten feet away on the wrong side of a slope. My prayers had been answered. The transceiver was working exactly as planned.

There was a murmur of disbelief from the crowd, which echoed the look of incomprehension on Harley's face. He went through his routine again and, as I held the flag, holed out to a huge sigh of relief from the crowd, followed by a huge roar of applause.

Larry Marsh was reinvigorated by closing the gap on Harley by two shots, and smashed a huge drive down the next hole. Harley was conservative again but was safely on the green in two. Marsh had hit his drive so far that he had a relatively simple pitch and made the most of it by putting his ball two feet from the hole. Another birdie. Harley was thirty feet from the pin, and I switched on my magic box again. I made sure he didn't get a birdie, but he tapped in for par. Only three shots between Marsh and Harley now.

As we walked to the seventeenth tee Harley could hardly interrogate me about his putter, even if he suspected me of any trickery. He looked at me searchingly, and I just shrugged. 'Just one of those things,' I meant to convey. I would destroy him on the next green.

If the fifteenth hole is rated as difficult, the seventeenth is enough to give most players a nervous breakdown at this stage of a tournament, let alone in the Open. At just over 460 yards, a long tee shot is needed to get you in the right position to play to the green. The hole is a dogleg to the left, and the left side of the fairway is littered with a dozen or more bunkers. If you drive safely to the right of the fairway you face one of the most intimidating shots in golf, across a great expanse of rough, made more hazardous by the presence of two wide and very deep bunkers. What a finish, as the television commentators say. 'A crucial hole for Brian Harley,' they were probably telling the viewers.

Larry Marsh really had his tail up and hit the perfect drive, down the middle and then fading slightly to the right side of the fairway.

There was just a hint of agitation in Harley's manner as he teed the ball up. He hit a rather skinny drive, no more than 230 yards, whereas Marsh was at least fifty yards ahead of him. I knew that Harley's tactic would be to hit a mid-iron over all the trouble and on to the sixty yards of fairway in front of the green, pitch on and hole out for a par.

He got onto the green as planned, even if his pitch was a nervous jab that left the ball about forty feet from the pin. Perfect. For my purposes.

I stood alongside the flag with my magic box turned on. Harley took several swings with his putter. The huge crowd was silent and motionless, a collective holding of breath. A huge sigh and a burst of movement as the putt sped on its way. People craning and ducking to see the ball, or just giving up and asking their neighbours.

The ball pulled up about ten feet short of the pin, to murmurs of sympathy from the crowd. Some shouted encouragement to Harley and the stewards called for silence. It duly fell as Marsh addressed his putt and stroked it towards the hole. It hit the right hand side of the hole and stayed out. A par for Marsh.

Harley had already played four shots and it didn't need a degree in mathematics or psychology to work out how important the next putt was. A cushion of two shots going down the last hole in the Open is not exactly comfortable, but it's bearable. Only one shot, especially when, three holes back, you had six shots in hand over your nearest rival, is not.

In complete silence, which seemed unbearable to me, let alone the two players, Harley crouched over his putt. It sped several inches wide of the hole, took a slope to the right and ended up about seven feet away.

Harley looked at me, as the crowd cried out in their excitement and anxiety. Surely their great British hope was not going to throw it all away? The colour had drained from his face and I thought I saw him shiver, as if struck by a sudden chill. He walked up to me and very quietly said: 'Get away from the hole, you bastard.'

He'd worked it out. He also knew he couldn't win.

He missed the next putt and tapped his ball in for a three over par seven.

The rest was anticlimax, though not for Larry Marsh who hit a textbook drive down the eighteenth hole. Harley was on the verge of collapse and took three shots to get to the front edge of the green.

As we walked off the tee Harley asked: 'How long have you known?'

'We suspected something weeks ago, but only put it all together about two weeks ago.'

'It wasn't the money, you know. I just wanted to win the Open. My little bit of immortality. To be somebody.'

'By cheating and murdering.'

'Killing Froggy and the other one was never part of the plan. That lunatic Summers did that.'

As we got near the green the crowd closed in behind the players but even their traditional enthusiasm seemed muted. This was natural since they had seen a British player on the edge of glory, only to see him draw back, seemingly unable to claim the prize.

On the green, Harley waved me away from the hole and took his last two putts in professional golf. Larry Marsh finished in style with another birdie, and took the greatest prize in golf.

Inspector Drew was waiting unobtrusively by the side of the green rather dashingly dressed, for him, in cord trousers, a roll-neck sweater and a darkish-brown checked sports jacket. It was fortunate that, amid all the hullabaloo that greets the finale of the Open, the players must hand their cards in to the officials, who have their own caravan near the eighteenth green. The players as usual have a cooling-off period to sit down quietly and ensure that their scores are correct. Although every shot has been witnessed by millions of television viewers and it is clear who has won, the players alone are responsible for checking their scores and signing for them.

To the amazement of the officials in the caravan and of Larry Marsh, Inspector Drew walked in, showed his warrant card and introduced himself.

'Gentlemen,' he said, 'as soon as Mr Harley has checked and signed his scorecard, I will be arresting him on suspicion of fraud and as an accessory to murder. When you hear what Mr Ludlow has to say to you and to show you I suspect that you will remove Mr Harley's name from this championship.'

I turned to Harley and asked him for the miniature receiver which he had secreted in his ear. He cupped his hand round his ear, felt gently with his little finger and it popped out. So did the eyes of the two officials.

Larry Marsh sat down wearily and said, 'I think I'm dreaming. Wake me up somebody and tell me I haven't won the Open.'

I showed them the tiny bug which, held between my thumb and forefinger, was only just visible to them.

'Harley has been using an illegal putter for most of the season. He started on the Safari circuit in January, I would guess, and the grand plan was to win the Open with it. Right so far, Brian?'

I looked at Brian Harley and he made a just perceptible nod of his head.

'The putter has an ultrasonic device built into it, which makes it virtually infallible. This bug, which he carried in his ear, is a receiver for the ultrasonic waves which are transmitted from the putter head. These are reflected back from the pin. When he did his practice swing with just the right amount of power to get the ball into the hole, the receiver would give him a certain sequence of sounds.'

Harley nodded his agreement and said: 'Yes, the bug would give out a continuous buzz.'

'And that was also the reason why his caddie was instructed to leave the flag in the hole even on very short putts of just a couple of feet or so.'

Larry Marsh had by now recovered his strength and asked the obvious question: 'But what about direction? That's even more important, especially on these greens.'

I held up Harley's putter. 'There's a microprocessor built into the head which is programmed to analyse the undulations of the ground. A pattern-recognition facility. It reads the correct line to the hole, just as humans do, but it doesn't make any mistakes.'

Larry Marsh was really interested now and, in between his exclamations and mild expletives, asked how the direction-finding signal worked.

'Harley swung the putter head down the approximate line between the putter head and the pin until a vibration in the putter handle told him he was dead on line.'

'Good God,' said Marsh, 'so he had a magic putter. He could hole out from anywhere on demand. And I'll bet that bastard Martinez is behind all this.'

At that stage Inspector Drew decided to intervene, and said. 'But he was clever enough not to overdo it, wasn't he? If he'd holed everything it would have been too obvious. And I suppose, Chris, that you jammed his system with your own transmitter, did you?'

I noticed that this was the first time that he had used my Christian name.

'No, that would have given the game away and he might still have won by using the putter normally. I used a little black box that received his ultrasonic waves and sent back corrupted information.'

The door opened and Oliver Moreton put his head in: 'What the bloody hell is going on? We're late with the presentation. The TV boys are creating hell out there.'

His belligerence slowly faded as he took in the scene. One of the officials took charge, made a final check of Larry Marsh's card and ushered him out. I heard him tell Moreton that Harley had been disqualified and would not be at the presentation.

Inspector Drew produced a radio from his jacket pocket. 'I take it, Harley, that you will cooperate fully with me. Am I right in assuming that both Jefferson and Martinez were in on the act?'

'And Summers, too,' I said.

Harley nodded miserably, and the Inspector spoke into the radio to his sergeant, who was instructed to arrest the others.

'Is there a back way out of here?'

I guided the Inspector to a service door at the back of the trailer. He paused and said: 'I'd like to see you and your brother and Mr

Greenslade after I've charged these various gentlemen and locked them up. Let's say seven thirty at your house. An informal statement from you. Oh and I'll take these.' He took the putter and the mini-receiver from me.

He almost smiled.

I felt drained of energy and feeling, but could hear the beginning of the presentation ceremony. I went outside to listen, in time to hear the bald announcement that Brian Harley had been disqualified from the Championship.

To my delight I heard it confirmed that Jack Mason had tied for third place with Jose Miguel and Bjorn Carlssen. Krantz was in second place, and the worthy winner was Larry Marsh. I looked up at the main scoreboard and saw that young Sam Ratcliffe had finished in the top twenty and that Jonathan Dyas had battled away to win the gold medal as the top amateur.

I fought my way through the crowds towards Jack Mason and found him half-surrounded by my family: my mother and father and Max. I shook him by the hand and he gave me an amiable bear hug.

'What a caddie Max turned out to be. He can read a putt better than I can. What a result, eh? And what a result for you, Chris.'

'Yes, the cup was well and truly dashed from Harley's lips, wasn't it?'

'What have you two boys been up to now?' asked my father.

'Saving the good name of golf,' said Jack. 'Come on, let's spend some of my winnings. Let's get into that clubhouse.'

He ushered us past the men who were guarding the entrance with a bluff 'It's all right, they're with me.' Jack had the natural authority which many large men carry around with them, and in we went.

We met Toby coming the other way. He was actually hurrying. Away from a bar.

'Come and have a glass of fizz, Toby,' Jack said expansively.

'Sorry, old boy, duty calls. The editor has not only cleared the back page for me, but half the front one as well. But I'll be with you in an hour or two. I'd taken the precaution of mapping out most of the story this morning.'

'Come to the house. Inspector Drew wants to talk to us.'

Toby groaned, but nodded. 'Chris, the delectable Sally is waiting patiently inside to greet the conquering hero.'

'Chris, are you all right, my darling?' She threw her arms around me and held me tight. 'And Max.' She gave my brother a hug, too.

'Don't I get in on the act?' asked Jack, and also got a hug and a congratulatory kiss on the cheek.

While I made the introductions to my parents, Jack surged off to the bar and in very quick time reappeared with a magnum of champagne and several glasses.

'There's another one on its way. Drink up. Here's to golf and to our two intrepid sleuths, Chris and Max.'

My father spoke up, half testily and half joking: 'I still don't know what this is all about. Is anyone going to enlighten me?'

'Brian Harley was a cheat,' I said. 'We managed between us to expose him, that's all. We'll tell you the details later. But let's enjoy our drink. This is, after all, Jack's moment. A marvellous Open for you, Jack. Congratulations.'

Jack's elbow was a blur as he tackled the champagne. His abstinence over the past two weeks certainly hadn't impaired his thirst.

We had broached the second magnum, with the help of several friends and acquaintances of Jack's who had come over to congratulate him, when Sally said, 'I think we ought to pop over to the house, Chris, and tidy up before the inspector arrives, don't you?'

'Well, the cleaner came in this morning . . .' I began, and felt a sharp but unobtrusive kick on the ankle.

'Yes, but we must put out the glasses and organise a few snacks.'

Max grinned and said, 'Off you go, Chris, we'll see you in an hour or so.'

As we dodged our way through the crowds, which were reluctantly drifting towards the exits, I asked Sally what the rush was.

'What do you think?'

'I'm not sure.'

'Nudge, nudge. Wink, wink. I want you on my own, Chris. We haven't been alone together for a whole week.'

We walked down the road towards the house through the gradually thinning crowds. Life is very sweet, I thought. I looked at Sally by my side and found her looking at me. We laughed. Two cats sharing the cream.

We swung briskly along the last hundred yards or so of pavement. Holding hands, we turned into the gravelled drive of Jack's rented house. As I fumbled for the key in my pocket amongst the loose change and my own keys for flat and car, I heard the crunch of gravel.

I registered that the noise was not coming from the entrance to the drive, so it obviously wasn't Inspector Drew arriving early. The steps were coming from the left, from the direction of the garden. Less than ten yards away the stocky figure of Brian Summers stopped. He held a gun in his hand and it was pointed at me.

# Chapter 19

'I've been waiting for you, Ludlow. I'm going to kill you, you bastard. Inside.' He gestured with his gun at the front door.

I noticed that his accent had slipped a bit since we last met. More Essex to it, I thought in a detached way. According to Toby, all the villains come from Essex.

I also thought my chances were better if I kept him out in the open. More space to manoeuvre than in the house. And maybe someone would turn up to rescue us.

I pretended to fumble again for the key and said: 'Look, Sally had nothing to do with all this. You can let her go, surely.'

I gripped her by the upper arm and stepped away from the door and into the driveway. I hoped she guessed what was in my mind.

'Not a chance,' Summers said. 'Into that sodding house.'

I had to play for time, and said: 'Why did you do it? Why did you murder those two?'

'Because nobody gets in my way and certainly not a couple of bums like that.'

'But you didn't have to kill them.'

'Why not? They're just expendable. And I enjoyed thinking up the appropriate way of knocking them off. And I enjoyed killing them. And I wasn't short of willing helpers either. If you've got the money and the contacts, you can do anything. You can buy anything. You can buy anyone.

'Now, get into the house.'

As he waved his gun menacingly again I shoved Sally out into the drive and shouted 'Run!' Despite the gravel underfoot, uncertain going as Toby later called it, she took off fast down the drive.

As I'd gambled, Summers was caught in two minds. In his heart of hearts, mean and miserable though it was, he probably didn't

239

want to kill Sally. He certainly wanted to kill me, but also wanted to savour the moment. A few bullets in the stomach perhaps, and see me suffer.

He half turned and aimed a bullet in Sally's direction. This was my one and only chance, and I launched myself in a diving, headlong rush in his direction. I slithered the last yard or so along the gravel, like a demented scrum half doing a particularly ambitious dive pass. But the surface was more painful than at Twickenham. Summers loosed off another shot as I took him low. My shoulder crashed into his hip and I grabbed him by the knees and hung on.

He had the strength of desperation and hatred. Struggling into a half-sitting position, he brought the gun up for another shot. I snatched at his wrist and bent his arm sideways, got some purchase with my knee and tried to smash him in the throat with my forearm. I only hit him a half-blow on the forehead, and he was still fighting to bring his gun to bear on me. Anywhere would disable me and then he could finish me off.

We rolled around on the gravel until I finally got a good grip of his neck with my right arm. I manoeuvred my way past his thrashing legs until I was on the left side of his body. While his free left hand was scratching and gouging at my face, I pulled him into a sitting position and bent his right arm backwards. I grabbed it with my own right hand and pulled it sharply across and upwards. There was a sharp crack from his shoulder and an even sharper scream from Summers. He dropped the gun and lay sobbing on the ground.

I left him there and limped heavily over to the front door. My knees and elbows and several other areas of my body were beginning to set up their chorus of complaint at damage they had sustained and my face was beginning to throb where Summers had clawed at it. Queensbury Rules had certainly gone out of the window this time, I thought. I headed for the phone to call the police, and turned back as I heard the crunch of a car turning into the drive at speed. The police had arrived.

Before the car stopped Sally had hurtled out of her seat and, for the second time that evening, was clinging on to me. No words. They weren't needed. I was safe.

Some elementary first-aid was applied to Summers' broken arm, and he was sent on his way to be charged with 'a number of offences', as it is usually put.

Inspector Drew was almost solicitous, ordered one of his men to make some tea, and apologised for losing Summers earlier in the day.

'Sergeant Aitken let Summers give him the slip,' he said grimly. 'We all guessed that he would head for an airport or a port. We didn't dream that he would hang about to exact his revenge.'

At this point, Max came through the door, and asked, 'Whose revenge?'

I explained quickly about Summers' unexpected appearance and said: 'Where were you when I needed you?'

'You can look after yourself, Chris.'

'Maybe. But it's painful. And you're better at it.'

Loud voices approached the house and in came Toby and Jack. They both stopped when they saw my damaged face and Toby said: 'Good heavens, Chris, have you been arguing with Sally already?'

We eventually settled down in the sitting room, and Inspector Drew got the meeting under way, after remarking that the scene reminded him of the denouement in an Agatha Christie play except that, as far as he knew, the murderer wasn't actually present. Although we all knew the background, some in more detail than others, Inspector Drew gave us a concise summary. No frills, police style.

He then looked sternly at Max, Toby and myself.

'You three have acted pretty irresponsibly. As I hinted several times to Mr Ludlow here,' he nodded at me, and I noticed that he had assumed his mantle of formality again, 'we more or less knew what was going on and who was involved. But we needed some hard evidence. Jefferson and Harley had impeccable alibis for both murders and we didn't suspect that Summers was so deeply embroiled in the scheme.'

'But it was much more than a couple of murders,' Max said quietly. 'It was a scheme to defraud the public of millions.'

'And to exploit the Open,' growled Jack.

'This is what I don't quite understand,' said the Inspector. 'If Harley had won the Open, so Martinez would have made a million or two for him and taken his cut, and Jefferson would have sold a few thousand extra putters. It's surely not worth the trouble of such an elaborate scheme.'

'No, it wasn't,' I agreed. 'But the scheme was much more ambitious than that. Martinez, Jefferson and Summers were set to make millions. After Harley had won the Open, they would have unloaded Supersight putters all over the world.'

Toby intervened: 'You must understand, Inspector, that most golfers are mad. They will pay any amount of money for a club that they think will improve their golf. Normally sensible businessmen, who are used to weighing up the pros and cons of every company decision, accountants who watch every penny on behalf of their clients, clever lawyers etc, forget all their usual caution when it comes to golf clubs. If they think a club will cut a few strokes off their score, they'll buy it.'

I continued. 'Brian Harley was set up to win the Open with an infallible putter. And it was. His putting average this season was about four strokes better than anyone else's. And, cleverly, Jefferson didn't hand them out to any other pros. I think that he just had a lapse of concentration when he gave Jack one of the putters. Jack went on and on about it, and I suppose Jefferson thought it would keep him quiet. He knew that he wouldn't change from his old blade putter, anyway.'

Jack nodded, and smiled.

'I've only really used two putters in the whole of my career. The one I've got now is forty years old and is a beauty. I can't understand these golfers who chop and change their putters. Putting is just a question of mind over matter. If you believe you can hole the putt, you probably will, and the reverse is true as well.'

I carried on. 'I say the scheme was cleverly worked out, because if other pros had used the putter without success it would have spoiled the story. And that story tomorrow morning would have been that Brian Harley won the Open by his brilliant putting. And the sales story would be that his brilliant putting was only possible because of the Supersight putter. So, roll up and buy one.'

'And the majority of the club golfers in the world would have been unable to resist it,' added Jack.

'So they sell a few thousand putters. That still doesn't make sense,' Inspector Drew said.

'Not a few thousand, a few million,' I said. 'The manufacturers sell about a million putters every year in Britain alone, and that's when there is no artificial stimulus to increase the market. It's at least five times as big in the States, and Japan is probably half as big as the American market. Then there's Europe and Australia. So you've got a total available market of well over ten million putters.

'And here's the nub of it all. Jefferson was all set to knock the putters out in Taiwan and Korea for peanuts. They could be made for less than ten pounds and sold for nearly a hundred. Even with discounts to the shops and with the commission paid to distributors, they would have made an absolute killing.'

The Inspector winced at the pun, and Max and Jack laughed out loud.

'How much, roughly?'

'They would have made an average of thirty pounds a putter,' Max said. 'If they clipped a modest twenty-five per cent of the world market, say three million units, they'd have made nearly a hundred million pounds in the first year.'

'Good God.'

'That would have kept them in Bolly for a while, wouldn't it?' Toby said. 'And if the punters threw the putters away after a few months, why should they worry? Putters aren't sold with one-putt guarantees, are they?'

'How much must it have cost to develop the putter?'

Max explained about his investigations in California's Silicon Valley, and his interview with the pseudonymous Dennis Quilter of Stellar Products.

'The answer is that the prototype didn't cost all that much. Quilter spent less than fifty grand on making two prototypes, one of which was used by Harley. Now that's just petty cash to Martinez. Remember that the techniques Quilter used have been around for donkey's years. Ultrasonics is after all the basis of sonar. The most obvious example is submarine detection. From your ship you send out a burst of ultrasonic energy. If it hits a submarine the intensity of the signal when it is reflected back to the ship tells you that there's something big down there. In other words, you can tell whether it really is a submarine or not, and how far away it is. Simple.'

'Yes,' Toby said, 'I vaguely remember a film when Curt Jurgens is being hunted down in his submarine.'

'That was *Run Silent, Run Deep*, wasn't it?' said Inspector Drew.

'I think so. But I remember the submarine detector. Ping, ping. Loud when they were close to the sub, and quieter as they lost contact. Great stuff.'

'That's it,' Max said. 'And of course bats use ultrasonics. They send out a stream of pulses and the return signals tell them where the objects ahead of them are and how big they are. So they can navigate quite easily in the dark and can capture their food in the dark. They recognise a reflected acoustic signature, of a fly for instance, and snap it up. They see with their ears, if you like.'

Max paused and Jack intervened: 'So that gives you distance, but what about direction? Over the humps and the hollows of the greens. That's the really difficult part,' he said with great feeling.

'Easy. As I've explained, ultrasonic devices can recognise patterns. Sonar can recognise different types of target. Otherwise you might spend your time sending depth charges, or their modern equivalent, down to destroy whales rather than submarines. Human begins use the technique all the time. They compare the signals they get back from an object, a ringing telephone say, with their own neural templates, which is just a complicated way of saying memory.'

'Neural templates. My God, have I got any of those?' Toby asked.

'Yes, even you. They enable you to recognise a bottle of Bollinger at fifty feet,' Max said with a smile and continued. 'So, the ultrasonic pulses transmitted from the putter head are reflected from the various contours on the ground and the return signals are analysed by the microprocessor. As soon as Harley swung his putter down the correct line he would get a response from the putter – in this case a slight vibration in the handle – and away he went. Another brilliant putt.

'It's another technique which has been around for decades. Fighter planes use what's called terrain-following radar. They can fly very low and automatically follow the contours of the ground.'

'The TSR2 was one of the first war planes to use it, wasn't it,

Max?' asked Toby. 'Cancelled by the Labour government in the sixties, you know,' he added.

'Before my time,' said Sally, Max and I in chorus.

With feigned disgust Toby left the room to find some champagne.

'How did you fool the magic putter?' asked Inspector Drew. 'I assumed you would simply use some sort of jamming device, but you said not.'

'No. That would have been the simplest method. I could have transmitted more decibels from a mini-transmitter in my pocket than the putter was transmitting, and Harley wouldn't have got any data back to help him. But he would have known straight away that something was wrong. And he might still have putted well enough to win.'

'I doubt it,' said Toby, who had re-entered the room with a tray laden with glasses and bottles of champagne. 'Without the psychological boost of knowing that he had an infallible putter, his game would probably have collapsed.'

'Well, anyway, I used a very sophisticated transceiver that Max found for me. It was programmed to send the signals back to Harley's putter with a ten per cent error. And a random factor was also built in. So that the information it sent back might be ten per cent short or ten per cent long.'

'Has this Dennis Quilter got any other magic clubs up his sleeve?' Jack asked.

Max grinned. 'I'm sure he could oblige. He actually had an idea for an intelligent club. A driver, for example. You would line your drive up on the distant flag and ultrasonic pulses would bounce off it. As the club head approached the ball the profile of the club face would change to ensure that, however off line the club head was swung, the ball would be hit towards the target. He'd redesigned the middle section of the club by building in a series of miniature solenoids, which would tilt part of the face of the club to ensure that the ball was hit dead on line.'

'Good God, I'll have a set of those,' said Toby, as he filled up the glasses again.

Inspector Drew stood up and prepared to leave, and Jack said: 'I don't understand these people. Well, I can understand Jefferson perhaps. He's not rich and he wanted to get rich. And Harley.

According to Chris he wanted the glory of being the Open Champion. But what about Summers and Martinez? They've got millions. Why do they want more? It can't be greed, can it?'

After a pause, Inspector Drew spoke. 'No, not greed. The money is just a means to an end, and the end is power. Certainly, in Martinez' case. The same with Summers, except that he's certifiable.'

'Worse than that,' said Toby. 'He cheats at golf. What's likely to happen to them all?'

'Who knows? Harley admits everything relating to the fraud, but claims complete ignorance of the murders, though he is adamant that it must have been Summers' doing. He is the original pawn in the game. I believe that his thoughts never went beyond the glory of being the Open Champion.'

'That's exactly what he told me as we walked down the eighteenth,' I said. 'The money he might have earned seemed unimportant to him. I almost felt sorry for him for a moment. As Graham Fearnley told me weeks ago, the one person who wouldn't make any big money would surely be Brian Harley.'

'What about Martinez and Jefferson?' asked Max, and Inspector Drew continued.

'Jefferson has got roughly the same story as Harley, and denies any knowledge of the murders. He claims that the scam was Martinez' idea. Martinez, of course, denies everything and says that he was the innocent victim of Jefferson's plan. He's just Harley's business manager and didn't realise he'd fallen in with a bunch of crooks, and so on. He might well get away with it, unless we can find hard evidence of his involvement.'

'What about Summers?'

'Well, we'll get him for attempted murder on Mr Ludlow's and Miss Drayton's evidence, but we've still got to prove that he organised the two murders. He will deny those in court, and we have yet to find the accomplices who helped him kill the two caddies. At the moment the charges are attempted murder and conspiracy. But a clever lawyer, and Summers will have one, may well get these charges reduced. It is up to us, the police, to find the evidence to make the charges stick, and a key element will be the evidence of Harley and Jefferson.'

The Inspector moved towards the door and said with an almost discernible smile. 'You Ludlows ought to be locked up. And you, Mr Greenslade, should be reported to the Press Council. But you did a remarkable job in the circumstances. I'll leave you all to enjoy yourselves. Oh and congratulations, Mr Mason, on your marvellous golf.'

We certainly did enjoy ourselves. After several more bottles of champagne had been demolished, Toby found a restaurant which was willing to take us. The party continued there, fuelled by Jack's enthusiasm and Toby's infectious style of bonhomie. As in the bar earlier, many of the customers came over to chat to Jack and to congratulate him on his sterling efforts in the Open.

Nobody wanted the celebration to end. Tomorrow was another day, when we all had to return to reality. But who cared about tomorrow?